M000211539

praise for **THE**

AN AMY PROWERS THRILLER

Amy Powers must go back in her family history to find the history of a small piece of cloth. Is it the famed Shroud of Turin or a fake? The results will impact the political power of a "General" who wants to dominate the world. As Amy Powers travels three continents to find the truth, the reader is in for a wild ride.

—Eric Cassel, economist

Once again, Katherine Burlake has woven a complex tale of intrigue with historical and cultural insights. This is a compelling read on multiple levels.

—Carol Vanderwark Nichols, California educator

Katherine Burlake's second novel in the Amy Prowers series is a winner. Katherine's mastery of world history and geography is showcased in the hunt for the Shroud of Turin and the multiple assassinations/murders that take place. Amy Prowers must come to terms with legacy of family beginning in WW II, their involvement with the Nazis, and her commitment to the Committee.

—George Skarpentzos, Foreign Service Officer

The Last Request *is the original weaving of a image in FABRIC. By using Fact, Fiction, Fable and the Global need for the Truth. My needs for reading, feeling and hearing stories that stirs my imagination were exceeded!*

—John Partilla, businessman

Amy Prowers is back. And her life is incredibly complicated. Nazis, the North African caliphate, power sources from ancient Egypt and pre-Columbian Mexico, Balkan monks, American oil, and the missing Shroud of Turin are all part of The Last Request. *Amy's late father sends Amy on a quest to find a priceless relic and to discover her hidden true self. Katherine Burlake once again has made history an adventure.*

—Mary Ellen Gilroy, Foreign Service Officer

THE LAST REQUEST

AN AMY PROWERS THRILLER

Carol,
many thanks
for your
help. Katherine
Burlake

KATHERINE BURLAKE

Edited by: Barb Wilson, EditPartner.com
Book Consultant: Judith Briles, The Book Shepherd
Cover design: Nathan Dasco
Interior and eBook conversion: Rebecca Finkel, F + P Graphic Design

ISBN softcover: 978-0-9989734-4-9
ISBN eBook: 978-0-9989734-5-6
ISBN audio: 978-0-9989734-6-3

Library of Congress Control Number: on file
Fiction | Political Thriller | Middle East

First Edition
Printed in the USA

Cast of Characters

Abbott von Hagen of the Gracanica Monastery, brother of the General, not sure if the Shroud is in the monastery or not.

Ace Prowers Amy's cousin, Geigner's brother, assists his Aunt Sonora Lleissle with her Committee in Berlin.

Akhenaton ancient Egyptian pharaoh, ruled for 17 years died about 1334/6 BC. Known for introducing the concept of one god. Lost in history unto the 19th century. Queen was Nefertiti. Some say his son was Tutankhamun.

Amy Prowers follows her father's last request to find the real Shroud of Turin and take it to the Cathedral in Turin, Italy.

Benton Prowers Amy's father, diseased, during World War II copied the Shroud of Turin.

Coptic's an ethnoreligious group living in Northeast Africa, in modern Egypt are the largest Christian denomination in Sudan and Libya, they are dominant in business.

Count Lleissle wealthy Swiss count, Sonora's husband, diseased.

el Ben Alemien tribal leader in North Africa, dreams of controlling North Africa and the oil.

el Habid Alemien son of el Ben determined to find the Shroud.

Geigner scientist working on tomb in the desert, Amy's cousin, Ace's brother.

General von Hagen brother of the Abbott, lives in Vera Cruz, Mexico, large oil holdings, wants to give el Ben the Shroud.

Gracanica Monastery is a Serbian Orthodox monastery in Kosovo, built in 1321 by Serbian king Stefan Milutin, in 2006 it was placed on UNESCO's World Heritage List.

Icons an icon is a religious work of art often called a painting, found in Eastern Orthodox Church, Roman Catholic and some Eastern Catholic churches.

Mayans a Mesoamerican civilization noted for art, architecture, mathematics, the calendar and astronomical system.

Marfkis el Alemien brother of el Ben, with Benton and Veilkov faked the Shroud of Turin.

Medak monk in Gracanica Monastery who assists Amy in finding the Shroud.

Rat Line escape routes for Nazis fleeing Europe during and after World War II, supported by the Catholic Church they lead to havens in Latin America.

Sonora Prowers Lleissle Benton's younger sister—aunt to Amy, Ace, Geigner.

Veilkov monk who with Benton and Marfkis copied the Shroud of Turin during World War II.

In the decades since World War II,
over 100,000 pieces of art, stolen, hidden
or forgotten have never been found.
THE LAST REQUEST *is a fictional account*
of what might have happened
to one such piece of art.

Prologue

The past is the future of the present.
An eastern proverb

1945

IN SERBIA

The train was late, and Benton Prowers was sure it was an omen. He turned to his partner, Brother Veilkov.

"We needed every minute to locate the Shroud of Turin and get it off the train."

With the passive assurance of a monk, Veilkov said, "The train must stop to fill up on water and coal. Takes a lot to cross our rugged Serbian Mountains."

Benton grunted, unconvinced. The Shroud of Turin was a small icon on a big train filled with treasures.

The snow crunched on the path as Veilkov's cousin, the yardman, arrived to service the train. A rumble sent a vibration through the frozen ground as the train, billowing steam and carrying a fortune in art and jewelry, slowly emerged from the darkness.

Nazi guards, on the stone bridge above the tracks, watched as the refueling began. The cousin moved slowly in the icy snow, trying to delay the departure without the guards getting impatient. Under the cover of the hissing steam engine, Benton and Brother Veilkov slipped around the stack of coal, where they were hiding, and headed for the last rail car.

No guards were on the train which didn't surprise Benton. The security guards thought the train was the local mail run.

"I hope the local partisan's right about a box with an *M* on it," said Benton.

Opening the door to the rail car, they came face to face with dozens of rows of crates stacked neatly on top of each other. *It's impossible,* thought Benton, as he and Brother Veilkov hurried through the car looking for the letter *M* imprinted on a crate. To his surprise, it was right in front of them. Veilkov's knife cut off the top. Inside was a small canvas packet.

Then they heard the hiss of steam as the train jerked forward. Veilkov quickly stuffed the packet in his knapsack, and the two men headed for the back of the car. As the train cleared the water tank, they jumped off.

The guards on the bridge above the tracks saw them and shouted, "Halt!"

Using the local dialect, Veilkov shouted back, "We pick up the mail."

The halt order was repeated, and they ducked down. Lying on the gravel next to the tracks, they weren't sure the guards could see them in the semi- darkness. Benton weighed their options to take out the guards.

A moment later the train was under the stone bridge. They heard a pop, the noise barely audible above the engine. Benton looked at Veilkov. Both were experts in building bombs.

"We know that pop."

The two men dove behind the coal stack as the train exploded under the bridge sending debris in every direction. The guards on the bridge were not protected: they had no place to hide.

When the clatter of debris stopped, Benton looked back at the wreck. "We are the only two men in the world who know the first icon, the Shroud of Turin, wasn't destroyed."

They emerged from the safety of their hiding place and turned to hike up the snow packed path away from the crash. "Yes," replied Veilkov, "and now it is our responsibility to protect it."

• • •

1946

GRACANICA MONASTERY

In the monastery's private alcove, monks prayed at all hours of the day and night to the icon *Christ in Glory*. Veilkov prayed with them, the Shroud of Turin concealed under his robe. He remembered the train crash the year before as if it were yesterday. He could still smell the fire and through the dust see fragments of burning paintings and jewelry. Now he waited, knowing his timing must be perfect.

One evening he was finally alone. Climbing up the four steps to the icons on the wall, he quickly hooked the packet containing the Shroud on the wire behind the icon, *Christ in Glory*.

Descending and kneeling again to pray, in the icon he could see, with an insight few can claim, his own death.

• • •

CHAPTER ONE

Reaching Out

My life has no beginning and no end.
My parents are dead, and the past is buried with them.
So why am I flying halfway around the world
to a monastery in Serbia?

APRIL 1990, OVER THE ATLANTIC OCEAN

From the window of the jet, Amy Prowers watched as the sky in the east turned black. She wondered if the sky above Serbia looked like this when her father died. *No, not died…killed*, she thought. She didn't expect a surprise when the will was read. Wasn't the past buried? Apparently not. Thinking about how he died made her mad and determined to follow through on his last request.

Leaning back against the seat, Amy sipped her vodka. If the real Shroud wasn't in Turin, contrary to what the world believed, there could be a scandal—for Italy, Serbia and the Catholic Church. Her father didn't care about scandals, but obviously he had been involved during World War II with one of historic proportions. Something from his past, some personal involvement, made it important to him for her to return the Shroud. She missed him more than she thought possible, and wished he'd told her more about his life during World War II.

Obviously, the past had not died with him. He was reaching out to her from his grave. Aunt Sonora said, "*Someone wanted Benton dead. Amy, you have to follow through on his legacy or something important in the past is lost forever.*"

Why didn't he just say where he hid the Shroud? Her father always had secrets, but hiding the real Shroud of Turin, obviously stolen… for what reason? Amy hoped the Abbot, whom she'd called from the states, would know.

Over the years, her father traveled every few months to the monastery to visit, she thought, old buddies from World War II. Now she wasn't sure just what he was doing.

If the real Shroud is at the monastery, I'll find it, and find who was responsible for his death. Amy smiled, remembering how her father loved puzzles. *This one may have cost him his life.* To her, the letter was the first piece of the puzzle, the icon book he left, the second, and going to the monastery the third.

The plane bounced in turbulence. Amy buzzed the stewardess for another vodka. Stretching her long legs, she looked out the window as the moon disappeared in a cloud bank. The sky became as dark as the ground below.

Amy realized she faced a window in her life. She had to stop wondering and open it for herself. She missed her father, but though he was gone, she knew she would do whatever had to be done to honor his last request. Hesitating, she opened the book, *Icons of the Balkan Monasteries.*

To her surprise, a small key, almost concealed, was taped inside the cover. An odd shape and size. She tore it off and held it in her hand, wondering what it opened. One thing she knew; the key clearly was the fourth piece of her father's puzzle.

Then the thought occurred to her that her father wasn't sure who would find his clues. Otherwise his letter would have simply told her where the Shroud was hidden. Being honest with herself, Amy resented being swept into her father's past. But whatever the key opened; she knew it would change her life because she was engaged in the recovery of one of the most sacred, historical relics in Christianity.

A thought from years ago flashed across her memory. Her first husband had called her a reluctant warrior. At the time she thought he was nuts, but today he could be right. She had a feeling she was in for a fight and one she was determined to win. She turned to the book, looking at pictures of icons. On the last page was a Biblical quotation from the Book of Revelations.

Then I saw another angel coming down from heaven, surrounded by a cloud, and a rainbow over his head: his face shone, and he held open in his hand a small scroll.

Amy skipped down to the last paragraph of the quote, underlined very likely, by her father.

God's veiled plan, mysterious through the ages, would be fulfilled.

She fingered the key, watching the stars in the darkened sky. Sleep came slowly. When it did, angels blowing trumpets filled her dreams.

• • •

CHAPTER TWO

The Gracanica Monastery

Inside her jacket pocket, she felt the brass key.
Why all the clues?

The road to the Gracanica Monastery spiraled up a mountain ridge and then curled down to the valley below. As she drove, and restless from the long plane flight, Amy again wondered why she was here. *It's time to stop this second guessing. Just follow Dad's clues.* She held the steering wheel of the car with one hand and with the other reached in her jacket pocket, reassuring herself she had the little icon book and the key.

Her plan was to find his buddy from World War II, a monk called Veilkov. He might be able to help her understand the icon book and lead her to where the Shroud of Turin was hidden. If not, the Abbot of the monastery, who her father had visited during his trips, certainly ought to know if the Shroud of Turin was in his monastery.

She was worried about contacting the two monks. *Secrecy always surrounds a monastery and for sure one this ancient,* she thought. Would they know the secret and assist her in her request?

Rays of sunlight flashed between the clouds, reflecting against the patches of snow among the pine trees on the mountains. The wild, narrow valley must have looked much the same years ago to her parents. The faint whistle of a train echoed against the slope. Could that be the train her parents took out of the Balkans at the end of the war?

She knew little of their life during World War II and nothing about icons or this monastery. Her father asked her several times to come with him on his regular trips to visit. She was always too busy, and now, sadly, it was too late. *Time to move on.* Reflecting on the past was not going to help her today.

Suddenly gunfire crackled across the valley. Raised on a ranch, she knew that sound and instinctively slowed. To her right a flock of birds rose from the trees, as if programmed in a pattern of flight. Was it hunting season? Was she in danger? It didn't matter; she had no choice but to continue to the monastery.

The road ended at a parking lot filled with tourist buses and guards. No one could miss the guards with *Monastery Policia* printed on their chartreuse jackets. She parked the car and watched the tourists walking into the monastery.

Looking up at the church towers, Amy recalled what she had read in the guidebook during her flight. *Historians believed the Gracanica Monastery had existed since the twelfth century. Years ago, the monastery was in Serbia, then in Yugoslavia as the Balkans changed rulers. Today, the monastery was in Kosovo, as if the average tourist knew that was the Balkans.*

When her father told her about his trips, he spoke about the people's different ethnic backgrounds and religions. He said they remembered every insult, and every church, mosque, or village destroyed in the last three hundred years. To her, such conflict seemed absurd. Why would anyone carry all that baggage around?

A cobblestone pathway led to a church with three spiral cupolas stacked upon each other. Among the trees, other cupolas atop monastery buildings could be seen. She followed the last group of tourists through the gate as their guide, a monk, explained the history of the monastery. He spoke English with an accent difficult for her to identify. She settled for the generic Slavic.

"Humans are God's expression of an icon of himself. A cloth wrapped around Christ's body and imprinted with his image created the Shroud of Turin, the first icon. To the Orthodox believer, the icon is a meeting point. Every Sunday, surrounded by icons, the believer becomes part of the liturgy."

She looked up at the cupola; the tiny round towers created the roof of the monastery. She had little patience with those who lived in the past. *This search*, she thought, *could be really tedious. I must stay focused.*

A gray-haired woman tourist, decked out in a pink polyester pantsuit and fitting Amy's image of tour bus travelers, raised her hand. Her question on the meaning of the word *icon* surprised Amy, since it was relevant.

She looked at the monk's expression. If he had heard the question a thousand times before, he didn't show it.

"The word icon is from the Greek and means 'image.' An icon is how God reveals himself to man. The icon represents a hierarchy of saints, with the top being Christ, then Mary, then whoever the painter chooses."

"When was the first icon painted?" she asked.

The monk's patience impressed Amy. How many times had he been asked these questions?

"There is a traditional and non-traditional view. According to tradition, the Evangelist, Saint Luke, painted the first icon—a portrait of Mary—in the first century AD. The non-traditional view is that the first icon is the burial cloth of Christ. The common name for the icon is the Shroud of Turin, after the cathedral in Turin, Italy where it resides."

Another tourist waved a travel book. "Local folklore says the Shroud—or the first icon as you called it—is actually in this monastery."

The monk took a deep breath, as if he'd been asked this question many times.

"Over the centuries, rumors abound, but I assure you only traditional icons are here in Gracanica. Watch your step. The flagstones on the path into the church are uneven. Remember it was built in 1321 by the Serbian King Milutin."

He didn't quite answer the question, thought Amy, as she watched the group follow him into the church. No one would remember the name of a Serbian king, but the tourists would certainly recall the first icon, or the Shroud of Turin. If local folklore said the Shroud was in the monastery, her father's letter could be right. It should be here.

Beside the doorway was a directory in English and Cyrillic, the local alphabet. She took out the small book on icons and quickly compared the title page to the directory. Two of the icons in the church matched icons in the book, the icon of the *Seven Angels* and the icon of *Christ in Glory.*

She opened the book and read the quotation neatly printed in her father's handwriting inside the book cover: *the tenth chapter of Revelations, see page six.* Carefully, she turned the old pages to the sixth page.

Then I saw another angel coming down from heaven, surrounded by a cloud, with a rainbow over his head: his face shone, and he held open in his hand a small scroll. But when the seventh angel blew his trumpet, then God's veiled plan, mysterious through the ages ever since it was announced by his servants, the prophets, would be fulfilled.

Why all the clues? The icon of the *Seven Angels* was in the book. Could that be the clue? If so, her father had made it simple. Find the icon of the *Seven Angels* and it would lead her to the Shroud of Turin.

She laughed out loud. *There was no way her father would make this simple. He loved symbolism, and Mayan symbolism was his avocation. Now he had her looking at icon symbolism.* She was ignorant about icons; their history and symbolism. Maybe the Abbot could give her a crash course.

Looking up at the gray stone towers and dark wooden doors, she wondered what force drove men to live in such a world of gray. Something within the monastery must have appealed to these men.

She turned back to the doorway and saw a monk—she guessed in his late forties—standing against the stone entryway. His blue eyes, blond hair and white skin stood out in a country of dark-haired and dark-eyed people. To her, his face and body language looked peaceful.

She had to stop this introspection. *It's ridiculous.* If he spoke English, he might be able to help her find the Abbot. Her skill at speaking German and French were mediocre; and she was doubtful he spoke fluent Spanish. Still, Amy approached him, opening the book to the picture of the icon of the *Seven Angels* and pointed toward the monastery.

"It is a thirteenth- or fourteenth-century icon, and yes, it's in the church."

His English was perfect and to her surprise he extended his hand.

"I am Stephan Medak, the Abbot's administrative assistant. He asked me to meet you, Miss Prowers, as he's going to Vienna for a speaking engagement. You asked him for help, and I am in his place."

She had no rational reason why, but she trusted this monk. The same instincts served her well in business, so why not now.

"I need to find one icon. I'm no expert, so I hoped he could help me. I don't know him, but for years my family has partnered with his brother, who is called the General and lives in Mexico. Over the decades the general has become a person whose judgement I value."

"*I found the human shape of God and my soul found its salvation.*" Medak spoke the words and said, "I forget who said that, but it describes the icon. Icons are not what they seem to be. Perhaps you've captured their meaning by searching out a special icon."

Amy thought he might be right but wasn't sure about finding salvation in an icon. She complimented Medak on his English.

"I studied in school and practiced with the Abbot and Brother Veilkov. Let me show you the icons in our monastery's church. Brother Veilkov is our expert, but he is on a retreat, so I am, as you Americans say, your guide."

Besides the Abbot, Brother Veilkov was the other monk she hoped could help her. What poor timing, with both monks out of town. Shouldn't they be at the monastery praying? She kicked herself again for not coming here years ago with her father. He had asked her often enough. Thinking about what might have been wouldn't help her now.

Following Medak along a flagstone path toward the entry to the church, her eyes rose to the stone arches towering above the doorway. She wondered how many carved stones it took to build the entry. The monks might live a simple life, but nothing was simple about the massive church, the centerpiece of the monastic complex. Huge from outside, but inside it was divided by gray stone pillars covered with religious figures. Compared to the sunny day, inside the church was cold and damp. More guards stood inside the entry to the church, adding to the dark mood.

Despite herself she asked, "Why all the policemen?"

"They aren't local police, but are UN forces guarding the monastery," said Medak.

With his answer, she could tell Medak knew what he was talking about.

"For centuries, this valley had a history of blood feuds among the population. Today it's a tinderbox populated by ethnic Turks, Orthodox Serbs and Catholic Croatians."

He spoke with an air of authority. Had he lived with the feuds or just studied the history? She didn't know and felt it was impolite to ask as she'd only known him a few minutes.

The policemen struck her as curious, and she wondered if that was how the monastery had escaped destruction over the centuries—being protected. The guards seemed calm, or maybe they were bored. She couldn't tell the difference. Each carried several weapons and the term "well-armed" described them.

Medak looked at the title of the book in her hand, *Icons of the Balkan Monasteries*, and launched into a discussion of icons and frescos.

"The paintings on stone surfaces are called frescoes. When the painting is on a wood board, it's called an icon. Both reflect religious scenes and are interchangeable. Your book is on icons, so we need to look for scenes and symbols painted on boards."

Amy looked at huge gray stone pillars covered with paintings; the walls were covered with icons hung on wooden slabs.

"Medak, why are there so many icons in the Balkans?"

"The history of the Balkans in the last century is one where hatred kills the innocents who are eager to be martyred. No matter who rules —the Turks, the Greeks, Communists—the message of icons never changes. Icons are a work of art showing the union between the painting and symbols. On a more practical level in past centuries, many of the people were illiterate. Icons are a picture and that helps them understand the Biblical message."

Amy thought his explanation interesting, realizing she was going to have to sift through a lot of information to find the Shroud.

"South of us, at every bend in the river, is a monastery. Most were built in the thirteenth and fourteenth centuries. Our monastery icons are said to be the finest of the fourteenth century. Due to good fortune or God's will, they were not destroyed, regardless of who ruled the country. I always think they remained untouched because the monks who painted them are unknown."

Seeing the icon on the church wall beside them, Amy saw one side was a portrait of the Virgin and child. On the other side was the crucifixion of Christ. The somber colors and gloomy atmosphere of the church did not appeal to her.

Medak was still talking.

"The icon is dark because the colors and lines are abstract. The message was important, and the light behind the painting shows a mystical depth that transcends time and space. The icon is different from western art, where color and nature are important."

Standing in the damp church, Amy thought about Medak's words. She realized if she ever hoped to find the Shroud among so many icons, she needed to be as honest as possible.

"My father was here before his death. He may have left something in this monastery for me. I have no idea where to look. I hope I don't sound nuts, but it's supposed to be the Shroud of Turin. The icon with the *Seven Angels* is my starting point, because my father mentioned it in a note he left with the book."

She opened the book and showed him the icon pictures. As he looked at the pages of icons, she asked the obvious question. "Did you ever meet my father?"

Medak told her that he saw Benton Prowers visit once or twice a year, and never understood why the American came. They drank coffee and wine and talked for hours. Neither Brother Veilkov nor the Abbot explained the visits. When the American left, Brother Veilkov was unusually silent in what was already a silent life.

"After one of the visits, I was curious. I asked Brother Veilkov how they knew each other. He told me they worked together in World

War II. Several years ago, another man from North Africa visited. They ranted about an el Ben Alemien. I remember because the name sounded like one of the famous battles in North Africa during the war. Then the man from Africa died, and they were sad. I never knew the connection. At the time, it just seemed like three old men reminiscing about the war."

Amy knew they were her father's wartime pals: Marfkis, whose tribe, the el Alemien, ruled most of the Sahara, and the monk, Veilkov.

"Maybe this could help you. The last time your father visited, he and Veilkov sat in the alcove with the two icons, *Christ in Glory* and the icon of the *Seven Angels*. They seemed transfixed. I suppose I'm trying to read things into whatever they did."

Amy felt discouraged. "I wish Veilkov was here, he might know exactly where my father hid the Shroud."

She was still troubled. Her father had never mentioned icons to her. Perhaps Medak had hit on the truth. Everything that happened here had to do with the war. *Could World War II be my starting point, not icons?* "The book also said tourists, and pilgrims came to see the popular icon of the *Seven Angels* and the icon of *Christ in Glory*, the two most famous icons at the monastery."

"They are both in the alcove at the far end of the church," said Medak.

As they walked past the stone pillars, Medak renewed his commentary. Amy thought the real message was in the silence of the monastery, but Medak's words helped her understand what her eyes were seeing.

"The symbol in the icon, a picture of Christ or the saints, is the icon concept of unity and universality. In the Hindu world, the Buddhist world, and the ancient Byzantine world, the temple is the sign of cosmology."

Amy looked up at an icon of a shadowed figure of a priest raising a chalice. Her icon book said each icon conveyed unconscious associations to show emotion. This was the mystical message, but to her they were just pictures of religious figures. If there was a message, it escaped her.

Looking at the icons, the silence of the chapel became a roar as she followed Medak down the church aisle. Maybe icons had a mystical side or was she feeling the spirits of the monastery across the centuries.

Instinctively, she glanced behind her, thinking in the movies someone was always watching from the choir loft. Not this time. She and Medak were alone in the corridor.

She noted the icons were painted on wood boards lining the walls, each with a different picture of a saint or of a scene from the life of Christ. Soft candlelight reflected against the walls, creating a haze of blues, greens and gold.

"*Well,* she thought, *At least the floor is still stone.*

Medak brought her back to today—or rather, to the fourteenth century.

"King Milutin built the church in the fourteenth century. He was the Serbian king and the church was part of his empire. In those days, icons were the center of Christian life, telling people stories of the saints."

Amy couldn't have cared less about King Milutin. "So many centuries and the walls remember them all."

Medak laughed at her sarcasm.

"History has been bloody here, because the country is always at war. Since old Yugoslavia broke up, fighting continues almost everywhere on some level. It is still not over. The UN soldiers you saw at the entrance saved the church but couldn't save the villagers' homes for any of the ethnic groups."

He paused, as if thinking about the war, and then pointed to the alcove.

"Here are the icons in your book, and where your father and Veilkov came to pray. The icons with the *Seven Angels* and *Christ in*

Glory are the most famous icons in our monastery. Both are original icons painted by unknown monks."

At last, thought Amy. *The right icons.*

Why had all the World War II buddies Veilkov, Marfkis, the North African, and her father, met here? Was it to reminisce? Some other reason drove him to visit. She doubted it was to pray, that was not part of her father's character.

She looked at Medak. "The Biblical quotes in the letter were specific to the icon of the *Seven Angels*."

Opening her book, she followed her father's note inside the cover, instructing her to go to page six. On the page was a picture of the icon of the *Seven Angels*. An angel was blowing a trumpet. She faced the icon.

What did her father want her to see?

Medak tried to help.

"The icon to the right, *Christ in Glory*, is considered by critics a masterpiece of Byzantine classical art. It's so special, Russian monks copied it for a cathedral in Moscow."

Amy turned to look at the icon with a dark image of Christ, his hand over his heart. At his feet were serpents, and in the background were angels. She turned back to the book and to the icon of the *Seven Angels*. An angel held a trumpet pointing skyward and a rainbow was over the head of another angel reading a scroll.

Unexpectedly, she noticed something odd, and bent over to see more clearly. Someone had taped a card to the wall below the icon. The writing was in Latin.

"Can you translate this?"

Medak bent over to look.

"It says that the fourth beast is the fourth kingdom. It is a quote from the book of Revelations that Veilkov put here after your father's last visit. I am not sure why he put this up, or why no one has removed it."

Amy looked at the icon in the book and then back at the wall. Opposite the page of the icon with the *Seven Angels* blowing trumpets was a picture of the icon of *Christ in Glory*. The two icons were on the wall of the monastery, just as they were in the book. Her father left her the book as a guide to his clues. She and Medak were missing something. They had the clues, but what was the message?

Staring at the wall, Amy noticed a rough spot as if something had been removed and took a step backward.

"Medak, is there an indentation on the base of the wall below the edge of the icon of the Seven Angels?

He dropped to his knees and ran his hand along the beveled edge of the niche.

"Could this be what you're looking for?"

His hand brushed the light dust off the baseboard revealing an address carved in the wood. How clever of Veilkov or Benton Prowers. Unless you were standing in front of the icon looking directly at the corner near the floor, you'd never notice the carved address.

"It's a street address; Eleven Stradum, Dubrovnik. I know that street. It goes through the main square, the Placa, in old Dubrovnik. The square is a World Heritage site with a monastery, a church, the oldest pharmacy in the world, and several other old buildings which I don't recall."

Amy opened her notebook and wrote the address down.

"My next stop," she said, with a confidence she didn't feel.

They walked down the corridor of the church, surrounded by hanging icons and painted frescos on the stone pillars. Amy hoped she was seeing them for the last time, but her intuition told her otherwise.

Outside the chapel, she heard birds singing and felt the hot sun reflecting off the mountain slope. Did time have no meaning? Her father and first husband would spend hours discussing the concept of time. At the time, she thought their discussions were trivial, but as she looked back at the monastery, she suddenly understood what they meant. What happened in the past, in that monastery, in those mountains? All of it had become a part of her life today and was behind the reason her father died.

"It's a pleasant time of the day for you to leave," said Medak. He whistled and a black nondescript dog appeared.

"If you'd like a walk, we can go back to the parking lot by another trail. The view is—how you Americans say, terrific—and the dog loves the walk."

The trail took them south to a view of rocky gray peaks and isolated mountain villages.

He pointed down the ridgeline to the river.

"See the wrecked bridge. It was blown up in World War II, and a train crashed in the river, destroying many art treasures. According to the villagers, the railroad cars were full of crates. No one knows exactly what was in them, but rumors were of paintings, gold, and jewels."

Amy looked up at the mountains, thinking of how her parents escaped from the Balkans on a train during World War II. For all she knew, they could have left on the train track in valley below.

The dog barked, bringing her back to today and the tree behind them exploded. She dived behind a tall pine tree with Medak right behind her, knowing it was gunfire. Peering around the tree, she could only see foliage.

And to think the world thought America was obsessed with guns.

Medak said, "It could be a hunter who doesn't know we are here. I'm going up the trail." Before he could move a tall blond man carrying a rifle appeared and came toward them on the path.

When the dog leaped out into the man's path, Medak said, "I know him; stay here." As he stepped around the tree, Amy wished she had a gun. As Medak continued speaking in rapid English sentences, she felt as if she had entered another era, like the Wild West. Her father always preached to *carry a gun*, and she could use one now.

She peeked around the tree, but Medak blocked her view of the man. She could see the rifle. It was an assault rifle not one used for hunting. Then the man was gone, disappearing into the trees as suddenly as he appeared. The dog growled and continued to look down the trail after him.

Medak turned to Amy, clearly concerned further puzzling Amy.

"The man says he's from Bulgaria, but I doubt he's a Bulgarian. His accent is odd, even though I have seen him around here. Claims he is hunting with a friend. Hunting is common for locals, but Bulgarians aren't common. He says he knows the Abbot and his brother, the General. I didn't want to worry you, but the Abbot said there could be trouble with strangers coming to our monastery. I think we should get to your car by another trail. He said the shot was an accident. But was it?"

It seemed an eternity as they walked until Amy saw the parking lot and her car sitting between two large blue and white travel buses.

Could security really exist in large numbers of tourists dressed in matching polyester pantsuits?

"Driving to Dubrovnik could be dangerous."

Amy sharply looked at him, because he sounded worried. Her eyes flashed as she felt the anger usually reserved for someone manipulating the family oil leases. She decided to reveal why she was on this quest.

"My father was an old man with not many more years to live. Someone killed him and I'm going to find out who did it and why. That is really why I am here."

For a monk, Medak looked agitated but continued knowing she need to be aware of the security issues.

"The road to Dubrovnik is guarded by UN troops, but rogue bandits roam the area."

He pulled out of his pocket a leather cord at the end of which hung a coin and handed it to Amy. Amy held the coin in her hand and looked carefully at it. Medak saw she was very curious.

"Brother Veilkov told me your father collected ancient coins for you. This is a so-called lucky coin that Veilkov gave me some years ago. He said it had special powers. The coin is old, from the era of Alexander the Great. When he conquered territories, he looted the countries' treasures, and minted coins in his image. No one can say if the coin was made during Alexander's reign or not. The Romans continued to make coins in his image long after his death in the third century BC."

Amy knew coins. To see what was unique about the coin, she'd need a research book and a magnifying glass, but she was polite.

At first glance the coin looked like the standard silver Greek drachmas used into the twentieth century before they were replaced by the euro. The unique coins had the same weight of silver, with a cow and a suckling calf on one side. The other side was more interesting, with a geometric design that many scholars believed represented the two stars Castor and Pollux, the twin sons of Zeus and the brothers of Helen of Troy.

"It is an elegant coin, a silver denarius, the Roman currency. My father had one of the coins made into a necklace for me."

She continued to look carefully at his coin. Roman and Greek heads looked the same, but the other side of the coin was different.

"This is the god Zeus seated on his throne, holding an eagle."

Medak was surprised. "You know the gods."

"When my father gave me the necklace, I looked up all the books on Roman and Greek coins I could find. There weren't many. This coin looks different, but I'm not sure how."

Medak pointed to a small letter on the coin.

"See the letter *M* under the throne. I have seen other coins with both Alexander's head and Zeus, but they don't have that letter. I wondered if that was why Veilkov called it lucky. I hope it protects you and brings you good luck."

Amy knew the coin was old but was less certain about the legacy of luck. Most artifacts carried either a tale of good fortune or a curse. To her, there was little difference. She thanked Medak, believing it would take more than a lucky coin to find the Shroud, if it did exist.

"I'll stay in touch." Amy waved goodbye.

"May peace bless your journey." Medak waved, feeling very little peace.

• • •

In Berlin, her aunt, Sonora Lleissle, was worried. She needed to find Amy. Wearing a black pant suit accentuated with a diamond bracelet and matching earrings, she strolled among the computers and tele-communications equipment in the office of her villa with the air of a commanding general.

She didn't have to know how the technology worked. Her staff plunked keys and got the information. Now she needed them to find Amy.

Her nephew, Ace, rolled his chair over to her with the printout of a map. A stranger would never have picked him to be part of the Prowers family. Tall like all the Prowers men, he weighed nearly three hundred pounds, none of which was muscle, and most was hanging around his waist. No one could recall why he was called Ace.

"She left the monastery and is likely heading to Dubrovnik with its international airlines. North to Zagreb, or east to Belgrade doesn't make sense. Dubrovnik is the jewel of the Adriatic Sea, so the guide-books say. My memories of the Balkans when Tito was alive are anything but guidebook copy. I doubt Amy is there for the scenery. It would be helpful if she replied to my texts."

Sonora let Ace's sarcasm pass. She figured he had earned it, after nearly having his leg shot off in some covert military operation, so secret no one could talk about it according to Benton. But now she needed more than a location.

"That part of the world could blow up any minute and she is right in the middle. Whatever she found in Benton's safe to make her fly off to the Balkans has to be important."

She paused. "I can't imagine what."

Ace didn't know how to reassure his aunt. The staff at the Colorado ranch said she cleaned out Benton's desk and left. What compelled her to take off for the Balkans? They were at a loss for ideas.

"She can shoot a gun, fly a plane, but likely will do neither. She likes to drive a fast car but that could be a problem on the mountain roads."

Sonora found little comfort in his analysis. "See if you can raise her on the satellite phone. When Benton was alive, the family had a rule; carry the phone whenever you left the country."

Sonora turned to look out the glass window at the gray sky over Berlin, which fit her mood. The weapon system in the southern Saharan desert was the real problem. She and Ace should be monitoring activity at El Kanitaoui and Geigner testing his ground-based laser, not worrying about Amy.

Going to Dubrovnik made no sense. It made even less sense that she would be running around alone.

Rarely did Lleissle think about her sister, Jarra, who disappeared decades ago in Southeast Asia. She wouldn't let that happen to Amy.

• • •

CHAPTER THREE

To Dubrovnik

She was uneasy.
This trip had gotten more complicated.

Clouds hung low over the gray limestone mountains as Amy drove to the Adriatic Sea and the port of Dubrovnik. Church towers rose in the gray mist, and the road twisted and turned through villages where markets were selling meat, vegetables, and pitchers of beer. Few people were on the cobblestone streets, but there were dozens of chickens and tethered goats. Before each village, armed UN officials stopped road traffic checking passports, though the official barely glanced at hers.

Amy checked the map. It was five kilometers to Dubrovnik and the President Hotel recommended by Medak. Mentally, she attempted to convert kilometers to miles, you divide by five and multiply by three. Or was it the reverse? Whatever, she was close, and the distance was less than five miles.

A road sign, in Cyrillic and English, said Dubrovnik, and she turned onto what appeared to be the main road to the city. Her eyes caught a flicker of blue in the rearview mirror. Was a car following her, or was she looking for trouble that wasn't there? She was uneasy, as her simple drive had gotten complicated.

The gray mist was lifting and through the haze, she could see the stone wall surrounding Dubrovnik. Beyond the wall, she caught a glimpse of the blue Adriatic Sea. For centuries, the city had been one of the most important trading centers in the Balkans. Today only the thick walls remained, carrying the scars of war. There were bombed-out buildings along the road, and she hoped Eleven Stradum was still standing. She recognized the cruise ships in the harbor, so something must be worth seeing in the city. Were the tourists looking at icons?

Iconology fit her view of medieval Europe, boring and filled with cities immortalizing the dead. She'd never understand how people could live in a town for hundreds of years and considered it an accomplishment.

She wondered what the key would open, perhaps a safe deposit box, that is if she could find the box.

• • •

Anton—who called himself the Bulgarian—gestured to the waitress and then to his empty coffee cup. Drinking coffee at the open-air cafe across from the President Hotel made for a dull afternoon. When he finished this cup, he would shift to a beer. Some days working for the General were just dull, and following Amy was definitely dull.

He enjoyed the surveillance in the mountains because he could shoot his rifle. Now, he was tired of the historic Placa, old-town Dubrovnik, and ready to move on. All Balkan countries looked alike to him, despite listening to the General's stories about his years here during the war. Dubrovnik, a crown jewel of the tourist industry, was to him a poor substitute for Mexican resorts.

The wind picked up and he pulled his jacket around him, though nothing could stop the dampness from seeping into his bones. He hated this weather and thought with longing about the young lady waiting for him in his room.

A car pulled up across the street to the entrance of the President Hotel. Amy Prowers stepped out. The General had told him she would show up. He paid the bill and walked a block down the street to his hotel, to enjoy what the General would call personal time. Amy, he knew, would order room service and stay in the hotel until dinnertime. She always did.

It was nearly dark when Anton awoke. He pushed the sheet aside, not wanting to wake up the young woman. He looked out at the skyline of Dubrovnik, feeling closer to the city lights of this strange city than the sleeping woman. It had been a pleasant afternoon, but now he had to follow Amy. She was an amateur and her lack of experience made his job easy.

On the skyway above him, he heard steps and saw a shadow move across the rooftops of the ancient city. Now it was gone.

He turned back to the room as the woman stirred. On the table stacked with American dollars, he added another large bill to the pile. She had been worth it.

• • •

Large wooden shields hung over the bar at the President Hotel. To Amy, they were reminders of the ghosts of dukes and duchesses from bygone years. She felt they were watching her. Even the musty odor in the air smelled like the past.

Then she remembered the man with the gun. Medak called him the Bulgarian, even though he said he didn't think he was from Bulgaria.

It didn't make sense. She had tried to see the man, but she couldn't through the trees. Why had he shot at them?

She felt the key in her pocket. According to the hotel clerk, the address was a bank, so the key could be to a deposit box at Eleven Stradum.

The bartender recommended the local drink, plum wine. "Some call it Rakia and others call it slivovitz. It's plum wine or brandy."

She sipped it slowly, at first thinking it tasted like cough syrup. But by the third sip she liked it and hoped it would help her sleep. She looked down at the small brown book she'd brought with her; *Icons of the Balkan Monasteries.*

Opening it, she flipped through the pages, looking at reprints of famous icons. The dark, heavy colors reflected what she saw in the faces of the Balkan people; direct, and penetrating.

According to the book, an icon reflected a sense of loss. In addition, its painter was never identified, nor the icon dated. She had to admit, the icon pictures had a timelessness that appealed to her. Being unknown allowed the icon painter's autonomy to express the deepest human emotions in their drawings.

She admired the artists for doing something on their own. Her whole life had been part of everyone else's, her father, her aunt, and her husband.

The bartender approached and looked at the book. "Are you here to see the Apparition?"

Amy hadn't heard of the Apparition. It sounded like something she probably wouldn't believe. Traveling taught her that everyone had a story to tell, so she asked.

"What's the Apparition?"

The bartender was eager to tell her.

"The sighting of the Virgin Mary at Medjugorje, a small-town east of Sarajevo where six children saw it, and all described the same face. The Apparition spoke to them, saying people must be obedient and faithful to pray for peace. The faithful must practice conversion, prayer, penance, and fasting—what seems today a medieval philosophy of repentance."

"When did this begin?"

"The children first saw her in 1981, and since then millions of pilgrims visited the shrine. It's a real economic boon to the village and will soon be as famous as other shrines like Lourdes and Fatima. Only the small wars keep pilgrims from visiting us ... bad for God, bad for business."

He smiled and moved to the other end of the bar to fill a drink. What he'd told her was amazing. No one could make this stuff up.

She remembered listening to her father talk about God's inability to intervene in the order of the universe. He thought miracles were just illusions. She agreed.

The singer crooned the strains of "I'll be Seeing You" in heavily accented English. Even the songs sounded musty.

She ordered another plum wine.

• • •

As she listened to the singing, an older man in a monk's robe approached and sat down next to her. She knew immediately it must be the Abbot, but the peace she saw in Medak's face was missing in his.

"Amy Prowers?" he asked, with a voice as strong as his square face.

"Yes, and you must be the Abbot."

"My train was delayed, so I came to find you. Medak said you were going to an address on Stradum Street looking for the Shroud of Turin. I'd go with you, but I have a speaking engagement at the iconology conference in Vienna."

He nodded at the bartender for a glass of plum wine. "These groups I speak to are the monastery's benefactors."

He looked so comfortable sitting in the bar. She remembered the General discussing his brother, the Abbot's work. His life in the monastery included travel to promote icons and raising funds. To her, he seemed much younger than the General.

He lifted his glass to her in a toast.

"Seeing you reminds me of your parents. Did you know I knew both during the war?"

She shook her head no. This was news to her.

"You look like your mother, are tall like your father, and fortunately, don't look like your cousins."

Amy had to smile. "I'm only tall if the year is 1880, or I'm an Asian. Otherwise, maybe I'm above average." She paused. This was no time for chitchat, so she came to the point.

"I need you to give me a crash course on icons. My father's last request was for me to find a certain icon. When he was alive, he talked about them, and I don't understand the connection, or why he wanted me here in Serbia. Can you give me a quick lesson, points to focus on? I recall you lecture at universities on icons."

She hesitated, then realized if she wanted to learn anything helpful from him, she had to be specific about what she knew.

"My father is using the icons in your monastery as clues to find the Shroud of Turin. Why the Shroud is so important, I don't know. I need your help."

At last she had come to the point. She hoped that told him she trusted him. She knew this was his avocation.

"I'll try to help you. When I lectured university students or the art groupies, many are in my class simply to be seen. I feel Amy, your motivation is different. Icons are a sociological imprint of the way people lived and viewed life in the Middle Ages. Through them, we see the evolution of social structure."

He was just getting warmed up. "Tradition holds that certain icons are sacred. The icon is a medium for those who pray. It translates divine power into something people can see in this world. Amy, look closely at the icon. The one that looks back at you is your spiritual twin."

Amy didn't like the art form, let alone believe an old painting was looking back at her. Yet she needed his help and couldn't tell him these dark, gloomy figures didn't appeal to her. She remembered her father's warning about whom to trust. Once again, she followed her instinct, believing the Abbot meant what he said. He was still talking, and she sipped her plum wine.

"When I was a young man, our family traveled to Italy and visited the Cathedral at Turin. There I saw the relic that changed my life, the Shroud of Turin, known among iconologists as the first icon. From that day, I dedicated my life to the church and to iconology. Sacred relics are supposed to have that effect on people, and for me that happened."

"You saw the Shroud?" exclaimed Amy, believing he was sincere. At the same time, she wondered where was the proof?

"Yes, and I remember to this day the portrait on the linen cloth. The face was full of suffering, yet there was peace, love, and forgiveness. Such harmony I knew was never created by human hands. For the first time, I saw peace in the world. That vision is the cornerstone of my faith. To deny the face of Christ is to deny he was a man and died on the cross. The Lord blessed me by a vocation in the monastic life where I could work in iconology."

He wanted to say, but didn't, without iconology he might have left the monastery at the end of the war. It was irrelevant to Amy why he stayed. He was a monk and committed to preserving the art form. To him, the two were the same.

"Scientific tests done in the early part of the twentieth century showed the Shroud couldn't have been produced by human hands or put on by paint or any of the techniques used in creating icons. When World War II began, the Catholic Church realized it had to be hidden from Nazis and Communists. The church leadership called our Abbot and entrusted our monastery to protect it. The former Abbot was an Italian, and I guess that was the connection."

He turned to Amy and apologetically shrugged. "I know the story may sound odd, but that's religious life."

Amy was silent but thought what the Abbot said was odd. It was the only word that seemed to describe not just what the Abbot said, but everything that had happened since her father died. Monks were silent, but the Abbot kept talking.

"When I became the Abbot, I didn't understand why Benton Prowers visited the monastery several times a year."

Amy smiled. "I don't know either. Please continue because I'm learning all the time."

"He and Veilkov were friends from the war. Your father knew Veilkov's work as a laser scientist in Vienna before being called to the monastic life. When your father was working on the excavation of the tomb in the Sahara Desert, he traveled in and out of North Africa to the monastery to see Veilkov. I thought he was consulting with him."

The glass of wine was empty, and he ordered another. Amy declined.

"One day your father and Veilkov told me how they had produced a fraudulent copy of the Shroud of Turin. As it turned out, they produced two copies and had the nerve to tell me how easy it was. I believed them, but always thought it had to be more difficult than they said."

He sipped his drink remembering.

"I was skeptical. Yet their story made sense in the context of that war, which was going badly for both the Nazis and the Communist partisans. Apparently, they drew a portrait on a piece of linen, poured gun powder on it, and ignited it. Sounds weird but the brown edges copied the outline. They ended up with two copies, one for practice and the one they called the copy. To protect the real Shroud from Communists and non-believers, the old Abbot sent instead a fake one to Turin planning to return the real one after the war. My brother, the General, knew the Shroud was in the monastery. The old Abbot gave it to him, to take out of Serbia with other artifacts. Why, we can only speculate. When the train carrying artifacts was blown up by partisans, everyone—even my brother—believed the Shroud was destroyed."

He paused to order more wine, and Amy began to really think the Shroud had to be hidden somewhere in the monastery, like a criminal hiding in plain sight. It was a mystery after the war, and it was a mystery today. *Did my father visit the monastery every year to pray to the hidden Shroud, thinking it had supernatural powers?* Maybe he did. Or was he asking Veilkovs' advice on lasers for Geigner's laser weapon in the desert?

The wine arrived and Amy brought him back to today.

"Medak said your book focused on the icon of the *Seven Angels*."

She looked at him, and opening the worn black leather knapsack, handed him the icon book, *Icons of the Balkan Monasteries*. He flipped the cover open, and began thumbing through it so quickly, Amy missed his hesitation inside the cover.

It was the wrong book.

The book Benton showed him once on a previous visit to the monastery had a soft-sided swastika inside. Called the Hakenkreuz, it was a symbol before it was identified with the Third Reich. The figure inside the cover was what distinguished one icon book from another. Benton could have switched the books, but if so, why? Then he realized the obvious.

The clues Benton left for his daughter to find the Shroud might have been misinterpreted. Where was the icon book Benton had shown him with the swastika inside the cover? That was the right book with the correct clues. The soft-sided swastika was the key. If only, he could remember the title? All the titles sounded the same, even to an expert.

"I'm sorry; I thought I recognized the title. Veilkov gave your father a book on icons and I borrowed it. It had a swastika, the soft-edged Hakenkreuz inside the cover. But there isn't a swastika in this book."

Amy was taken back. "My father's book had a swastika?"

He smiled, remembering the past, his mind on World War II, and gave the book back to her. "This swastika has a long history in many religions from Europe to the Middle East to the Far East. The original Hakenkreuz had soft sides making it look less harsh."

She realized she had to trust him; knowing that being a man of God didn't mean he was an honest broker to anyone outside the monastery. Now was the time to share the other clue her father left her. What mattered was finding the Shroud. So far, neither the Abbot nor Medak had been of much help.

"A key was also taped inside the cover of the book."

She handed him the irregularly shaped brass key. He had seen a key like this before, but where? He couldn't place it, yet it was so familiar.

"I should be more help, only it escapes me. It looks like a bank deposit box key."

"My father's icon book led me to icons in your monastery. Below one of the icons was an address in the old city of Dubrovnik, that of a bank according to Medak and the hotel clerk. Tomorrow I hope to find the safe-deposit box. Regardless of what's in it, I'm on the train to Berlin. My Aunt Sonora will never forgive me for being in Europe and not seeing her first. I'm sure the Shroud is hidden somewhere. My father didn't create these clues—and the symbolism—without a purpose. Of course, it would be nice if the real Shroud is in the bank box."

"I agree," said the Abbot, who changed the subject.

"My brother, the General, says you're a very good businesswoman. You make a lot of money."

She laughed. "He's made my family a lot of money and is a good teacher, especially on oil leases. With oil leases and tankers, everyday there is a new decision. My father however was only interested in finding the wells."

The Abbot looked at her, now feeling she'd manage with or without his help. Amy finished the glass of plum wine and looked like she was ready to leave, then stopped.

"Abbot, one thing my father didn't tell me was why the Shroud was so important. I understand it's a famous religious artifact; supposedly the burial cloth of Jesus Christ. Medak called it the first icon. None of that tells me why it is so important to anyone but the Catholic Church and other Christians. Can you tell me why?"

The Abbot was impressed. She had asked the right question and put her finger on the problem.

"Amy, do you know the history of North Africa?"

She shook her head no, wondering what Africa had to do with anything.

"North Africa is, to most people, tank battles in the Sahara Desert in World War II. Your father was a visionary who saw the problem with oil and Islam coming decades before the Arabs had the world's attention. Today the Coptic Christians, an ancient sect of Christians, are scattered throughout North Africa and the Middle East. Few realize the power they have in the entire region. In Egypt, they own the water along the Nile River Valley to Aswan.

"Today as in the past, water in the desert is worth more than gold. The Coptics own the land along the Nile and are a splinter group of educated professionals; doctors, lawyers, etc. They also control the agricultural industry in Egypt, and food is power. It is often overlooked that Mohammed instructed his converts to Islam to live in peace with the Christian population. It amazes me how that is forgotten today.

You see, el Ben as their leader with the Shroud, will unite the Coptics and his el Alemien tribe."

To Amy, what he said made sense. "My father was a friend of Marfkis, the former leader. He told me he was a dedicated humanitarian with a sense of history. When he died, everything changed. My father said if el Ben joined with the Coptics, he could rule like the prophet from the Atlantic Ocean to the Red Sea. Never, though, did he mention the Shroud."

"He was trying to protect you," said the Abbot. "The Shroud is the key to owning North Africa. After Marfkis died, your father did everything he could, including hiding the real Shroud, to prevent el Ben from his dream. He saw him as a totalitarian force controlling a significant part of the world's oil resources, but not for the good of humanity."

"Thank you. Now I see the importance. Sleep, however, is what I need. Jet lag has kicked in."

She said good night and the Abbot stayed, slowly sipping his wine.

Amy was bright and naive with little idea of what she was getting into. Did she realize what happened in Yugoslavia—to her parents, to Veilkov, to the General—during the last days of World War II?

In her smile, he saw the idealism and character of her father. Those were not qualities in her mother. Otherwise, her brown hair and light brown eyes were a copy of Hanna's. Did she have her mother's rigid commitment to finish what she started? Was she as cold-blooded? If the answer was yes, she'd find the Shroud.

He knew the Shroud survived the train crash because Benton and Veilkov gave him an extra copy of the Shroud. Copying the Shroud was harder than the two men thought, as the burnt image had to be just right. By accident, they'd made two, and asked him to hide the second fake. The other forged shroud was in the Cathedral in Turin, Italy.

Brother Veilkov had to know where the real one was, but so far had kept the secret to himself. Now, so many years had passed, he wasn't sure he'd ever find out where.

Looking into his glass of plum wine, he saw a reflection of his past. Who would have thought that today, Benton would burden his only child with the past? The past had caught up with Amy; now, after all the years, his own past had caught up with him.

In the beginning, it had been simple. He and his brother at the university became experts on iconology. Hitler learned about the General's work and directed him to oversee the restoration of the icons at Lambeck in Austria. As the war gathered strength, the General was in charge of collecting icons from all over Eastern Europe, a job that kept him from serving on the front lines.

Today, another leader desired to dominate the world, or so Benton Prowers had thought. To the Abbot they were all the same; el Ben or Hitler. It didn't matter. He sipped the plum wine and whispered, "I just want to enjoy the flavor of this evening."

The flavor was the continentals at the end of the bar, speaking quietly in French, of the small tables of Greeks, Turks, and the Dutchmen. He reveled in the feeling of being alive today, in an atmosphere that reeked of a bygone era, as he ordered another glass of plum wine.

• • •

CHAPTER FOUR

Clues

You have a key to one of our older boxes,
but they are not numbered very clearly.

Amy walked along the cobblestone streets through the Placa, the main square in the old city of Dubrovnik, wondering how many centuries the cobblestone streets had been here.

The morning mist slowly lifted above an array of church towers. Around her, sleepy shopkeepers opened their stores. Up and down the street, vendors were setting up stands filled with fresh vegetables, fish, and meat. On the corner was an open-air café packed with locals drinking coffee and smoking.

Last night's conversation with the Abbot was now in the past. She had to focus on what her father was trying to tell her and find the bank.

The owner of the café on the corner knew a little English and a lot of sign language. His arm pointed to the right and his hand held up two fingers.

"Two blocks down past the old pharmacy, and bank there."

She thanked him and headed in the direction his arm gestured. As she turned the corner, she saw a large gray stone building. It didn't take imagination to envision it was a bank. The address listed on the front of the building, fortunately in English was Eleven Stradum.

An olive-skinned man, unlocking the chain-link grate covering the front doorway, opened the door for her. She walked into the marble edifice and looked around, trying to find someone who spoke English. She had never considered using a minicomputer to produce instant electronic translations, but now she wished she had one.

The man who opened the door caught up with her. Any other time she would have been embarrassed to be treated as a tourist, but not today. She was relieved he spoke English.

"Miss, may I be of service? I am Sebastian."

Amy showed him the small key. He looked at it closely, and his face lit up as he recognized it.

"This type of key is for what we call closed boxes, ones no longer in use."

She followed him through a large steel gate and down a marble staircase to the floor below.

"Is this still the bank?" asked Amy. She was sure Sebastian was full of information. Surely having the key would show him she deserved a history of the bank.

"Yes, this is the old bank. Once it was a custom house and stored the country's archives. Now it's a bank again. For over two centuries, even with many uses for this building, the safe-deposit boxes remained. You have a key to one of our older boxes, but they are not numbered very clearly, ah."

The rows of boxes were wooden and went to the ceiling. He pulled out a flashlight to highlight the carved numbers. Amy wondered how safe the boxes were, and then realized the walls, floor, and ceiling were made of marble. How could she criticize safety if the vault had been in use for two hundred years?

"Ah, I think it is up there."

Amy looked up, about twenty feet to the top of the room. Sebastian pulled the wooden ladder to a row of boxes. She handed him the key, thinking the ladder wasn't strong enough to hold him. But, Sebastian, a fit young man, confidently climbed up.

Balancing on the wooden rungs, he took the bank's huge key ring, passing by several odd shaped keys and finally put one in the box. He took Amy's key, placed it without difficulty in the other slot and climbed down the ladder.

"It fits," he said, sounding surprised. "Please close the gate when you leave."

Slowly Amy climbed the ladder, focusing on each rung. At the top, she turned the key and pulled the box out and opened it, thankful it was light. The gleaming empty steel sides of the box stared back at her. A small envelope was in the bottom. She took the envelope out, put the box back in its slot, and carefully climbed down.

Sitting on a small stool in the vault, she opened the envelope. *Oh God, not another letter,* she thought.

Seeing her father's handwriting was no surprise. Forcing her eyes down the page, she saw the first word.

"Welcome."

The word *welcome* was generic to anyone and since he hadn't addressed it to her, apparently, he wasn't sure she would find it. She sighed in disgust. There was another Biblical reference; another clue. Then she realized his clues meant he wasn't sure she would be the one following them.

"The Book of Revelations says it so well. 'But in the days of the voice of the seventh angel when he shall begin to sound, the mystery of God

should be finished, —and said Go and take the little book which is open in the hand of the angel which standeth upon the sea and upon the earth'.

"*The end of the war was a relief but left me with an obsession. I felt the hand of God was upon me, in the form of the seventh angel. It must have come from Revelations, which I was reading. I believed the angel was meant for me. All these years, the responsibility for producing a false Shroud at the end of the war, never left me. I tried to ignore it by studying Mayan cultures where I saw myself as the Balamob, the guardian of the forest. Somewhere, the seductress is waiting beneath the Ceiba tree, daring men to their death.*

Amy looked up at the wooden boxes surrounding her. Why now, why here did he mention the Balamob and the Ceiba tree? She knew they were common Mayan references, but she was not sure how to interpret them.

"*The time clock of history rapidly unwinds and lately I felt the seventh angel calling me again. Not to prophesy, but to warn the world of those who do. I hope I have kept the trust. I have been fearful of the fourth beast from the Book of Daniel. When I read the chapters, I saw the fourth beast devouring the earth, trampling it down and crushing it. And as I've watched the politics in North Africa over the years, the angel's voice in my ear became more urgent.*

"*Now I've given the Shroud of Turin a real "SHIELD." Proverbs says, 'Keep your heart with all diligence, and remove thy foot from evil.' God willing, I have.*"

Amy took a deep breath. The seventh angel must refer to the icon of the *Seven Angels,* one of the icons in the icon book. The Biblical references bothered her; and why was the word "shield" in all capital letters?

Her father, an amateur archeologist specializing in Mayan culture, knew the word *shield* was associated with Mayan rulers. What did he know of the Bible? What was the connection with icons, Mayans, the Bible, and politics in North Africa? They had to connect. The problem was how.

Folding up the letter, she saw her father's handwriting on the back. She peered at the writing in the dim bank vault.

El Ben is a follower of Sun Tzu, the Chinese philosopher who said a weapon and symbol were needed for war. To el Ben, the weapon is at El Kanitaoui, and a symbol is the first icon. The next sentence was written in quotes: "*All men can see these tactics whereby I conquer, but what none can see is the strategy out of which victory is evolved.*"

What am I missing? My father might understand the Chinese quotation and its meaning to el Ben, but I don't. Geigner was supposedly searching for the pharaoh's tomb at El Kanitaoui, but he has built—or was close to building—a laser weapon.

There were too many symbols, angles to the search. The point had to be el Ben, with both the weapon in the desert, like Sun Tzu said, and a symbol, the Shroud.

She held the note tightly in her hand, as if the paper itself could tell her what her father meant. Like her mother, he had lived in his own world.

A gulf of loneliness spread over her as she realized she was lost in a world of puzzles created from his past.

• • •

Leaving the bank, Amy walked through the old city of Dubrovnik. The merchants actively hawking their wares added a dimension missing earlier in the morning. Steps headed up the stone wall that surrounded the city. The climb was long, but the view was worth it. Each corner of the wall had a tower or some type of fortification, making the city a fortress.

That morning, the hotel clerk told her five hundred years ago, Dubrovnik was a small city state, and bitter rivals with Venice. Today, he said, the city was a haven for tourists, who came to see beaches, mountains, and in summer months, the music festival. The limestone walls stayed gray-white, as sea breezes blow away the pollution. The medieval buildings remained, but the only power was the tourist dollar.

She looked out at the placid, almost flat Adriatic Sea, wondering how many times merchants of old stood in this same spot, watching and waiting for their ships. Dubrovnik had an aura of history that reeked of stories untold. Maybe there was something to being centuries old after all.

The clerk said the people never thought the glory days of Richard the Lionhearted and the Middle Ages would end. The city declined as a power on the Adriatic Sea, fitting Amy's belief that no government, no ruling class, lasts forever.

She believed individual lives created a pattern, a culture that became the basis of ancient civilizations. She had no faith in leaders; which she was sure she inherited from her grandfather, who, in 1920, founded the group called the Committee. Working behind the scenes, they used their wealth to influence world politics based on their personal political philosophy. They made millions during World War II and throughout the past decade.

Maybe there was a point to the Committee, now run by Sonora. Her aunt had tried for years to involve her in the group, saying it was her legacy. To her it was politics, power, and money. She had no interest in joining and had never understood the need for power that consumed the lives of the members of the Committee. She would not let it rule hers. The family business, the Prowers legacy, was her life. If she joined, could she change the direction of their policies? Did she *want* to change them?

Maybe, she thought.

Stone stairs curled around the side of the wall to the beach. She followed them down to the white sand glistening in the sun. From where she stood, the sea appeared to be higher than the shore. One minute the sea was calm, then the blue water turned into a rocky swirl of waves battering the shore. *People were like the sea*, she thought, *having an ability to change like chameleons.*

Behind her on the mountain, ancient houses were built one upon another and interspersed among them was a stone wall. A church sat on top of the cliff. She picked up a handful of sand and watched the grains fall through her fingers.

Something was not quite right. Her father rarely mentioned icons, or Yugoslavia, Serbia, the Balkans, whatever names were in vogue for this part of the world. True, he often made trips to the monastery to see Veilkov, which she thought was business for the Committee, because the monk was a member. Her father loved Mayan culture, its symbolism. So why did the clues direct her to icons? Why, before his death, had he wanted her to visit the monastery?

"You should come with me to the monastery. The Balkans have a history of their own."

Amy was not impressed. To her, they were little countries wrapped in religious feuds.

"Seriously, you have to be there to see and feel the different cultures."

"Dad, they had three hundred years of religious wars. What's to be seen?"

"Maybe only to see those wars are still being fought."

Belatedly, she realized he was still fighting his own war. She should have been eager to go with him, but there was always work. Now it was too late, and she had to interpret his clues on her own. She shivered, remembering the Bulgarian in the mountains and her father's death.

There was no telling what might be ahead of her. And what about the monk, Veilkov; where was he?

Her father left so many clues to deceive others, but I'm the one he deceived, she thought. The Mayan symbolism in his letter made sense because, for decades, Mayan culture was what he had researched. The term *shield, the guardians, the gift from the sun,* were words common in the Mayan culture. This symbolism didn't fit with icons. Her parents had been in this country over sixty years ago. Could something that happened then, have caused her father's death years later?

She wished Vince was alive. Her first husband always seemed to understand these abstractions. Vince got her father hooked on Mayan ruins. Then they started searching the world for remnants of lost civilizations. After Vince died, her father and his nephew, her cousin Geigner, started the excavation in the Saharan desert.

Looking down the long white beach, she agreed with the hotel desk clerk who told her the beach was romantic. She walked along the sand, untouched since the tide went out. The sun cast a red hue on the sky that broke the clouds apart and scattered the rays north and south along the horizon. The trails of the jets from Belgrade and Rome filled the sky leaving an orange streak.

Her eyes rose to the hotels and houses on the cliffs along the beach. She needed to get out of here and see her aunt Sonora and her cousins who always believed yesterday was being lived today. The search for the past was costly, with her father and Vince both dead under unusual circumstances. If she was right, perhaps her life was in danger. The realization didn't make her fearful, only more determined to find the truth.

In the east, low clouds were descending from the mountains to the beach. The last time she had walked on sand this white was in Mexico, visiting her father and a team of archaeologists excavating a Mayan ruin. She could still feel the sand between her toes.

She had become involved with one of the archaeologists. Since her third and last husband's death, he had been the only man in her life. Maybe when the windows of the past were closed and the Shroud found, she would find the time to rekindle their spark.

• • •

Anton handed the desk clerk an American hundred-dollar bill. *Why did they always want dollars?*

"She is leaving on the morning train to Berlin, transferring in Vienna. No airline flights, Italy is on strike."

Anton thanked him and went to find a phone. Phone connections were a problem, especially cell phones. The landlines in the back of the lobby worked best, and he got through to Mexico on the first try.

The General listened, saying little, and then issued new instructions, thinking how much trouble the Prowers family could be.

"Go to Berlin and delay Amy. She will be coming to Vera Cruz for the archaeology conference. Prowers was here before he died and could have hidden the Shroud. I still think it's at the monastery, but I will have my staff ask around to see if there is any gossip on it."

• • •

To Amy, the train stopped at the border to check passports for what seemed an extraordinarily long time. Sleep was not possible, even when the vibrating train stopped. She hadn't called Sonora, knowing how peeved her aunt would be when she told her she had gone to the Balkans without a phone call. Now she needed her aunt and cousin to hopefully shed light on her father's icon clues.

"*Where was the satellite phone?*" She knew that would be Sonora's first question.

How could she tell Sonora she just forgot it? She hated sounding disorganized. Sonora would say she could be kidnapped, but that was only if someone knew who she was. Amy looked at her clothes. She thought the beige nondescript jacket and pants, along with her non-designer knapsack, made her look like any other traveler. No one would think she had money.

Through the window, she watched passengers boarding the train. They pulled their gray and brown coats around themselves as the wind from the mountain pass blew through the station. To her, it seemed strange to be in a country that was still today fighting wars from the past.

She recalled something the General had said to her on a recent visit to Mexico. To him, the meaning of war depended on an individual's view of the world and some countries were always at war trying to carve out their destiny. Americans saw the world as black or white, when it was really gray.

She could hear his voice. "If your country had seen more shades of gray like Churchill, the world wouldn't be in its present mess. America would rule it all and life would be simpler." Looking out at a gray world, she thought that might be true.

The whistle blew. There was a last-minute rush of passengers and then the train slowly began moving toward Vienna. On the steep slope, the train billowed clouds of smoke created by diesel fuel past the windows and the cars vibrating on every tie. As it slowly moved up the mountain, she wished she had taken her chances with the airline strike.

The colors of the Adriatic progressed in shades of blue green to the horizon, where again the sea turned dark blue. She watched as the tracks began to wind along the coastal mountains. A stone bridge loomed ahead, crossing a rugged tree-lined ravine. The views slipped by, and she was reminded how the countryside along the railroad had developed.

Turning toward the aisle of the train, separated from her compartment by glass windows, she saw the Abbot walking slowly looking in each compartment.

What now, she thought, surprised as he opened the compartment door.

"I got on at the last stop out of the city. This is the only train to Berlin, and it connects through Vienna, so I knew I'd find you."

He took a gold cigarette case out of his coat pocket.

"Do you mind?" he asked.

"Feel free," replied Amy, waiting for the reason why he was on the train.

"Your aunt phoned, looking for you."

Amy shrugged. "I know, I should have called her before I left the States."

"She mentioned that and told me she and Ace are in Berlin for a meeting of the Committee. I canceled my trip to Vienna when I remembered something about the bank and the key. The deposit boxes at that bank go back to the eighteenth century. There's a new and an old section to the bank. Some of the boxes, particularly the ones in the older section, are built with a sliding bottom drawer. They are over a hundred years old and the key opens more than one box. Many years ago, I saw one of the keys, the same type you had in the bar."

He went on to explain that without a box number, they would have to try the key in all the old boxes. Amy realized she had to tell him about the letter in the deposit box. He might know the meaning of the symbolism.

She handed him the letter from the box at the bank and watched him read it rapidly.

"Your father has woven the text with many clues, but to me, the little brass key is still important. What he meant with the icon and shield references, well, we must go back to the bank in Dubrovnik. The key might open another box. I know that sounds crazy, but in the past century they did. We can change trains at the next stop."

Amy knew he was right. If he'd had a mobile phone, he could have called her, and she would never have left Dubrovnik. Seeing her aunt would just have to wait until she'd found out if the key opened another box.

• • •

If Sebastian was surprised, when he saw Amy and the Abbot coming in the front door of the bank, he didn't show it. Nor did he seem surprised when they asked to see the large vault with the safe deposit boxes again. As they walked to the staircase, Amy found the silence created by the marble floors and walls roaring louder than words.

Neither the Abbot nor Amy objected to Sebastian climbing up the ladder to retrieve the box. He brought down the box and Amy opened it. The drawer was empty. The Abbot ran his hand along the sleek sides and bottom. It was one piece; there was no false bottom. He turned to Sebastian.

"I seem to remember some of these boxes had false bottoms. Even more interesting is that if the key came from a churchman, it could open other boxes. Some church keys could be used in more than one box. My old Abbot told me the unique system limited the number of keys. Unfortunately, he is no longer with us and the old bankers are also dead."

Sebastian hesitated, but the Abbot was a clergyman who knew about the duplicate boxes. It was best to go along with him.

"Today the bank doesn't admit that was the practice. However, we have an older section of deposit boxes in the vault below. These boxes date back to the turn of the century. Only the nobility and churchmen had such boxes, and often a key could open more than one box."

Amy handed Sebastian her key. "We have all the time in the world."

Sebastian walked out of the vault, and opened a door leading to a narrow marble staircase. They descended to a floor below the main vault. Sebastian took the small key, glanced at its number and turned to a recess off the vault, leading to a smaller vault with stacked wooden boxes.

"It may not take that long. As the keys were returned, the duplicate boxes were removed. It is rare anyone opens one. If the key opens a second box, it should be in this room."

They were nearly to the last row before there was a fit. At first the key stuck, then it opened. Slowly the Abbot pulled out a brown leather bag and unzipped it. Even in the dim light of the vault, the jewels glistened. All three of them were silent for a moment.

Then Amy, in spite of herself, reached out to let the multicolored gems fall through her fingers. Clearly, the bag contained a fortune in emeralds, diamonds, rubies, and gold.

The Abbot reached into the bottom of the box and pushed. As he pressed on the bottom, there was a squeak, and the false bottom came out. Alone in the hidden compartment was a newspaper. Carefully, he opened the paper, and they stared at a diamond necklace framed in ruby chips.

The jewels were exotic. Then their attention turned to the newspaper. The date was June 1960. Amy knew that date. It was the year her mother died. While it was a relief not to find another letter, she realized they might never know who put the jewels in the box.

"I know this necklace," said the Abbot. "It is part of the crown jewels of the Italian monarchy and dates to the fourteenth century. Supposedly they were lost during the war. The Italian government officials came to our monastery with pictures, which is how I recognized them. The officials were trying to verify if the jewels were lost in the train crash. The find is historic, but I doubt that your father risked his life for jewels. Sebastian, you can turn these over to the proper authorities to establish ownership. Contact me at the monastery if there are any questions. I will keep the Prowers family apprised of the status."

Amy readily agreed. "My family doesn't want antiquities we don't legally own, but who could have put the jewels in the box?"

"I don't know," said the Abbot. "But Amy, we both know Benton didn't write a letter or leave clues for you to find jewelry."

• • •

The Abbot and Amy found a café and ordered strong black coffee. *No lattes,* he said, and Amy agreed, needing the real thing. She sipped slowly, waiting for him to explain what finding the jewels could mean. After spending some time with the Abbot, she understood that the mettle of this clergyman was like that of her father and mother, a mold that seemed to breed secrecy. Now she needed to hear the truth. The Abbot didn't disappoint her.

"I'm convinced the address carved at the base of the icon in the monastery was clearly meant to lead you to the vault in Dubrovnik, but it wasn't to find the Shroud. Benton kept the whereabouts of the Shroud a secret, because after Marfkis' death, he feared el Ben would find it. He understood world politics and believed that the next Great War would come if the Shroud was in the hands of the one, he called the fourth beast, el Ben Alemien. He hated el Ben and knew Ben wanted the Shroud more than anything. This was your father's greatest fear. Sun Tzu has a quote that says it all: '*All men can see these tactics whereby I conquer, but what none can see is the strategy out of which victory is evolved.*'

That was the quote her father had written on the back of the envelope from the letter in the vault. *How can everyone be living by that quote,* thought Amy.

After all the years and all the secrets, she had to be honest. Secrecy was getting her nowhere. Reaching into her bag for her father's letter from the vault, she remembered all the energy she had poured into trying to figure it out.

"My father wanted me to have this letter, so I think it is a clue to the Shroud. I've read it several times. When you read it, you may find something in it I have missed."

She handed him the envelope, wondering how many letters her father had written with clues. Turning to watch the thunderheads over the Adriatic Sea catch the last rays of sunshine, as she had on the plane, wondered what the next window of her life held. She was heading into the darkness—not of the night, but of the past. She learned from Vince that in ancient civilizations, signs were not necessarily the truth. Somewhere, in the darkness of the past, was the truth.

She watched the Abbot skim the letter until he reached the Biblical verse and read it out loud.

"'Then I saw another angel coming down from heaven, surrounded by a cloud, and a rainbow over his head: his face shone, and he held open in his hand a small scroll.'"

"This is your business, Abbot. What does the Biblical quotation mean?"

He thought a moment. "I'm not sure, but I believe it might be the clues in your father's letter confirming the Shroud was not destroyed and it isn't in the cathedral in Turin. Veilkov and your father could have hidden it at the monastery or in Mexico. I can only guess which one?"

"You think he may have taken it to Mexico, because of the Mayan references in his letter?" asked Amy.

"Yes." The Abbot was explicit. "He came to the monastery to move the Shroud to a safer place. He was heading to Mexico and could have taken it with him, where it would be far from the hands of el Ben. Your father called him the fourth beast. Now *that* is Biblical. We need to hope it wasn't with him when his plane crashed."

Amy was thinking of possibilities.

"I have to be in Mexico next week for a meeting. If he took it to Mexico, Jaime, our hacienda manager, will know where he went and might have hidden it."

"Before Mexico, you have to go and see your aunt. Sonora may know more about all of this than you think."

He paused. "You realize Sun Tzu's quote is important. '*All men can see these tactics whereby I conquer, but what none can see is the strategy out of which victory is evolved.*' That's what it is all about, Amy, tactics and strategy."

Amy was sick of the quote. "How do you tell which is which?" But the Abbot was right. She had to see her aunt and try to explain why she didn't call before she left the States. *Relatives*, she thought, even though she knew Sonora had her best interest at heart.

• • •

CHAPTER FIVE

At el Kanitaoui -
an oasis in the Saharan Desert

Veilkov wanted to make this trip since the excavation began.

"Green one, online, red one, online, ready, fire green, ready, fire red."

Geigner watched the simulation program on the computer screen as the laser beam fired at the line of decoys dropped by the helicopter. He typed in a series of commands on the keyboard. The screen showed the beam as it destroyed the decoys.

El Ben's sons broke into laughter as a toy plane and a pilot doffing his hat filled the screen. To them, the weapon worked like a video game. Harold Geigner knew otherwise. In the real world, the program to aim the beam needed to be verified.

Did he regret his creation? Yes—the regrets came after his uncle, Benton Prowers, and the leader's oldest son, Marfkis, died. He realized the laser weapon in el Ben's hands wouldn't be used to advance science, but for personal gain.

El Habid, the leader's favorite son, brought him back to today.

"My father will be pleased with your work. He will congratulate you when you see him in Tripoli. Awesome describes the weapon system. It is the will of Allah. He brought you here to search for the tomb of Akhenaten and our linage to the Egyptian pharaohs. What you found was unexpected but it's better—a laser weapon to rule the world. *Allah Akhaba*, God is good."

But one man at the console didn't repeat the praise to Allah. Harold Geigner was silent, his mind searching for a way out of the nightmare he had created.

• • •

Jets with airline logos Geigner didn't know existed were parked everywhere on the tarmac at Tripoli International Airport. The names on the side of the planes were from Eastern Europe and small African countries. Tourists came for the climate, white sand, and sky-blue water, and the government catered to them with cheaper beach vacations than other Mediterranean resorts, making North Africa the motel mecca of the Mediterranean.

Geigner wasn't on vacation. He had to ask el Ben for a favor and conceal his real motive from the leader. He spotted El Habid, who stood a foot taller than other locals. His robes billowed as he bowed to greet Geigner.

"*Salaam alaikum.*"

"*Walaikum assalam,*" responded Geigner.

"Tomorrow we see my father at his desert retreat. Tonight, I have arranged special entertainment at Café La Rouge, your favorite place, yes?"

"It is." Geigner smiled. "Serves the finest cuisine in North Africa. Some think it's French, but no one cares as it is the best food."

Not to mention, thought Geigner, *the extra courses which included some of the most uninhibited women in the world.* El Ben, who followed the teaching of the Prophet, allowed western culture in his cafes. The economy trumped religious beliefs. Hypocrisy, Benton had called it, but they both knew the cabarets provided a source of revenue in dollars and euros needed to fuel the government's grand plans for building an empire.

"*Shokran.*"

"*Inshallah*, Geigner, God willing."

• • •

Geigner lost track of the courses served during the evening meal. They finished eating and coffee was served as the dancing began.

Geigner watched the shimmering motion of the belly dancer with little interest. Belly dancers had to be physically fit, never out of shape, and he admired their bodies, but tonight something seemed wrong. The capital hadn't changed in the three years since Marfkis died. He missed his friend, who had been like a brother.

The whining wail of the flutes and goatskin drum stopped abruptly. The dark-skinned girl lifted her head from the floor and bowed. The dance floor spotlight was turned off and the cafe resumed its bustle. Customers ordered more drinks and waited for the next dancer. Some started smoking a hookah, as it was often called, or a hubbly-bubbly.

To Geigner, the flavored water pipes had more names than the wind. The true question was what was being smoked; flavored tobacco, the shisha, or something stronger. He didn't know or care to experiment.

"More coffee?" asked el Habid.

Geigner shook his head. "I'll go back to the hotel. It's been a long day." He didn't say he had a stop to make.

El Habid started to rise, to accompany him to the hotel.

"Please stay. I can find my way back. Enjoy the night."

El Habid smiled, pleased to stay.

"As you wish."

Geigner left the crowded café and turned down a darkened street, heading toward the hotel. During the day, the street was part of a bustling Kasbah—a market—but now seemed to be swallowed by the desert night. Rounding the corner, lights from the booming business in the cafés reflected off the stucco walls onto the street. A taxi moved slowly down the narrow street. The driver, smoking a cigarette, leaned out the window. Geigner motioned him over, reaching into his pocket for the address of the *maqbara*, the graveyard where Marfkis was buried. The hotel clerk had written it in both French and Arabic.

A few minutes later, the taxi stopped at the edge of the city on the graveled plains of the desert. Geigner climbed out of the cab, paid the driver, and looked around. In the darkened sky, he still could see the top of the mosque next to his hotel. The taxi pulled away with gears grinding, leaving him with the silence of the desert night. He walked between the broken stone walls forming the entrance.

Muslim cemeteries didn't have head stones, just mounds of dirt. Any lump could be Marfkis' grave. He walked on the dirt path between the lumps and spotted a marker in the center of the graveyard. In Arabic and French, he saw Marfkis' name engraved on a cement memorial with a bronze plaque dated the day he died. The plaque must have been erected because of the affection his countrymen felt for Marfkis. Still, Geigner found it strange there was such a marker, unusual in a Muslim country.

I know, he thought, *how much you hate to be here.*

Marfkis would rather have had his ashes scattered across the desert, but his brother, el Ben, must have put up the marker. Geigner knew the reason; El Ben needed the tribes to remember Marfkis' because he couldn't match his popularity.

He looked again at the marker to examine it but stopped. A man was walking toward him from the archway over the entrance to the cemetery.

"Mr. Geigner, el Habid sent me. You are in danger and you must get back to your hotel. Ossery's men looking for you. We can protect you at hotel, but not on the open road."

Geigner knew Ossery was el Ben's advisor on the stars. In another country, he would be an astrologer, but Islam didn't allow soothsayers by any name. Only el Ben could rationalize the teachings of Islam with astrology.

"El Ben say if you get to his desert camp, it is Allah's will. Ossery say stars say you bad for el Ben. Advised him to terminate you. Ossery's men looking for you."

As they hurried out of the cemetery and into the narrow street, the headlights of a car came down the side street, moving slowly toward the mosque.

"I have gun," said the man.

Geigner shook his head. "I won't need it. Give me a lift to the top of this wall. I'll get back to the hotel on the rooftops. Coming?"

The man smiled.

"You are infidel. I am holy man. I'm visiting the mosque. Ossery has no reason not to believe me."

He leaned over, and Geigner stepped up on his shoulders, pulling himself to the top of the wall. Dropping to the path below, he was glad he'd stayed in good physical condition. When he was nearly across from the hotel, he climbed back on top of the wall and looked down on the street, thinking Ossery's men had to be at the hotel entrance.

A car was below him, across from the hotel. Three men were walking away at the end of the street.

Geigner climbed down the arch of another doorway to the empty dirt street below, and quickly crossed to the hotel entrance. The desk clerk looked relieved to see him.

"Can you call el Habid?" he asked.

"Yes, go to the room and wait, safe now."

"*Shokran.*" Still, Geigner wasn't confident in the claim of safety.

• • •

El Habid turned on his side so the girl's fingers could massage oil into his back muscles. Slowly he raised one arm and stood up, confident in his body, and reached out for the woman, who had disappeared in the shadows. He walked to the curtain and pulled it aside. The exotic, olive-skinned woman was standing on a white marble slab beside a pool of pure blue water.

She said nothing and dropped her wrap, silhouetted against the pool. He thought no one was born with these looks. Had cosmetic surgery reached the Arab world? He reached with one hand for the bottle of chilled champagne and slid the other across her breasts, down her buttocks and thighs. She took the champagne from him, and casually poured it into glasses. She emptied the rest of the bottle in the pool and pressed her body against his. Silently, he thanked Geigner for letting him stay in the Kasbah.

There was a knock on the door. He pulled himself away from the girl and opened it to see his men.

"It's Ossery. He wants Geigner dead."

"No surprise," said el Habid, not sure why the American was a threat. But then, Ossery was a crazy man. If only he could make his father understand.

• • •

Geigner was awake. He blamed the *qahwa*, the Arabic coffee, not the threat from Ossery. The hotel was an armed camp, filled with el Habid's men. He needed fresh air and stepped on to the patio of his hotel room. Below him the souk was preparing for another day.

Looking over the city, he heard the silence. It haunted him at sunset when the mosques called the faithful to evening prayer. He felt part of the history of the desert. Benton told him how this desert culture formed Marfkis' character. His uncle recounted stories about World War II and the cafes of Rome where he and Marfkis thought Mussolini and his inept government were a joke. Both despised Hitler and pondered what an alliance with Germany would mean to the Italian people. Marfkis, he said, always liked Americans. Real people, he said.

Today, Marfkis' name was revered in North Africa, especially in Egypt, where the leaders of the Muslim Brotherhood respected his memory as one of them. Geigner knew that when his friend was alive, he spent every day wooing some tribal group. Marfkis was charismatic. People came to him as he was one with them. El Ben didn't have the magic of his brother. He used his brother's name to make his own dream of ruling from the Atlantic Ocean to the Red Sea a reality.

El Ben respected Benton's advice, and Khadafy, the dictator of the country, trusted el Ben. Over the years, when a political decision was needed, Marfkis asked for advice and now, so did el Ben. Now they looked to him. *I show respect to el Ben, but I don't really know where his head is.*

Geigner walked across the ceramic tile to the edge of the patio. The curling edges on the roofs of the mosques reached skyward. The sound of music and voices told him the cafés were closing for the night. He tipped his head back and looked up at the sky, filled with stars.

How long did anyone have in this life? It didn't matter; he was living out his destiny. Were Marfkis and Benton somewhere in that eternal darkness?

"You preserve in the night," was what Benton would say.

As the sand cooled, a light breeze blew in from the desert. Blowing across the roof tops, it seemed to grow stronger. Everyone who lived in the desert understood the nomadic nature of sand. The wind cleared everything in its path, making every day a new day. Uncle Benton always said that travelers arrive at the desert and there found life.

His first discovery was the ruins; the second, building the laser beam; and finally, designing the computer program. The next step was critical. Without his computer program to direct the beam there was no weapon. Now he needed Veilkov to visit El Kanitaoui to confirm the accuracy of the calculation that guided the program. If it worked, the land-based laser could be built by anyone.

The evening wind was picking up and he hoped it would blow the past out of his mind. For now, he had to concentrate on his meeting tomorrow.

· · ·

Seated in front of the tent, Geigner looked at the silver *tassa*, the cup full of goat milk. He sipped it slowly, so as not to choke. The taste was sour, but it was a show of respect to drink it. Arabic coffee, his favorite, came next. He leaned back against the cushions on the flowered Oriental carpet, trying to concentrate, not only on what el Ben said, but what he didn't say.

El Ben lifted his arms. A slight breeze caught his blue and white thobe, the desert robe, billowing like a canopy. Only his closely cropped black hair didn't move, nor did the single gold, banana-shaped earring hanging from one ear. What it symbolized, Geigner had no idea.

The leader began to speak in English. Geigner wondered how many of the tribal leaders sharing the coffee understood English. He knew the words meant little; it was the performance by the leader that was important.

Despite the aging lines in el Ben's face, it was the face of a young man. Geigner wondered if a youthful appearance was what true faith provided. He watched El Ben looking at him wondering if he was still confused about who he was or what he believed.

El Ben begin to speak. "The weapon you have built is our fortune when the oil is gone. I praise Allah for sending you to our country."

He raised his hands to heaven.

"It is said by the Anglo world that all the world fears time, but time fears the pyramids. An Arab proverb? No, it is an infidel's definition of the Arab proverb. The pyramids were never meant to be worshipped. They are large stones, overdone, but a graveyard. The real force in North Africa is the Prophet Mohammed, peace be upon him.

"It has long been my dream, and I believe my destiny, to rule the empire of Islam that existed from the west coast of Africa to the Red Sea. It is the will of Allah. You see, Geigner, time fears the pyramids, but history fears me. I need both the weapon and a symbol to realize my dream."

As he listened to el Ben, Geigner wondered how he planned to depose of Khadafy. He reached for the pot to pour another cup. This could be a long day. The smoking pipes were sitting alongside each person. El Habid picked one up. Geigner shook his head no. The coffee would be enough stimulus to deal with el Ben, or rather, to show he was listening.

"My brother Marfkis shared this vision. Geigner, you and your uncle built the weapon at El Kanitaoui, but the Shroud of Turin is needed to fulfill the prophecy and rule as Mohammed did. It is the symbol. When I present the Shroud to the head of the Coptic Church, I will have the political and financial support to rule North Africa.

"How do I know it is not in the cathedral at Turin? Marfkis told me how he, Benton, and Veilkov faked the Shroud. When I first heard the story, I remember saying it is better to rule in hell than serve in heaven. I thought it fit the picture of so-called Christians, faking the burial cloth of Christ. The plight of Christianity is its own hypocrisy."

El Ben stopped in mid-breath as a cloud of dust appeared across the desert sky. "My friend, you will have to wait a moment to continue our discussion."

Relieved to have a reprieve from the lecture, Geigner thought the cloud could be an SUV. Then as the dusty haze receded, he saw half a dozen tribesmen on camels. Their bright blue robes and turbans identified them as Tuaregs, the blue men of the desert. His host rose, and with a wave of his hand, indicated Geigner should wait. The Tuareg were allied with the Alemien family and he would not insult them by making them wait.

To Geigner, the men looked small until he realized these camels were some of the largest, he had ever seen. No wonder they could cross the desert. Without the discovery of oil, el Ben and his tribe would still be nomadic camel and goat herders, traveling from oasis to oasis, generation after generation roaming the desert. Today his tribe's land crossed three countries; Tunisia, Libya, and Egypt. They controlled the desert by controlling the oasis's water and allowing all the desert tribes to use the water. Marfkis once said the oasis was where he and his brother learned what ran the world—power. Oil and water brought them power, but the tribes remained.

The culture of tribal discussions was never quick. Geigner poured more coffee. From his pocket, he took out the coin Marfkis gave him so many years ago. It was always with him. Marfkis said it was one of three lucky coins. Benton and Veilkov had the other two. Benton and Marfkis were dead. He knew Benton had given his coin to the General in an oil deal. He had no idea where Veilkov's coin was.

Desert nights lead to talk and one-night Benton told him the story of the old man. In the mountains north of Belgrade at the closing days of the war, the old farmer claimed the coins possessed mystical powers. Geigner remembered being surprised Benton believed the old man. Benton, unlike Veilkov, never believed the Shroud of Turin had any mystical powers but played along because so many others believed. He could hear Benton's words.

"I told Veilkov, Marfkis, these coins are from the Roman period when Christ lived. We each have one."

Benton told him a few months later he was waiting on a train platform, flipping the coin. A gypsy selling flowers at the station watched him. Suddenly the woman became frantic, grabbed Benton's arm and tried to speak to him. Benton had the stationmaster translate the dialect. Geigner could hear Benton's voice when he told the story.

"The old woman says your coin is from the gods. Bring fortune and long life to those who bear them. Says she see many times in her dreams."

Benton said he looked carefully at the coin, asking the old woman whose face was on it. She replied, "Pontius Pilate."

He said it was more likely the face was a little-known Roman general and remarked that they all looked the same. Benton claimed he later found out the face on the coin was Alexander the Great, a Greek. Whatever the country the coin was from, Benton asked if Geigner believed in stories of luck. Geigner said he wasn't a believer but kept the coin because Marfkis had given it to him as a gift. Still, he wondered if Marfkis and Benton would still be alive if they'd kept their coins.

Who cares today, thought Geigner. The Shroud was far more important. Benton had told him the three comrades made a replica of the Shroud during World War II. A religious zealot, Veilkov was sure the Nazis or Communists would destroy the Shroud, so Benton and Marfkis agreed to help their friend create a counterfeit Shroud.

Over the years, while drinking coffee over campfires, the Shroud stories continued. One-night Marfkis told him why the Shroud was important to his family, and to their dream of uniting all the North African Muslim countries under one leader. He also told him neither he nor his brother, el Ben, wanted to rule, just control—like the water from the oasis. It was then Marfkis gave Geigner his coin, saying Muslims didn't believe in symbols.

Geigner thought the so-called power of the coins was like the Shroud. They were symbols of perceived powers.

The flaps of the tent billowed in the wind. The desert was heating up in the midday sun, and he wished he was in the tent. Then as suddenly as they came, the visitors mounted their camels and headed out over the desert.

El Ben must have read his mind as he and his tribesmen returned to the tent to avoid the heat. They sat down on the woven carpet in the tent. Huge fans made the desert heat comfortable. As they drank coffee, el Ben finally came to the point of the visit.

"We followers of the Prophet Mohammed, peace be upon him, do not worship idols. The Shroud of Turin is an invention of the Christian world, but it's necessary to rebuild the Prophet's dream. With it, I will cement the alliance with the Coptic Christians of Egypt."

He looked at Geigner. "You are not working for the General on this one, are you?"

Geigner shook his head. "If I was, I wouldn't be here."

"What about Sonora and her Committee? I know the General is not fond of that group."

"I have nothing to do with my aunt's Committee. May distrust it as much as the General does."

El Ben knew that was true. No one liked Sonora's Committee made up of pompous do business who under the pretense of doing good, made fortunes for themselves. His gaze turned to Geigner. "Do you know what makes the Shroud and the alliance with the Coptic Christians so important?"

He answered his own question.

"Most people have heard of the Red Monastery, the Coptic monastery on the Nile River. They don't realize the Coptic Christians go back to the first Christian Church founded by the apostle Mark. The Coptic remains while Egypt's leaders come and go. When regimes end, we have opportunities to take over the government. We don't need to hold a position in the government, we only need the power to control those who rule. Power lies in land, money, and symbols.

He paused long enough for Geigner to speak.

"I understand why the Coptics are important. But why the Shroud of Turin?"

"It is hard to see, I agree," said el Ben. "To the Coptic, an ancient Christian sect, the Shroud is like finding the face of Christ."

He shrugged. "Who really knows? It's a symbol of what might be."

"So, we are dealing with a symbol?" asked Geigner, still a little confused as to what the Shroud was.

El Ben poured more coffee.

"It is a symbol, my American friend. We need symbols for unity. Otherwise the people of North Africa are nomadic tribes, wandering in the desert. Without structure, we will have revolutions, bloody ones. Many people on both sides will die. There will be no rule of law. Bandits and thieves will rule."

"The Coptic religion was practiced during the time of the Prophet; peace be upon him. He protected them. My family has done business with the Coptics for centuries as they control the commercial wealth, shipping out of Alexandria the agricultural products from the Nile River. To Christians, the Shroud of Turin is more than a symbol. They revere it. They believe it changes lives. Does it?"

"So…" said Geigner, "It doesn't matter if the Shroud is real or not."

"I agree, but we are unbelievers. The Coptic leaders will give their people repentance from the past and hope for a new future. It is the mysticism of the Shroud. No other symbol can compete with that. It's helpful if it is real. The Coptic will do carbon dating. My gesture will fail if it's false, and there will be bloodshed."

Geigner did understand. He could see how a symbol could be a power to unite the religions and Bedouin tribes of North Africa. *And,* he thought, *the weapon I have created gives him the power.*

None of this pleased Geigner, but he held his emotions in check. El Ben continued his monologue, or a speech for the tribal leaders. He again wondered how many spoke English.

It didn't matter; his audience appeared to be riveted to his words, even if they didn't understand English.

"The justice of the Prophet was on Marfkis. When he died in the desert, it was the will of the Prophet, peace be on him, for me to lead our people to the dream of conquest."

Geigner agreed with what el Ben said, but his intuition told him el Ben had more to do with Marfkis' death in a hunting accident in the desert than Allah. He focused on el Ben's words.

"I must tell you what few know. I am not, as you think, self-promoting. Our family's roots go deep in this shifting desert sand. My grandfather and his father, along with others in 1928 formed the Society of Muslim Brothers, today called the Brotherhood."

He spoke the Arabic words for the Brotherhood, Hizb al-Ikhwan al-Muslim, and then, Al-Ikhwan. Switching to English, he quoted the motto of the Brotherhood: 'Allah is our objective, the Prophet is our leader. The Qur'an is our law. Jihad is our way. Dying in the way of Allah is our highest hope.'

Geigner sipped his coffee and thought about el Ben's analysis of the Brotherhood and the el Alemien family. Some four thousand brothers left the North African countries, but not the Alemien family. They stayed and formed a bond with the Coptic Church. Other

Brotherhood members missed this opportunity. When members of the Brotherhood assassinated President Sadat in 1981, the group was banned. Today members had seats in Parliament, as well as professional organizations funded by the el Alemien family.

Geigner knew the history was important and understood why the Coptics were important.

"Geigner, the ideas of the Brotherhood were the force that shaped Islamic beliefs for the past decades. Many of the brothers cooperated with the Nazis in World War II and that's why the Brotherhood is so strong in Germany today."

Taking his lighter out, Geigner slowly lit a small cigar, wondering if this was why Benton had believed in the Brotherhood. His uncle and grandfather knew the Brotherhood's leaders in Egypt. If Benton had those contacts, so did Sonora. Both were against the extremism of the organization but believed the Brotherhood should be part of mainstream politics in Egypt. That was the Prowers' clan solution to extremists; bring them into the fold. He was a Prowers, but his beliefs were different. To him, extremists had to be eliminated.

El Ben was still talking. "One Chinese general said it so well. You need a symbol and the—how you say, clout. Geigner, the clout is what you have developed at El Kanitaoui. But I still need the symbol. The symbol will tie the Coptic to me and no one in the Brotherhood will be able to stop me. I need your help to find the Shroud of Turin."

Geigner agreed immediately, almost without thinking. He saw his opportunity because of the older man's obsession with the Shroud.

"With my uncle dead, there is one man who may know where the Shroud is; Veilkov the monk. Let him visit me at El Kanitaoui. By allowing him into the country to revisit the desert he had first seen in his youth, I might convince him to tell me where he and my uncle hid the Shroud."

Geigner stopped before he said the obvious; if the Shroud existed. He still thought there was a good chance it had vaporized in the train crash. Neither Veilkov, nor his uncle, were above acting as if it was still around, just to create confusion.

El Ben understood more than Geigner realized. "Never did I think your uncle's death was an accident. So, let the monk visit." El Ben smiled. "Let him lead us to the Shroud."

Geigner took a moment to sip coffee. No one felt right about Benton's sudden death, though there were no facts to show it wasn't an accident.

"Maybe the djinns, the spirits of the desert, killed Benton, but no one knows. El Ben, you're right. Veilkov may be our last best source to find the Shroud."

The leader looked a moment at Geigner; they understood each other. He turned to his son el Habid and instructed him to plan for the monk to visit the ruins.

"You and el Habid go back to the city. Ossery has said best for me not to fly so I think the same for you. This evening will be pleasant. The desert in the twilight shows a new life."

With a gesture, he waved away the servants, who disappeared into the folds of the tent. This time, el Habid motioned Geigner to follow him. Geigner looked back at el Ben, sitting alone amidst the pillows on the Oriental carpets. It was prayer time in the light of a fading desert sunset.

Geigner looked out across the flat graveled desert surrounding the sandy oasis, perfect for tanks in the battles for North Africa in World War II. Today, how many remembered the lives lost on all sides in the war? The revolutionaries looking for regime change had no memories. Had any of the regimes in the past decades thought about World War II? He doubted they had. So much blood was shed and for what?

El Habid, pretending to look at the desert, was watching Geigner stare at the surrounding plains. Why, he had no idea. Here at the camp-site, the soft tan-colored sand mixed with the gray hard dirt of the desert. One was important for beauty, the other allowed his father to bring in every modern convenience to the desert tent; most importantly, fans to cool the air.

His love of the desert was natural for a Bedouin. It was in his DNA. There was no reason for the American to stare over the sand. There were scorpions, which he thought was natural, the small desert gazelle, and always the jerboa or desert rat, the Anglo words. On rocky ridges, camel trails could still be found. All that remained from World War II was an occasional Jeep buried in the sand or unexploded bombs. None of this was important now.

El Habid needed to shake Geigner from his reverie.

"Sheikh Ahmed Ossery is not fond of you. He tells el Ben you have no faith in Allah. And worse for you, a short aura. You will not be around to see the end of—how you say—the ball game. Ossery say same thing about Khadafy. His time is short."

"Habid," said Geigner, "I should have died years ago in Vietnam. My time has been borrowed from the universe since then. You can tell that to Ossery. Now tell me your part in this era of revolution."

El Habid grinned.

"You know well. One day my time will come. Your right about Ossery this time. El Ben pay him no attention. He say he need your help. Ossery finally agree. He check auras this morning and tell el Ben yes. You be better for el Ben to do business instead for old German. My father trusts you."

What trust, thought Geigner. Neither el Habid nor his father knew that at El Kanitaoui, Veilkov could confirm his calculation on aiming the laser beam. That was the purpose of his visit.

As they headed to the waiting SUVs, Geigner looked at the sand to the east of the oasis. It wasn't smooth any longer but had blown into small mounds. *How strange,* he thought, and started toward the mounds to get a closer view. He couldn't believe what he was seeing.

Suddenly, an arm reached out and stopped him.

El Habid spoke. "There is no reason to go closer."

Geigner turned away willingly. He was close enough to see piles of human skulls bleached in the sun and stacked about a foot high. Were they enemies of the state, or part of el Ben's religious rites? Whatever— it didn't matter to him. In his mind, he was already thinking about where his uncle could have hidden the Shroud.

We spent so much time together, I should have asked, he thought.

The answer to him was simple. Benton wanted Amy to go to the monastery because Veilkov knew where to find the relic.

That is it. Veilkov knows where the Shroud is hidden.

Regardless of where the Shroud was, his responsibility was to verify the calculations with Veilkov and run a new test. He would call the Abbot to set up the trip for Veilkov. Ace had sent him four texts to come at once to Berlin. He'd tell Ace he would come after Veilkov's visit to El Kanitaoui. Then he might have something to tell his brother and Aunt Sonora. Nothing was more important than the calculations.

He shook his head. How could people he trusted and loved be so tied to an ancient artifact that might be a fake, or even the real one?

• • •

CHAPTER SIX

At the Gracanica Monastery

Man is the most dangerous of all animals.

The Abbot woke up in a sweat. It was always the same dream. Benton Prowers handed him a baby. He shook his head, trying to clear the memories of the past. In the monastic life, he lived a peaceful existence. The routine for him was a commitment to a lifestyle, not to a religion. With confidence few clerics agreed on, he believed man designed religions. He believed in a God who led him to believe in himself.

In monastic life, he found the freedom Benton Prowers sought for a lifetime and never found. He looked through the window at the beginning traces of a sunrise. It was a surprise to get Geigner's call and to learn el Ben had agreed to the visit. Veilkov would be here this morning and, the Abbot knew he'd be pleasantly surprised to be going to El Kanitaoui.

What would have happened if he and Amy hadn't gone to the bank vault in Dubrovnik? Too many questions and the Abbot had no answers. He knew in the monastery library there was a copy of the Shroud. It had been there since Benton asked him to hide it at the end of the war. Had Benton lied? There were so many lies, so much misdirection. For all he knew, the Shroud he had hidden in the library so many years ago was the real Shroud. Whatever; he would say nothing. The so-called copy would remain in the library.

He rose and stretched his long frame. The sun had nearly risen. He had a full schedule, which included a lesson with Medak, still his student, and then a plane to catch. His next speaking engagement on iconology was in London.

Over the years, these trips balanced his vocation to the monastic life. Often, he was asked to speak because his monastic lifestyle gave him credibility as a teacher and critic of icons. His life had been devoted to restoring the icons or frescoes, as some called the medieval Byzantine paintings.

He glanced at the pages on the table and began to prepare his lecture.

Today, in the twenty-first century, the icon is a neglected branch of European art history and is in the midst of a major evaluation as to their artistic merit. Icons are in demand for museums and for private collections. Critics laud them as a high art form. Icons are fashionable. It was not so when I first began my lectures after World War II. There was little interest in icons. A century before, Peter the Great had the Russian populace thinking of icons as an art form. The German poet, Goethe, suggested icons be viewed for their message. Goethe's contemporaries were judging icons by the aesthetic standards of the Italian Renaissance.

"Icon painters, like the Impressionists, are concerned with light. The Byzantine sees light as radiating from a source behind the painting and illuminating it in the way the rays of the sun glow through stained glass.

The Abbot stopped thinking about the words. He was paraphrasing Veilkov in describing the icon *Christ in Glory*. Veilkov spoke often about the robes of Christ shimmering with gold lines, like delicate shafts of light from the center of the icon, Christ, to the corners of the icon representing the world of his creation.

In the past months, that icon was Veilkov's obsession. Veilkov never mentioned the icon of the *Seven Angels*. True, the address Amy and Medak found was below the *Seven Angels*, but with Benton's gift for deception and misdirection, the correct icon might be *Christ in Glory*. Maybe after Veilkov visited the desert, he would tell him where the real Shroud was.

Outside his hermitage, the sun was starting to rise through the mist covering the mountain peaks. Gone with the dark night were bolts of moonlight that crossed his sparsely furnished hermitage. In the valley he could still see a few lights. Then he heard a step and spoke even before the knock on the door.

"You're on time, as your message said."

"I hope the coffee is hot, Abbot. I drove most of the way but climbing up here from the parking lot reminded me of my lack of fitness."

They both laughed.

"You're getting old," said the Abbot.

"I am old," said Veilkov and gladly rested on one of the wooden chairs.

It wasn't only the exertion from the walk, but the tedious drive from Belgrade to the monastery. He noticed the pistol hanging from the Abbot's brown robe.

"There are still dangerous animals in the mountains?"

Neglecting a direct answer, he replied, "Man is the most dangerous of all animals. I learned that truth traveling the world protecting icons from destruction by their natural enemy, man."

They sat on the terrace and the Abbot poured coffee from a silver pot. He had to find the right moment to ask Veilkov about the Shroud.

Veilkov broke the silence with a question of his own.

"Have you researched the bearded heads Geigner and Benton found? Are they icons of Akhenaten? I never understood why only two of the gold heads had beards. The others found in the tomb didn't. Do you think it was a dissident craftsman?"

The Abbot laughed. "Perhaps. While in Vienna, I asked an expert in symbolism."

"What did the expert say?"

"Not what we might expect. The mystery remains as far as I am concerned. The good professor decided the drawings on the walls indicated there was a drought. It's hard to see the configuration of the tomb being used as a rain-making machine. But until recently, I would have thought the concept and purpose of a laser weapon just as absurd."

"Not to el Ben," replied Veilkov. "He loves the desert. It would never occur to him that he needs rain. He has oil. With the Shroud and the laser as a weapon North Africa will be in his control. Tribes and the Coptics will finally be unified politically."

The Abbot listened, pouring a second cup of coffee. It was from Kenya and the flavor was blended perfectly. The Arabs were people of the desert, disciples of Mohammed and though united through religion, politically were fragmented like straw. After a generation of observing the Bedouin, the Abbot was still unsure where they stood. Directly into this complex mess, he was sending Veilkov, confident the monk could handle it.

Over the years, the Abbot had learned to sense a man's destiny. Geigner's was to die in the desert; of that he was certain. Veilkov, he sensed, did not have long, either. It was his feeling based on his years in the monastery. Nevertheless, they are now essential pieces in an on-going political chess game.

"El Ben has agreed to let you visit Geigner."

He didn't wait for a response. Veilkov would show no emotion, though he made it known he had wanted to make this trip since the excavation began.

"You agreed?"

"Yes, but take Medak with you; safety in numbers. I think you should go through southern Egypt. Avoiding the cities in North Africa will be safer, less questions."

Veilkov also preferred the southern route into the desert. That area was where local folklore believed Alexander the Great was buried. Many Egyptologists had spent their lives in that part of the Sahara searching for his grave. Medak, who was once his student, would be a good companion; though if he knew the Abbot, there was another reason for the young monk to accompany him. If the laser weapon Geigner was developing worked, verification by an expert of the computer program that ran the weapon would be needed.

"You know, Abbot, about the treaty between the superpowers to reduce strategic arms."

The Abbot was not surprised Veilkov was knowledgeable about current events. Unusual for a monk, but then Veilkov wasn't like most monks.

Veilkov grimaced.

"The weapon in the tomb, is an opportunity for blackmail by third-world countries who aren't a part of the treaty. Did you know there is a terrorist training camp down the road from our retreat house on the Greek border? I have seen them. In the camp are so-called trainees from all nationalities."

"Your right about the treaty," said the Abbot. "Look at what the free world spends on defense. In the next five years, the U.S. will spend two trillion dollars on defense. This upsurge has convinced me, after years of resisting Sonora's arguments, to join her Committee. The members believe warfare is the most natural condition of diplomacy. Their objective is to end the need for another war to end all wars and send another hawk to heaven."

The Abbot had no real desire to participate in the Committee, but he needed a group to support him. In the past, it had been the Yugoslavian leader, Tito, who appointed him Abbot over the objections of the Orthodox Church. With Tito dead and the country breaking into independent countries, he needed another protector. Committee membership would serve that role.

As the Abbot poured Veilkov more coffee, he realized how much alike the monk and Benton were. Both were idealists, a trait the Abbot considered a weakness. He believed Veilkov had hidden the real Shroud. If he was wrong, then Benton had hidden it in Mexico, and Veilkov would know where. His problem was how to get Veilkov to tell him.

"Now Veilkov, you know Benton thought Marfkis' death was a sign; not just to him, but to the world. Change was coming and Benton believed he had a responsibility to his family and to humanity. He despised el Ben and was sure he'd killed Marfkis. An eye for an eye is what Benton wanted. How this connects back to the monastery or why Benton came back, I have no idea."

Listening to the Abbot seemingly ramble, Veilkov thought, at last he knew the real reason the Abbot approved his visit to Geigner's site in the desert.

The Abbot thinks I know where the Shroud is. This was another strategy by the Abbot to have him reveal where the real Shroud was. He wished they had never given the Abbot one of the fake Shrouds.

Benton believed it was necessary. The war was on and no one knew what was coming next. Neither he, Benton or Marfkis wanted the Shroud to disappear forever. The fake Shrouds ensured that.

Veilkov sipped more coffee, then spoke.

"Benton felt a part of his life was left in these mountains. He visited almost every month until his death last year. We talked about the war and the train wreck. When Marfkis died, what happened during World War II took on new meaning to him for his vision on the fate of the world. The Committee and Sonora allowed him to think whatever he did was critical to the world. Benton and the General had a lot in common, as each over-estimated their importance in world affairs."

He paused as they both sipped coffees, realizing he might as well bring up at least part of what the Abbot wanted to hear.

"Benton believed Marfkis told his brother the real Shroud, supposedly at the cathedral in Turin, Italy, was hidden in this monastery. Hard to believe Marfkis told el Ben, but he obviously did. All the players here in the war—Benton, Marfkis, you, and I—knew the Shroud at Turin was a counterfeit."

The Abbot interrupted Veilkov. "I still have the copy you and Benton gave me."

Veilkov showed no emotion at the Abbot's comment, nor did he ask where the Abbot had kept the copy, they gave him so long ago. Instead he became philosophical, asking if it was the symbol or the belief in the symbol that men desire. They both knew there was no answer to that question.

The Abbot realized Veilkov had told him nothing. He tried again, using another tack.

"Ossery, the advisor or astrologer, whatever you want to call him, told the el Alemien brothers he had a vision; confirming the Shroud was a fake. That was the final sign. I doubt it was a vision; more likely, he heard the rumors and made them fact. It was not a secret that both brothers, never got along, but always shared a dream of a united North Africa, the old empire of Mohammed. Ossery had a dream where he saw the brothers riding a camel across the sands from Morocco to the Red Sea forming a grand alliance in North Africa, just as the Prophet Mohammed had done.

"We know the Shroud of Turin is the key to making that dream a reality. It's the symbol that will tie the Coptics and the Alemien family together. So where is the Shroud—in Mexico or here? And it must be the real one, as the Coptic will carbon date it to prove its provenance. My thought is if we don't find it, el Ben will.

"When he called yesterday, Geigner told me he promised el Ben he would find the Shroud. And now you're going to his country and you may know where it is."

Veilkov knew the Abbot wanted to know where the Shroud was. There was no need to tell him. It was safe, that was enough. He ignored the comment.

"You know, Abbot, how much I have wanted to make that trip. My thanks to you."

Veilkov realized the Abbot didn't have the whole picture of life in the desert and obviously didn't see el Ben as any crazier than the Abbot's brother, the General. He sipped coffee, and the Abbot made another try.

"Since the death of Marfkis, el Ben's son, el Habid has been sticking close to Geigner. El Ben asked Geigner to find the Shroud of Turin. With Benton dead, I think he sees the Prowers family as having some intrinsic relationship to it. If the Shroud was not destroyed when the train blew up, where has it been hidden? Benton and Marfkis are dead; that leaves you, Veilkov."

To ignore a direct answer he said.

"Abbot, where would I have hidden the Shroud? I would like to hold el Ben accountable for the deaths of Marfkis and Benton. But what can I do?"

Now the Abbot was a puzzled as ever, but it was obvious Veilkov as usual wasn't going to tell him.

They were silent for a moment, sipping coffee. The Abbot thought of a line describing a Dostoevsky character: *he had succumbed to the dread spirit of death and destruction and was now free to bring death and destruction to everyone and everything he encountered.* The Russian novelist from another century could have been describing el Ben or Geigner or Veilkov.

"Veilkov, if you're right, Geigner's search for the Shroud is an odd way of repayment, and even odder since he knows Sun Tzu's quote. El Ben needs both the weapon and the Shroud."

Veilkov knew the quote and the meaning. He and Benton had discussed it more than once. *All men can see these tactics whereby I conquer, but what none can see is the strategy out of which victory is evolved.*

The Abbot continued. "El Ben has consumed Sun Tzu's philosophy, and made it his own. His interpretation is the Shroud is the tactic which the Brotherhood, the tribes, and Ossery see. But el Ben has a strategy no one can see, and that is to develop El Kanitaoui, the tomb of the ancient Pharaoh, as a weapon."

They sat in silence for a moment. Then the Abbot said, "What's going on at the tomb could be important; and one more reason I would like Medak to accompany you as a witness, if you will."

With the Abbot's blessing, Veilkov departed, leaving the Abbot to ponder what was at El Kanitaoui. The Shroud was the symbol, while the tomb, the laser weapon, was the means.

Geigner had done the right thing by getting permission for Veilkov to visit the tomb. Obviously Geigner needed Veilkov's expertise in laser research.

Watching Veilkov disappear down the trail, the Abbot realized that if el Ben was looking for the Shroud, so were others. He was sure Veilkov knew where it was and hoped he lived to tell someone.

Until today, he found ignoring the past easier than remembering. Now it appeared el Ben was allowing no one to be ignorant. If the Shroud was involved, Veilkov would have to face what had happened to that train in the mountains so many years ago. For years, only his memories were a reminder of war. Now it appeared payment was due. He just wasn't sure who was paying whom.

• • •

CHAPTER SEVEN

Berlin

All this talk on the past isn't getting us anywhere.
We need to focus on today and
why Benton went to Mexico after the monastery.

Fog hung over the village of Dahlem outside Berlin. Ace hoped Amy remembered Grunewald Bahn was her stop. Otherwise, he'd have to drive into Berlin to pick her up at the main Bahnhof. The thick fog made all driving dicey.

Looking out the window of the truck, he could barely see the railroad tracks. Surrounded by the Grunewald forest, the largest green area near Berlin, the only sound to be heard was the rushing water. The Havel River couldn't be far away. This city had seen so much death and destruction. He loved it, though he often heard the voices of the ghosts. There was no way to silence them.

It was all coming back, he thought. *The old feelings of being in the game.*

Maybe he was addicted, not to danger, but addicted to the thrill of not knowing. When he was in a war zone, each minute was an event. Today, his life had moments of interest, but no adventure and no danger. Then Uncle Benton was killed.

He laughed at his own paranoia as he felt the bulge under his jacket. Since Benton's death he carried a Glock revolver, his weapon of choice in Europe.

As usual, he was early and with time to kill headed to the newsstand. He bought a copy of the International World Tribune, a conservative newspaper. Sonora would never approve, but he liked to read all points of view. The headline in bold print announced the President's peace proposal. On the bottom of the page was a small column on Libya.

He skipped the peace proposal, which he knew would be political-speak and contain little substance, to read that Khadafy was threatening retaliation against the United States. A plane from the Mediterranean fleet strayed into Libyan air space and set in motion the usual verbal displays of outrage. He noticed el Habid Alemien was Khadafy's spokesman.

What had Geigner thought about the threat? He'd bet his brother didn't know. No interest in politics was one thing, but what was worse, his brother didn't care. His life was consumed in building the laser weapon in the old pharaoh's tomb. *He ought to know by now if it was, or wasn't, Akhenaten's tomb. His brother had been digging in that tomb for at least a decade.*

The rest of the article discussed how the US Senate voted to delay granting Khadafy fifteen F-15 jets. El Ben's son, el Habid, speaking for Khadafy, labeled the delay an irresponsible conspiracy. To Ace, it reaffirmed that Khadafy was supported by the Bedouin tribes, including el Ben. He didn't care what the world thought, yet he wanted the weapons. With his country rich in oil, his actions were a problem for the rest of the world. None of this gave Ace any confidence his brother was safe, because he knew his brother would never leave the desert.

• • •

For hours, the train had travelled through the rolling green hills and the small villages of northern central Germany. The perfectly trimmed yards were so neat, Amy found herself looking for trash. Surely the Germans must have trash. Berlin was near, yet she couldn't see city lights. She knew the thick forest and fog prevented the city from being seen.

The intercom crackled, announcing the train stop. She understood German, though she couldn't speak much. No time to enjoy the city and its museums, because once Ace and Sonora read the letters, thought about clues, she'd leave for Mexico. If she didn't show up for the annual meeting of the Mesoamerican Archeological Society, the General would be calling to see why.

She'd like to visit Geigner and get his take on the letters, but she wasn't going to the oasis of El Kanitaoui. A couple of visits to the site to see her father had been enough. In those days she felt safe; today, she wasn't so sure.

Ace was waiting for her as she stepped off the train. He didn't look out of place, even though he was dressed for a hike in the Alps. She was sure he had gained more weight, if that was possible.

Her cousin was Sonora's favorite, because her aunt liked her liquor strong and her men tough. It sounded like a line from a third-rate western movie, but Sonora never made any apologies and Ace's life pleased her. Then he was injured leading some type of covert government operation —just what, nobody knew—and he never said what he did.

Amy thought he was too tall to be in an elite military group, one whose initials she never could remember. Even in those days, *fast* and *agile* were not words to describe him. Her father told her Ace planned operations and was rarely in the field. She never had a reason to doubt her father, but she never totally believed him either. Something about the way he said it didn't ring true. Now, she looked forward to Ace's help on trying to figure out the meaning of her father's use of icons and Mayan symbols as clues.

"Good trip?" Ace asked, sounding cheerful.

"Yes, and I could use a drink, and some of Sonora's chef's great food."

Ace laughed. "The villa is stocked with the finest wine and brandy, but German draft beer is best at the local Gast Haus. Besides, Sonora is taking a nap, and don't want to wake her. It's the only thing she does her doctors prescribe."

• • •

Ace looked down the long-mirrored bar of the Gray Wolf tavern, and ordered two tall lagers, while his cousin explained what was in her father's letters and how she was going to Mexico. He knew she believed it was her responsibility to follow up on her father's last request.

But his gut told him the last days of World War II held the key to what Benton had been doing before he died. After reading her father's letter, Amy went to the Balkans to find the Shroud. That was what el Ben wanted, the symbol, not jewels in a bank vault. Misdirection was a favorite ploy of his uncle's, and to Ace, Amy going to Mexico was misdirection. He needed to hear what Amy thought.

"Ace, my father was an expert on the Mayan culture, not icons and Bible verses. When he talked about trying to keep the beast from the Shroud, he meant el Ben. All this talk on the past isn't getting us anywhere. I need to know why he went to Mexico after visiting the monastery. He could hide the Shroud at a Mayan site or at the villa. I don't think he would trust it to Bernardo or any of the hacienda staff, but they might know where he went to hide it. What if he had the Shroud with him when the plane crashed?"

They sat in silence, sipping beer, each going over Benton's trip in their mind. Neither believed he had the Shroud with him on the plane. Both had questions, but no answers.

"His trip to Mexico could be for deception. He could have hidden the Shroud or left it in the monastery." She shrugged. "Who knows? My god Ace, I miss him."

Ace understood her frustration. "Your father wanted you to find the Shroud, because he believed you would keep it out of el Bens' hands. So, it has to be some place you can find it."

Amy agreed.

"My father loved the Mayan culture. Today, the descendants of the Mayans, who live in the Yucatan, keep the culture alive in everyday customs. Living in isolation in parts of Central America, they touch the natural world and believe the soul lives on in the animals of the jungle; jaguars, pumas and coyotes. There was no mystery in their disappearance like so many conspirators say, but famine, war and disease. Sometimes I think these theories are just to sell books.

"For me to switch to a new set of symbols using icons is difficult. I was young when my mother died. We never sat around and chatted about Europe. Now my parents' deaths are dragging me back to their past. I know some philosopher said we never escape our past. When my father died, he left unfinished business, which seems to be me finding the Shroud of Turin. When I find it, I'm taking it to the Cathedral in Turin."

Ace laughed, finding humor in her realistic appraisal of her father. "Does anyone facing the past, really know what to do? When it happens, you will know what to do. I mean, you're a Prowers."

Amy was less confident her bloodline would give her an answer but saw the irony in his comment and smiled. "If we don't laugh, we cry, right? Day after tomorrow, I'll be in Mexico at the annual reception for the Mesoamerican Archaeology Society. I'll ask our employees at our hacienda if they have any idea where the Shroud might be, and if not, I'll be back here."

Ace ordered another round of drinks, while the music of a three-piece local band played the song, *The Winner Takes It All*. Amy heard the words about winning being a destiny, and how the God's tossed the dice. That was her life. The past of her parents was like throwing dice. Her destiny was her parent's past. Once she found the Shroud, she would have her own life back again, and choose her own destiny.

"Vera Cruz is going to be dangerous. If the General thinks you know where the Shroud is, he will go after you, friend or no friend. To stay a player, he needs to be the one to give el Ben the Shroud. You've been at the monastery. He will figure you know something."

Amy laughed. "Why does everyone worry about the General? So, he was a Nazi. My father often said we are all Nazis, and my mother was a Nazis. I like to think she was just a pilot, but the truth is she idolized Hitler. Remember the picture of the two of them in our study on the ranch."

"I remember the picture," said Ace, "they were standing in front of the Reichstag in Berlin. Right?"

"Yes, she loved that picture, but you know, to me she was just a mother. I didn't focus on where she had been or what she might have done. My mistake maybe, but I didn't know she would die so soon and then I never found an opportunity to ask my father. Usually you find out more about your lineage when your older. Living in America, Berlin is a long way away."

He knew Benton never apologized for his wife Hanna, an unrepentant Nazi until she died. He and Sonora were sure the General treated Amy like his heir because of Hanna. He taught her how to manage mineral leases, because she had the right blood in her veins.

"A former Nazi is still a Nazi. Be careful."

"I will. He is king."

"You just lost me, Amy."

"The Mayan culture is the cult of the ruler. My parents could have been Mayans, but I never bought into the ruler concept."

"Not you?"

She shook her short brown hair and her face took on a look of determination. Ace thought she looked like her mother.

"I will never follow a leader, so no one can accuse me of being a Nazi. As for the General helping me, it is all about money and in a way a business friendship. Since the 1950s, we've owned a sugarcane plantation in central Mexico which you know is one of the largest in the world. We sold it to him, but not the rights to the oil leases. The search for oil isn't over. We own the rights and an agreement with the major oil companies gives us a cut of revenue on any new discoveries. The General is needed to help with the leases and on managing our joint fleet of oil and liquid gas tankers. He deals often with el Ben. Takes a man, you know."

She didn't add what they both knew. Transporting oil was how the Prowers family made their money. It was the only major business decision her father ever made for the family to hold the majority shares in the tanker fleet, not the General. The General couldn't live forever, though sometimes it seemed as if he could. In the future when he was gone, Ace might have to represent the Prowers family in negotiations with el Ben or his family.

• • •

When they left the tavern, what was left of daylight had nearly disappeared and the fog had partially lifted. Amy could see the lights of Berlin in the darkened sky. The road followed the Havel River, winding through the Grunewald Forest. Wind from the storm blowing in from the North Sea rattled the pickup truck, but its weight kept it on the road. Amy was reminded how durable a good American pickup was.

"Where is the Mercedes?" she asked.

"It's in the garage. Believe it or not, this truck is green. Sonora is trying to go green and I insisted on a truck, even in Berlin."

Amy laughed, thinking of her aunt as an environmentalist, and Ace needing a pickup.

They rode in silence, listening to the wind. The road broke into a clearing with the Grunewald Forest on the left and the Havel River to their right. His eye caught the lights of a car behind them and he turned the mirror to cut the glare. The car had room to pass but didn't.

The road turned again, a long wide curve, and they felt the first bump. Then the car bumped them again.

Ace turned the wheels to meet the skid and loose dirt swirled up around the side of Amy's door. She felt helpless remembering what her father preached—*always carry a gun.* This was the second time in days it had come up.

"Under the seat," Ace shouted. "There's a gun and I have one in a holster but it's under my arm."

He was struggling to keep the truck on the road.

"Got it." Amy wasn't surprised. A Prowers household, even in Berlin, would have weapons. The holster held a Glock, a gun she had fired at the shooting range many times with her father. She clipped the magazine in ready to fire.

"There are some turns coming up as we go through the park, and the drop-off is steep. Hang on."

Amy was listening while trying to figure out how to take a shot at the car without hitting her cousin.

The pickup shuddered as they were bumped again.

"Give me the gun."

Ace lowered the window. As the car pulled up beside them, he fired through the window, directly on a trajectory to hit the driver. The car shot in front of them. Instead of slowing and taking the other lane, it flew up off the pavement, paused in midair, and in slow motion, dropped back onto the road. Then it speeded away, as its lights faded into the night. Neither of them had a clue who was in the car.

"Sonora won't be pleased when she hears about this, ah incident," said Ace. "But then we aren't either, right?"

Amy agreed.

• • •

CHAPTER EIGHT

The Next Generation to Lead

The irony was, she knew her brother never believed
in the mystical aura of the Shroud of Turin.

Behind Sonora, the sky was as dark as the woods. The fading sunset
cast a red glow low in the sky and faded into the clouds, leaving Berlin
in a gray haze. She loved the city and felt at home in the villa, though
it was a hundred years old. Benton said it was outdated. To him, the
Prowers family could live in a hotel with the services at their fingertips
when they were in Berlin.

Sonora ignored him and kept the house. Tonight, she wore her
diamond and emerald rings and a matching necklace contributed to the
air of elegance. Others might think the Prowers money paid for her to
look young, but Sonora was a natural beauty. Dying her gray hair blonde
was her sole vanity.

An oil painting of the family hung above the fireplace. Benton, Hanna, and Amy, barely old enough to stand up, were on the prairie posed beside the derrick of an oil rig. To Sonora, the painting said it all. The Prowers family had herded cattle for over a hundred years; however, today, the revenue from minerals beneath the land allowed the ranch to prosper. The Prowers family was one of the largest landowners in Colorado, Texas, and—what few knew—Wyoming, and Montana. Underneath the land their cattle grazed on were pools of oil, gas, and other minerals.

She and Benton profited from the vision of their father who bought and sold land while keeping the mineral rights. Trained as a chemical engineer specializing in petroleum products, the old man used to tell them stories he had heard of a giant meteorite landing in the Gulf of Mexico thousands of years ago. He was convinced early in the 1920s there was oil in the Gulf. One day the drilling rights would be very valuable. Years after he died, geologists found the oil most of which was controlled by the Mexican government. Neither Benton nor Sonora ever forgot his stories of those early days.

When their father died, she and Benton took over. As a team, they weathered the highs and lows of oil and natural gas prices. Their companies managed leases, pipelines, and made millions. Money was available to finance Hanna's research on breeding stock and hybrid wheat and soybeans. Today Amy managed the Prowers family trusts and legacy leases from her grandfather. With the General, she negotiated with oil companies to drill and collect royalties from the leases. The leases were all over the world, only the General insisted on remaining in Mexico. The old man was afraid of being picked up by any one of a dozen humanitarian groups ferreting out old Nazis. Mexico didn't allow extraditions.

Sonora was proud Amy had a head for business but was sorely disappointed Benton was never able to get her to accept her social responsibility. Maybe the letter he left with his will for her to find the Shroud of Turin was his way to get her to accept her families' political responsibility.

At least her niece didn't have her head in old ruins, like Benton or Amy's first husband. Her second husband was a good friend and became a player on the Committee. Their divorce Sonora found inconvenient. He stayed on for a time as a consultant until his father had a heart attack and he was needed to run the family feed business. He died of an unknown tumor a few years later. Sonora still missed him. No one—not even Amy—ever mentioned her third husband whose head was in the clouds and literally lost in the clouds in one of the mountain ranges in South America. All three were dead and, though unfortunate, Sonora felt their deaths gave Amy time to concentrate on Prowers family interests and be a player on the Committee.

She wished Benton had been honest with Amy about his past and her mother's. Was he a coward or just didn't want to burden his only *child? Now it was too late. Still, she had not given up hoping Amy would* one day accept her obligation to the Committee. So far, Amy had resisted her arguments.

She paused to pour another half glass of brandy. Her niece and nephews had no children. Would the Committee end? No, it would go on. An unbreakable trust left by her father to fund the work would ensure the continuity of the Committee.

Amy was a Prowers, and she must be the next generation to lead. Ace and Geigner would need her. When she was gone, it would take the talents and time of her niece and nephews to lead the Committee's work.

Sipping her brandy, she realized Benton must have known his life was in danger or he never would have left all these clues. She shook her head, realizing the clues were because he was afraid el Ben's men would find the shroud, not Amy.

The irony was her brother Benton never believed in the power—the so-called mystical aura—of the Shroud of Turin. She never asked him where the real Shroud was because she didn't believe it was important. Now, given the role of the Shroud in North African politics, she cursed her own complacency for not asking him especially after Marfkis died. He was the one Benton trusted.

She was worried about the General's influence on her niece. Thankfully, he couldn't live forever. She smiled, knowing she had won; if winning meant knowing the truth. The General was living with lies. He had no idea the Shroud was saved from the train crash. But that wasn't the only secret. He didn't know about the baby Veilkov's family raised in Serbia.

Benton and Hanna were reluctant to discuss the child, even when she badgered them with questions. One evening, after consuming many bottles of wine, they told her that Eva Braun's baby was the child of an officer of the Wehrmacht killed while running messages out of Berlin to the Eastern Front; not Hitler's heir, as some speculated.

With few details, the type that drives history and gossip, Sonora became a spectator and enjoyed watching the General peck away at what he thought was the truth over the years. No matter what the truth was, the General would think the lost baby was Hitler's heir.

To her surprise, Hanna and Eva Braun settled into a comfortable life in America and Mexico. What a shock when they died in a plane crash in Spain. Benton told her the women were going back to the monastery to find the baby.

What karma, she thought, *to live through so much turmoil in the war, and then be gone.*

Were the two women at peace? Sonora didn't know, but believed her brother was, because Benton spent his life preparing to die. She, on the other hand, was determined to outlive the enemies of her family, especially the General.

The old man was a fraud, claiming medals for battles on the Eastern Front when he never left Vienna, yet he had the nerve to resent Hanna who was awarded the Iron Cross by der Fuhrer for her work as a test pilot.

Her brother Benton and Hanna were so alike. Both focused on today, but with their minds living in the past. Hanna had an instinct for managing the ranch, and Benton let her. At first Sonora always believed that was how he justified pursuing archaeology digs.

She looked at her watch. Where were her niece and nephew? They should have been back from the train station by now.

The doorbell rang and the maid opened it seeing a delivery truck. Usually packages arrived at a post office box not at the villa. She carried it down the hallway to the Prowers security chief.

"What is going on?"

"This package arrived by delivery truck and addressed to Amy. I cannot make out the return address."

"Let me see it. We need to clear the package and open it for you."

Sonora's security men were used to the staff ignoring them, but at least this time the maid brought them the package.

"I know, I know," she replied. "You're right. The return address is unrecognizable. When you're done, put it out on the desk. Amy should be here shortly."

As he took it to the secure room where packages were checked, Sonora looked out at the dark foggy night wondering what could be in the box.

• • •

CHAPTER NINE

The Middle East is Always In a Revolution

We must find the Shroud before el Ben and the General.

Amy and Ace arrived moments later. After listening to the road incident, Sonora realized, though a serious attempt had been made on their lives, nothing could be done. Amy and Ace proved they could handle themselves. What was worse, she was sure more incidents would happen before the Shroud was found.

The wind rattled a window as the fire crackled and a log rolled off the top of the pile, scattering sparks across the bricks. Amy grabbed the tongs and moved the log back on the fire.

Sonora jiggled her glass and a maid appeared.

"This time, make it bourbon and branch, and bring me the bottle. Bourbon has always been the American rancher's drink," she said to no one in particular. She nodded to the maid and pointed to the desk in the corner.

"A package arrived addressed to you, Amy. It was delayed because of insufficient postage. None of us recognized the handwriting, so our security staff cleared it."

The maid retrieved the small brown package from the top of the mahogany desk and handed it to Amy.

Amy didn't recognize the handwriting or the postmark, except she knew it wasn't German. She opened it and found herself looking at another very thin book on icons.

She read the title; *Beyond the Face: A Commentary on Icons, Symbols, and Illusions*. It was in English, but the author was a Greek with fifteen letters in his surname.

"Well, at least it isn't another letter." She looked at Sonora. "When you read the letters, you'll see what I mean."

She thought about the book the lawyer had given her at the reading of the will.

"The other book, titled *Icons of the Balkan Monasteries*, read like a tourist guidebook. When I looked at the icons in the monastery, I could never figure out what I was supposed to find. I hope this one has more detail."

Amy sounded like she'd found nothing, but Sonora knew they must be getting close to the truth. Benton loved puzzles.

Opening the book, Amy saw inside the cover a drawing of the Hakenkreuz, the soft-sided swastika. "The Abbot said to look for it. He thought icon books with the soft sided swastika inside the cover were clues. Otherwise, the book was just another description of icons."

She flipped through the book, looking at pictures of six icons, and a short narrative in English which said ancient scholars considered it to be the finest artistic examples of icon symbolism.

"Amy, let me take a look at the book."

Ace held it up to the light, pulled the pages back, running his thumb along the binding. At least one page had been torn out. All the icons listed in the contents had a picture, except the icon *Christ in Glory*, which must have been torn out.

"What's so special about this one?" asked Ace.

"I know that icon, *Christ in Glory*," said Amy. "It was in the Gracanica Monastery and painted by an unknown monk in the fourteenth century. In it, Christ is holding his hand over his heart and serpents and snakes are coiled around his feet. The author's interpretation was that the serpents at his feet represented evil. The icon was a message to man that he must remove his foot from evil."

They looked at each other and Amy asked Ace, "What are you thinking?"

"Maybe it's nothing, or maybe the icon *Christ in Glory* has something to do with the Shroud. The excavation at El Kanitaoui and the Shroud are both important to el Ben. Benton told me el Ben lived by Sun Tzu's philosophy on war. His favorite quote was, *all men can see these tactics whereby I conquer, but what none can see is the strategy out of which victory is evolved.*

"Sounds tricky or slick, but it makes sense. If el Ben has both the Shroud and the laser weapon, no one will contest his authority to rule North Africa. The weapon gives him the power and the Shroud the spiritual link with the Coptic; which, in turn, gives him access to Coptic wealth."

Listening to him, Sonora understood why the Abbot said Veilkov needed to visit the desert. There could only be one reason. Veilkov could verify if the laser weapon really worked. The irony was, with Benton dead, he might be the only one who knew the location of the Shroud.

"The Abbot called me and said Veilkov and Medak were going to visit Geigner in the desert. A visit by Veilkov to evaluate the laser site means Geigner is very close to making the laser weapon operational."

On that point, they all agreed.

The wind was howling through the crevices around the windows, a signal that the storm sweeping across the north German plain had arrived. Amy could tell her aunt was not ready to call it a night. Ace opened a bottle of Amy's favorite, an Argentinean red wine.

Sonora raised her glass of bourbon in a toast, "Benton was obsessed with the fourth beast that brings war and destruction. He never trusted el Ben. So, he hid the Shroud, putting his life in danger, and now your life, Amy.

"The Middle East is always in revolution. Marfkis' dream when he died was to emulate the Ottoman Turks who ruled for three hundred years, by uniting an Arab nation to rule from the Atlantic to the Arabian Gulf. His brother El Ben has the same dream."

She paused long enough to sip her bourbon.

"The Nile is the key to controlling Egypt. Few realize a pocket of Christians live in the desert and have protected old monastic sites along the Nile since the time of Mohammed.

"The Muslims overthrew the Byzantine Empire, but the Coptic churches remain. The old imams, the holy men, know the Coptic have the financing for their political aspirations. They control a significant portion of the wealth of Egypt, while the Muslims control the political power. It has been an unholy alliance dating back to the apostle Mark.

Egyptian leaders and political confusion come and go, but the alliance with the Coptic remains just as Mohammed protected the Coptic centuries ago. They are safer with the Muslims than with the Christians."

She paused, reached for the bottle of bourbon, and continued talking faster than before.

"As bad as el Ben is, the next leader is always worse than the last. I am not as against him as your father was, because I am more of a realist. Dealing with one dictator is easier than trying to control all the tribe and ethnic factors in the region."

Talking about Coptic and laser weapons frustrated Amy. She attempted to redirect the discussion back to the Shroud as she pulled out the note her father had left in the bank.

"I also have the letter left with his will."

Sonora knew what needed to be done.

"Ace, you can analyze the letter and note on your computer programs and see if they make any sense? You know how Benton's mind worked. The Nazis kept lists on everything, and it may be possible for you to find out what artwork was destroyed in the train crash. If I recall, no one looked closely at the crates buried in the rubble. Some stuff, including the Shroud, could have been saved.

"We have to find the Shroud before el Ben and the General. I don't trust either of them and wise men should fear them. The question is, do we have all the clues Benton left? I'll read the letters Amy brought."

For a moment, they sipped their drinks and looked at the logs blazing in the fireplace.

"O.K." said Ace. "I'll use a data mining program to look for patterns. If I'm lucky, we might figure out Benton's clues and find the Shroud. At best, we'll get a handle on whether the monastery or Mexico is most likely where he hid it. The Shroud is out there, somewhere. I'm sure because Benton was sure."

"Data mining; sounds like a weapon," said Sonora.

"It's all part of the analytical program one of the Committee members got for me."

Amy was as dubious as Sonora. How could a computer program figure out her father's clues? Still, anything was worth a try.

• • •

Ace headed for Benton's study. Stepping inside, he looked at the rows of books, remembering it was his uncle's favorite room in the Berlin house. Along one wall were the heads of a bear, an elk, and various birds. Some would say it was a real man's room. Benton was dead, but Ace felt in this room his uncle was still alive. For that reason, it was now his own favorite place to work.

The room reminded him of how the present moved in and out like the wind. Only yesterday remained in his memory. He didn't know how Benton was killed, but his inner gut, that he trusted through so many special operations with the military, told him the plane crash was no accident. The General had to be behind it. The plane had refueled at the General's private airport in Mexico; his staff could have tinkered with the plane.

Above him on the wall were family photographs Sonora had brought from the States. They were old and he never thought about their meaning. Today, the one that stood out for him was a black and white picture of a house.

He peered closely at the faded label on the bottom: *The Bergdorf, Hanna Reitch and Eva Braun's favorite picture of Hitler's home.* Hanna would stare often at the picture. One day he asked his uncle what Hanna was thinking when she stared at the picture? Benton said she was remembering those Germans who said Hitler needed to die to end the war. He said Hanna never forgave the military for his defeat. The Fuhrer was dead; yet she loved remembering the early days, the speeches, the parades, and the idealism of the Third Reich.

Ace turned back to the computer screen and sipped his drink. His brother, Geigner, was like their mother, Jarra, focused on an illusion, and a belief in the Asian folklore Benton and Vince talked about. Who had ever heard of the force fields, selected points on the earth immune to gravity? What a story.

Amy's husband, Vince, believed it, and died in northern Pakistan searching for such places. Was it another suspicious death? Now, according to the Abbot, his brother Geigner had asked Veilkov for help. That meant he was close to making the laser in the tomb operational.

Ace knew if the chamber was capable of being a land-based laser, a new problem arose, especially for Geigner. How does idealism take a stand when a new weapon is created in the hands of an unstable ruler? He and his brother were alike in one respect. They trusted no one.

Now his Uncle Benton was fixated with icons, Mayan, and Biblical symbolism. He created clues to where he hid the Shroud, believing Amy would understand the clues and find the Shroud. There was no mention of El Kanitaoui in his letters.

Because he trusted Geigner with the site, thought Ace.

He turned on the computer to a data mining program, designed to detect patterns and trends. One of the businessmen on the Committee had given it to him. The irony was a businessman had developed the program, not the military. Whatever—it was what he needed to analyze the letter and note.

The game was getting dangerous and he hoped Amy was up to the task. The Balkans and Mexico were tricky places. He wasn't sure he and Sonora could protect her.

• • •

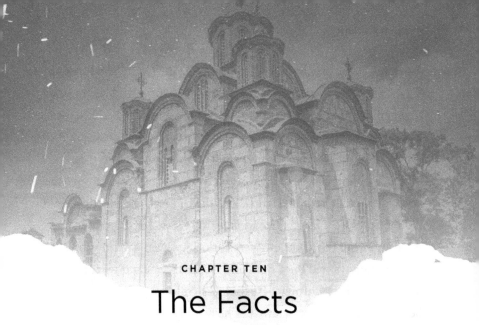

CHAPTER TEN

The Facts

Sonora hesitated, but realized
Amy should know all the facts.

Amy sipped brandy, its flavor accentuated by the rich, comfortable surroundings of the Berlin mansion watching her aunt read the letter from the will and the one she'd found in the bank.

"Brandy is healthy." Amy smiled, "Our cook once told me my Mother claimed the brandy was for medicinal purposes but kept the bottles out of sight whenever a doctor came to the ranch. The premise that brandy was healthy was German folklore, but who cared if she enjoyed it."

Sonora looked up from the letters at the bottle of *Asbach Uralt*. "Ace and I drink as much as your mother and Eva. It was your mother's favorite, and years ago you could only buy it in Germany; now it's in every liquor store from New York to Texas."

She finished reading and put the letter on her lap.

"My dear, so far we have nothing specific. Is the Shroud at the monastery or in Mexico? In the days after the war, no one realized the importance of the Shroud. Your father was working undercover,

I suspect, because of his fluency in German. The Count and I met him in Egypt where we were to catch a freighter to Mexico. We'd been working on a remote excavation of ruins near the Libyan border. Frankly, we were glad to leave because the area had gotten so dangerous.

Benton was waiting for the same freighter. He was very careful about revealing Hanna and Eva's identity. Looking back, I think what a coincidence that Benton, Hanna, Eva, the General, and my husband, the Count, and I were all on the *Meridian*. My sister, Jarra, had been at the excavation, but flown back to New York. Ships were too slow for her.

"Benton wanted the Count and me to understand what Hanna and Eva had been through. He told us a child was left in a village in Serbia. I wanted more details, but he would say little. I was never close to either your mother or Eva. It was your father who told me after the plane crashed in Spain in 1960, the women were on their way to Serbia to find the child."

Sonora hesitated, but realized Amy should know all the facts. She was never sure what Benton might have told his daughter. Today the baby could be more important than anyone thought.

"Benton told me years later that Eva's tears were for a young officer who ran messages in and out of Berlin. When the soldier was killed in the fighting outside Berlin, Eva agreed to leave with Hanna. Their departure needed secrecy to protect Eva. No one knew how the partisans would react if they suspected her relationship to Hitler. Hanna helped with the cover story.

"Amy, you know from seeing Eva at the ranch that she was much smarter, and shrewder than everyone believed. Benton once said she had the ability to see those who would use her and swore, she would never be used."

Amy knew what her aunt said was true. Even though she was often away at boarding school, she liked Eva. She was fun. Her mother was never fun; all business.

"Only the three of them knew what happened to the baby. I know there was a baby, but don't know if it was a boy or girl. The baby wasn't on the boat. So, it either died or was left in the Balkans.

"Today the child, even if it's alive, isn't so important except maybe to the General. What's important today is the icon, the Shroud of Turin. The General wants to use the Shroud to make a deal with el Ben and be a leader in a new oil boom. Benton would have done anything to prevent el Ben from finding the Shroud."

"One night your father told the Count and me, how he, Veilkov, and Marfkis made a counterfeit of the Shroud. Now I wonder how many copies are out there. I seem to remember he said they made several attempts to get it right. He said it would take an art expert to tell one from the other. He used the words 'it was so easy.'"

Amy sipped her brandy, thinking all she needed to make this worse was more than one Shroud floating around.

"Sonora, to me, the key to controlling this part of North Africa was oil, not religion. Politics was business and so was religion. I just learned about the Coptic connection from the Abbot when he was explaining to me why the Shroud was important to el Ben."

Amy poured both another glass of brandy, as the cook appeared at the door followed by two haughty, nondescript cats.

"Need anything else?"

They both said no. The cook left and the cats stayed. One climbed up beside Amy for a scratch behind the ears and the other lay down beside Sonora.

Amy petted its head. "I suppose these fat old cats have to be inside."

"Right," said Sonora. "Otherwise the foxes will have them for lunch. We brought five cats over from the ranch. Cook adores them. They love her tasty food and are as happy in Berlin as they were on the ranch. The city is lovely, and I hope you will take some time to enjoy it."

"You know I love the city, but if I'm not in Mexico at the Meso-american Archeological Society's annual meeting, the General will be angry and wonder what I'm up to. My trip to the monastery confused me. I wish you'd come with me to Vera Cruz."

Sonora had no desire to go to Mexico and said so, but assured Amy she would keep working with Ace on the letters for clues.

"Amy, remember the General still hears the marching feet and the sound of drums. Some poet said the greatest poison ever known is Caesar's laurel crown. Which is another way of saying power corrupts. I understand how the General feels because I miss the crown, too, but he will get his hands on it over my dead body or my family's. He is a die-hard racist, and more than likely knows something about your father's death."

Amy understood her concern.

Amy knew the Shroud was one part of el Ben's plan, the other was the success of the weapon her cousin Geigner had built in the desert. Sun Tzu's quote said it all. The leader wanted a symbol and a weapon.

Sonora wasn't finished.

"Toward the end of the war, the partisans blew up a train. It wasn't the first train they wrecked, but what was on it was priceless. The Shroud was on the train and the General believed it was destroyed. Benton and Hanna owed their lives to Eva, who insisted on leaving the train and staying on in the village. Why she didn't want to leave, no one ever said. But it had to be because of the child.

"Years ago, I decided Hanna and even Eva, were alike in one way. They destroyed the lives of those who loved them. No one gave them more than Benton, both of himself and of his money."

A nurse, part of the villa staff, entered carrying Sonora's medication, but she waved it away.

"No, I want to be alert if Ace comes up with some conclusion from his analysis. My God, I realize I am obsessed like the General. Only I want to keep him from finding the Shroud."

Just then Ace stuck his head in the room. "The computer is still searching but I have found something in the material we have been collecting for the Committee."

They both looked at him wanting to say hooray, what is it.

"It's amazing what Geigner has done. If the weapon works, it will confirm the mythology that surrounds the mystical points on the earth, showing the points are not a myth, but scientific fact. This is what Vince was searching for when he died years ago in the Karakorum Range in northern Pakistan."

"You're right," said Amy, watching Ace as he continued to pull out photographs.

"Take a look at what is odd about the oasis at El Kanitaoui. The size of the buildings and the radar dish show there is an extensive installation at the base of the mountain. This is where Geigner is excavating the archeological site believed to be the tomb of Akhenaten. Lleissle International, along with other conglomerates, ship computers and scarce minerals into el Ben's country. The only visible activity where they might be used is in this excavation. Aerial photography can't help because the main site is inside the base of the southern mountains. We can't see into these mountains but are sure it is some type of weapon. Maybe Veilkov can tell us when he returns."

To his aunt and cousin, he pointed out if Geigner had perfected the laser weapon, el Ben would own the ultimate weapon of destruction if he decided to use it. The irony was that the search to provide el Ben with proof of his ancestral ties to the Egyptian pharaoh had instead produced a universal weapon that might pre-date known ancient cultures.

Today the question was, did the weapon work and could el Ben blackmail the world with Geigner's weapon. Certainly, the weapon made all the weapon treaties in the world irrelevant.

Sonora listened thinking the key to any political system was the people who supported the rulers. When el Ben died, she doubted el Habid and his brothers would be able to hold the pieces of their father's tribal land together. She wondered what Benton would do if he was here.

"It almost seems like the good old days when Khadafy went out in a patrol boat with a machine gun to take a stand at the so-called *Line of Death* against our Mediterranean fleet. We thought it was a joke. Then we proved he was supporting terrorist units. Eliminating the terrorists or using an economic boycott are actions that never seemed to work."

Amy was silent, listening to her aunt.

"Sonora was finally getting around to why she wanted Amy to visit her in Berlin.

"We need you on the Committee as someone with your natural cover as a wealthy, and—though I know differently—naïve volunteer. We have serious work ahead. Our family has always believed the individual citizen has a public responsibility. Our fortune and the Committee provide us with a unique role to play."

Amy was annoyed. Now was not the time to be contemplating her public responsibility. She had to get the conversation back to the Shroud. She looked at Ace for support, but he was silent.

"My father's letter and the icons are enough," protested Amy.

Sonora said the obvious.

"I admit the Shroud is a distraction, and quite important, or Benton would not have surrounded the search for the icon with so many clues. We have been given the responsibility to understand and accept it."

Sonora shifted in her chair and as she did, shifted the subject.

"The quintessential problem today is whether the ruins at El Kanitaoui are a tomb or a weapon directed at other nations through outer space. It is a laser system, but can the Arabs run it without Geigner?"

Sonora was on a roll. She looked at Amy as she spoke.

"I admire Geigner for standing up and following his ideals. There is a quote from Ecclesiastes that I think describes him today. *There is a little man who is said to save a city, but no one remembers his name.* That, I believe, is my nephew's karma. He will always be trying to save something, even from himself, and no one will remember his name. Then he found those gold heads and became fixated on them.

"He picked the name 'Aaron's Beard' for the gold heads found in the tomb at El Kanitaoui, because Aaron was Moses brother. I question the Biblical accuracy of that fact. In the time of the Pharaohs and the Egyptians, only the Jews had beards. Aaron was responsible for leading his people, the Israelites, to the Promised Land. Many believe he was Akhenaten's half-brother. For whatever reason, Geigner kept the name 'Aaron's Beard.' The gold heads are also hollow, which for some reason I found interesting."

Amy listened, but wasn't going to overdo the emphasis on karma. Since the wars in Iraq, she wasn't too sure today whose side had the right karma. As for the golden heads, to her, they were another artifact, the kind found in a Pharaoh's tomb. The desert, centuries ago, could have looked quite different, and might not have been as extreme as the tomb looked today in the middle of a sea of sand. The Pharaoh could have lived at El Kanitaoui.

Sonora picked up the book that was anonymously sent to the villa.

"The index of this little book you just got in the mail suggests the icon is in the Gracanica Monastery. It repeats the Biblical quote your father put in his letter, 'remove thy foot from evil.' And the author says the icon *Christ in Glory* has seven angels in it. The book also refers to the icon as having serpents, which mean death, at its feet."

Amy looked puzzled a moment, then followed up on her aunt's thought.

"The book with the key the lawyer gave me said the icon was the *Seven Angels*. At the Gracanica monastery, the two icons were side by side. *Christ in Glory* was right next to the icon of the *Seven Angels*. I believe whoever sent the book was someone who knows where the Shroud of Turin is. The person could be anywhere since the postmark is obscure. The letter from the vault in Dubrovnik was filled with Mayan symbolism. The Mexican Archeology reception may turn up something interesting."

Sonora pointed out the obvious.

"True and as much as I hate to admit it, a reason to go to Mexico is that a no-show at the reception would alert the General something unusual has come up. In addition, the Mexicans see you as the heir not just to Benton but in part to the General, if he ever chooses to die. To skip such an event would be an insult and have a negative impact on our oil business."

They both knew they had their roles to play.

Sonora sipped her brandy and looked at her.

"I always feel a sense of reality working with the Committee. I remember a saying I picked up, from where I can't say. It is that even when we are a year old, we don't have many years left. I guess I remember it because of its unshakable truth. We have so little time, and then we are gone. Each of us dies over and over."

She paused.

"Shall we drink a glass of brandy to the sands of time in this life?"

In reply, Amy raised her glass. She would find the Shroud, not for the ghosts of her father and Vince, but for herself.

• • •

PART II

CHAPTER ELEVEN

Southern Sahara Desert

So far, no proof has been found that
the cavern at El Kanitaoui is his tomb.

From the patio of the Saint Macarius, Monastery, Medak watched the
swift current of the Nile River, flowing north to Cairo held in place by
rows of sand dunes on the east and west sides. Dozens of local boats,
feluccas, loaded with people and goods, headed up and down the Nile.
He suspected this was the last he and Veilkov would see water.

The outline of the monastery could be seen above the flat desert.
From studying monasteries around the world, he knew this was a
Coptic monastery. It was unique, as it sat atop an ancient Roman ruin
dating from the eighth century.

The mother house, established in the fourth century at Wadi El
Natrun, fifty miles northwest of Cairo, was where Saint Macarius the

Great built the first monastery for hermits who wanted no part of civilized life. With seemly endless water from the oasis, they grew wheat and olives, providing adventurous travelers with food and water. After surviving World War II, the desert surrounding the monastery became too civilized and they moved south to the new monastery of Saint Macarius. Today the monks kept to themselves, but shared food and herbal medicine with local villages and Bedouin tribesmen.

Medak and Veilkov sipped tea, waiting for their driver. Except for the Nile River, they could be at any oasis in the heart of the Sahara Desert. A woven mat covered the beige earth, and Medak could feel the early rays of the sun against his skin. A cool breeze and shade from palm trees made the morning pleasant.

The silence was broken by the roar of two jets, flying just above the floor of the desert. The air vibrated as the jets pulled high into the crystal blue sky above the Nile River. Veilkov watched as they disappeared on the horizon.

"When you live as a monk, you see the weapons of war as man's fantasy. In the words of some wise man, the more we go on, the more we return," said Veilkov, who found himself remembering World War II.

He was pleased to be back in the desert, even though memories he thought forgotten were coming back to him.

"Medak, after the war with German and Italian deserters roaming all over the desert, Benton Prowers, his new wife Hanna, and their friend Eva Braun, were waiting for a freighter to Mexico. I was to stay in case Benton needed help.

"Benton's half-sister and her Swiss husband, a count, who spent the war excavating ruins in the southern desert, were also waiting for the freighter to Mexico. I couldn't believe they led a life inside a war zone, but apparently, they did. The freighter was delayed, and they decided to make a short trip into the Sahara, inviting us to join them.

The women weren't eager to go, so Benton stayed with them, but he insisted I should go with the count and his wife."

Veilkov paused a moment, as if remembering.

"Medak, it was fantastic, a word I rarely use. Few people know that deserts have more mountains than anyone realizes. In the cliffs above the large oasis near Zelten, we found royal discs and more talatat. Those stone tablets were useless until the Rosetta stone enabled Egyptologists to decipher the language. Using computer technology, Egyptologists took the talatat—some 45,000 pieces, now in museums in London, Paris, Berlin, and New York—and pieced together the story of the Egyptian rulers. Until we found them, the only known discs were in the tombs of nobility along the Nile River. The finding told us nobility were buried here."

They sipped more tea as the red sun rose in the east, bringing the heat of the day. One of the monks came to announce the driver was a little late, but on his way. Medak leaned back and waited for Veilkov to continue the history lesson.

"Nefertiti, Akhenaten's queen, with the future King Tut and her daughters, moved to a palace on the northern side of the city of Amarna. Akhenaten and his queen built the city to worship the disc god, Aten. The people, the nobility, and especially the clerics at Thebes, never believed in the concept of a single god and were not pleased.

"After Akhenaten's abdication as pharaoh, the people returned to worship Aten and other gods. There is no evidence he killed himself or was killed, and supposedly died two years later in 1377 BC. A tomb was built for him in the Valley of the Kings, but there was no evidence it was ever used, or a mummy ever found. Many scholars believe he lived another twenty or twenty-five years somewhere.

"I agree with Benton, Geigner, and now el Ben. They are convinced Akhenaten lived at the oasis of El Kanitaoui," said Veilkov.

What Veilkov said next was a surprise to Medak. He didn't know the monk was so knowledgeable on Egyptian pharaohs.

"Akhenaten fought with the military and Egyptian nobility concerning their worship of multiple gods, so he moved to the El Kanitaoui oasis. There, in the solitude of the oasis, he practiced the religion of the sun disc god, Aten, but left many unanswered questions. His rule lasted only twenty years. There wasn't much time to build lasting monuments like the tombs of other pharaohs along the Nile and in the Valley of the Kings. His monument was what nature provided, the cavern in the mountains. The current Bedouin tribal leaders are determined to use his tomb to prove they are descended from the pharaohs."

Veilkov paused, remembering the rubble they cleared from the cavern when he and Geigner discovered the sarcophagus at el Kanitaoui. He wanted Medak to understand some of the history and some of the fables. Medak was a willing listener.

"So far they haven't found real proof the cavern at El Kanitaoui is his tomb. But the cavern is unique. For starters, it's one of several places on the earth that have minimal gravitational pull or are not as influenced by the force of gravity. This phenomenon of nature is known to few and denied by many. Benton and Vince, Amy's first husband, ran around the world for years looking for these spots. Vince died trying to find one in the Hindu Kush in Northern Pakistan.

"You might be surprised. I was. El Ben is a believer in so-called spots on earth immune to gravity and calls the tomb at El Kanitaoui his gift from Allah. If the anti-gravity theory is true, Akhenaten would have known about the phenomena. He knew the desert expands in time and space. One day his mummy might be found, not an empty sarcophagus."

He told Medak about the destructive force of the wind. "Called the *khamsin*, it blows for "only two months each year from the south."

"That's a lot of wind damage for blowing only part of the year. Today the Sphinx is disintegrating in the pollution of a Cairo suburb. Other temples dated about the same should have the same erosion, but don't. There is also more weathering at the Sphinx base than at the head, which defies the wind erosion theory.

"Egyptologists concluded that the Great Sphinx of Giza was much older than the temples and buried longer than five thousand years. When Napoleon found it in 1816, it was buried in sand up to its head. That is impressive, since the sphinx is immense at two hundred and sixty feet long and sixty-five feet high. By 1936, archeologists had excavated it completely out of the sand."

He paused as if remembering. "The fundamental feature of Egyptian civilization is that it was complete at the beginning, it did not develop," said Veilkov. "To them, death is not an end but a transformation."

Medak watched him sip tea and gaze across the desert, as if it hypnotized him. Now he heard the silence of the desert.

They were still sipping tea, thinking about the past. when their driver pulled up. Accepting the blessings of the Coptic monks, they climbed into the Jeep and headed west across the desert in the hands of a short, turbaned local driver named Abu.

• • •

The blacktop road ended, and the Jeep headed down the dirt road running parallel to what had once been a narrow railroad track. Strewn across the sand were rotting wooden rails, testimony to the railroad built by the Germans and Italians in World War II.

Abu steered the Jeep, driving carefully in the soft dirt as the road had become a track. They started early and would end late to cover the nearly 400 miles to the oasis. At the top of the ridge, the driver slowed and pointed south to a faint outline of dry desert mountains, their destination and El Kanitaoui.

• • •

Medak found the trip to date fascinating and was grateful to the Abbot for allowing him to make it. To be here with his mentor was something he never expected. However, in the back of his mind he felt there was more to it; nothing specific, just a lingering doubt as to what their real purpose was in the desert. He wondered what the Abbot knew about El Kanitaoui.

Medak thought Veilkov, who usually never talked, was out of character. The desert seemed to open him up.

"Rainfall has been nonexistent in this area, and there is only one oasis, Bardai, between here and Chad. Lack of water kept the Germans out of the southern desert. Before World War II, German geology expeditions trekked across the desert searching for new routes to the Niger River. The commander visited the monks in the monastery, Gabal El Uweinat, and later sent the monastery a note he had penned from the top of one of the highest peaks in the Southern desert."

"The Tibesti Mountains," said Medak.

"Right. There, the Bardai oasis was surrounded by sandstone towers and volcanic lava flows. One crater named Waw en Namus, or 'Mosquitoes,' was filled with water. Wild date palms grew surrounding it in temperatures over one hundred and twenty degrees. On a later visit, with Marfkis and his helicopter, Benton and I flew over it. From the air, it appeared perfectly round, like a halo, and the most beautiful spot in the southern Sahara. Marfkis landed near the edge and we walked up to the rim of the volcano. There was absolute silence. Such silence is a sound beyond imagination."

Veilkov knew Medak understood silence. He was a monk.

"The immense size of what the Egyptians built always amazes me. Today, the area where the tomb arises was once an inland lakebed. The space program has taken photographs that prove this was true. El Ben, using the excuse of searching for water, asked NASA to get photos to aid in the exploration of oil, but got a no. The Americans saw through it and said their space program wasn't there to prove el Ben's ancestors were Egyptian pharaohs.

"Most of the tombs of the ancient pharaohs in the Nile River Valley over the last centuries, have been looted by grave robbers, with more burial artifacts in the Louvre and the British Museum than in Egypt. Geigner and el Ben believe the cavern at the oasis is Akhenaten's tomb. I agree. But it is easy to go off on tangents. The desert does that to you."

"Akhenaten is an ancient Egypt fad?" asked Medak.

"Yes," replied Veilkov.

"To date, his claim to fame is that he was King Tut's father. On his own, he was a progressive ruler who initiated the concept of only one god, the god of the sun. Amarna is the word for Sun."

Veilkov continued.

"Once when Geigner visited the Gracanica Monastery, he brought a gold head with a jeweled crown about eight inches tall. The man had a beard. He said he had found five heads scattered around the site, believing them to be gifts to Akhenaten from the Amorites, a tribe near Israel. Egyptian rulers were always smooth-skinned. None ever had a beard. He called the heads 'Aaron's Beard.' The Abbot checked out the heads with his religious experts, but nothing ever came of it."

The dirt road turned to blacktop.

"Where was the border?" asked Medak, thinking there must be guards.

Abu smiled a toothless grin. "We crossed it many kilometers ago. Libya has much money and the roads are very good."

CHAPTER TWELVE

El Kanitaoui

The stone tablets, the talatat, found along the Nile River
told the story of what happened centuries ago.

Geigner pulled the jeep to a stop among the tents and goats munching on desert grass and cactus. He pointed to a dirt trail heading up the mountain.

"Now it is time to climb. If it wasn't for the glare of the desert, we could see El Kanitaoui below us."

He led Medak and Veilkov, refreshed from a night's sleep in an air-conditioned trailer, along the narrow ledge on the desert mountain.

Geigner was lost in his own thoughts. He looked again at the valley below, then back up the mountain at the stone tomb. He was looking at a laser weapon, no mummies and without a soul. Odd that after two decades or more in the desert, he still believed in the concept of soul. What he no longer believed was that he was still in control of his life.

Veilkov and Medak were his insurance. Once Veilkov verified the calculation, he would hide it inside one of the gold heads, called Aarons Beard. The head would never be picked up by el Ben's security force, who were marginally competent and only looked for weapons. Medak was the perfect courier to take it to the monastery. For a backup, he would send the calculation to Amy at the villa in Berlin, coded in the margins of Vince's manuscript on *Strogatz and The Legend of Escobar Cay*. No way would the manuscript be seen as a coded message to his cousin.

They climbed about forty yards to a rock stairway curving down into a cavern. The rough floor made walking difficult. The ceiling and walls were the same smooth surface as Egyptian tombs. Medak admired the ancient architects' ability to be both symmetrical and artistic. Mathematical precision was one of the fascinating aspects about ancient civilizations.

The workers had meticulously cleaned out the natural cavern, but an earthquake and half the mountain falling on top of the tomb slowed the pace. The quake probably kept looters from finding the chamber. Khadafy also caused slowdowns, because every time they found another room, a chamber, the workers were sent to Tripoli for prayer and a celebration.

The three entered a large symmetrical rock chamber. Medak and Veilkov saw what Geigner meant. The light of the flares showed the room was a perfectly formed square. There wasn't a rough surface to be found. Geigner pointed a flashlight at the drawings on the walls.

"The stone tablets, the talatat, found along the Nile River told us the story of what happened centuries ago. Many of the stones were taken by explorers or grave robbers. If we could find them, they might tell us what Akhenaten was doing in this chamber. We think it was Akhenaten, since the paintings on the walls of the tomb are the same as those found in the tomb in the Valley of the Kings of his queen

Nefertiti, and their children. Egyptologists believe the two young men in the procession are King Tut and his brother Smenkhkare."

Geigner's flashlight scanned the wall, and the three of them looked at the strange stilted figures in family scenes. They were not an attractive family by today's standards. However, the effort to create this tomb and paint these figures far surpassed many of the burial sites Medak had seen on a trip to Egypt before entering the monastery. The ancient Egyptians royalty were obsessed with afterlife. They devoted their time today, to ensure they would rest in comfort, forever.

Medak looked at the drawings. A riverboat with its mast in full sail and a peacock sitting on the bow caught his attention. He held up the light and looked carefully at the drawings. There were men with beards on the boat.

"The picture is a retreat from the city of Aten?"

Geigner was noncommittal.

"Perhaps; Benton and I gave it a lot of thought. Based on what we had seen in the tombs along the Nile, we decided the drawing was of prisoners from Syria or Hittites who were forced into labor for the Egyptians. They were workers with beards who carved this tomb."

They turned their lights to the sound of grating rocks where several Bedouin, anticipating their arrival, were removing the stone doorway to another room. There was a haze from the film of fine dirt that fell as they walked through the opening to another large room.

Geigner felt like he was on the edge of a discovery every time he entered. He used to read accounts in journals of the Egypt Exploration Society on finding tombs. Then he had felt like a trespasser; now he was one.

"We have found four other tunnels, but none appear to lead to another sarcophagus. They are dead ends, almost as if they were dug out and then filled in. These dead ends are where we found the heads, we call Aarons Beard."

The light revealed an empty stone coffin, a sarcophagus. Geigner brushed the light dust from the engraved side of one of the coffins. It was a gold carving of a man wearing a beard. Geigner translated the inscription.

"*The hawk has gone to heaven; another sits in his place.* This is a favorite quote of Khadafy's. No one ever knew where it came from, and many always thought he made it up," said Geigner, as if everyone knew all of Khadafy's sayings.

"When Egyptologists opened a tomb along the Nile River that they thought was built for Akhenaten, it was empty. However, there were quotes on the walls usually associated with the changing of the ruler. And these quotes are the same."

Geigner told them Akhenaten's tomb along the Nile River wasn't grave robbed, just never used. Akhenaten abdicated; he wasn't killed, just disappeared. The Egyptian nobility eradicated all evidence of his rule. Writings in several tombs referenced him, but no tomb had been found with either a mummy or the trappings that would have been part of a pharaoh's afterlife preparation.

Geigner motioned to the Bedouin standing at the entrance to hold their lights up. Medak and Veilkov could see the theme showed a ceremony, with the same stiff figures, repeated over and over, carrying food, riding on chariots and carrying chests supposedly filled with gold.

To Medak, how the ancient Egyptian, a people of such obvious artistic ability, could spend a lifetime simply repeating the same figures on the walls of the tomb, was amazing. He looked at the inscription on the far wall.

Geigner translated again.

"It is part of a prayer to Aten. So far all we have found is a part of the Great Hymn. Maybe this is an extension to it."

He read the inscription.

"May the Good God live who takes pleasure in truth, Lord of all that Aten encompasses Lord of Heaven, Lord of Earth, Aten the Living, the Great who illumes the Two Lands, may the Father live."

"There was a mummy here?" asked Veilkov.

With a look of disgust, Geigner nodded his head yes. "For years the mummy has been in at a lab in Tripoli. El Ben refuses to allow any testing. The Asians made forensic pathology an art many years ago. The western world calls it a science. Sonora gave a pathologist from Cairo an airline ticket to come and visit El Kanitaoui, but el Ben still refuses to let anyone analyze or carbon-date the mummies. He says it has something to do with Islamic law and desecrating bodies."

Without testing the mummy, they all knew there was no way to verify if it was Egyptian nobility or not.

Geigner continued, "If this mural on the wall is Akhenaten you can see he took only the clothes on his back, jewelry, and one of the carved statues of the gold head with the beard to the next life. In contrast, the tombs in the Valley of the Kings were filled with gold offerings to take on the journey to the next life."

They looked again at the drawing on the wall of the tomb. "The ruler is this rather oddly built man here."

Geigner flashed the flare to a large male figure that looked like a clown. He tapped the wall.

"Akhenaten was believed to have some type of thyroid problem that gave him the large head and stomach with spindly limbs. It is not the body of a warrior. I believe he was more of a spiritual intellectual which is his true legacy.

"The man with the beard is called Aaron. Scholars believe he is the brother of Moses, while others think he was Akhenaten's half-brother. His servant is carrying the disc, representing the god Aten. Because he wears a beard, it means he is not Egyptian, so we dubbed it Aaron's beard. These wall drawings are the only evidence we have showing a disc in the tomb.

"We found other heads at the base of the second part of the excavation, but none with a beard. Ten years ago, the earthquake blocked us in many places, but not in the main chamber which is the essential part of the entire excavation."

They turned to walk a short distance back down the passage, then turned down a rocky corridor. Medak had missed that passage the first time. It led to another row of steps and to a corridor that went deeper inside the cliff. After about twenty feet, it turned, and they were standing on an open stone platform with a view of the desert below.

Stone-hewed carvings aligned in even rows surrounded them. Geigner walked to the edge of the stone platform and pointed back above them.

They climbed up a metal ladder to a smooth stone chamber. Veilkov estimated it was at least one hundred feet long. Half of it was in the cliff and over many centuries, has defied earthquakes. That was why Geigner wanted him to see the site.

Geigner was watching Veilkov. He needed to know what the old monk was thinking but decided the moment could wait.

"Now you see the second part of el Kanitaou's mystery, what we call the weapon. What is this chamber we asked? We had no answers. It looks like a radar or beacon light for a runway in the desert below.

"At night, the views of the stars from this chamber seem to transport you to outer space. Remember, during the last years of Akhenaten's rule, the Egyptian empire was falling apart. Queen Ti came to his palace in Amarna to provoke him into action. After her visit, his wife Nefertiti moved to the north end of Amarna on the Nile. Whether Nefertiti wanted Akhenaten to go to war or not may be lost in the stone talatat forever. But we do know he lived alone in isolation with the god Aten, then abdicated and disappeared. I believe he moved here to communicate with a higher being."

"This fits your belief, Geigner; no Jesus, no Mohammed, just a higher being. What about el Ben?" asked Veilkov.

"El Ben believes in one god, Allah. His goal is to prove his lineage to the Egyptian pharaohs. On this ledge we found two of the gold heads of Aaron. They were complete with his carved beard. But the real purpose of the cavern escaped me until I remembered your background, Veilkov. You were a scientist. Benton told me you worked on lasers and the concept of accelerated electrons when the science was just beginning."

Geigner paused, waiting for Veilkov to think about what he had said, then continued his explanation.

"Benton and I tested this odd chamber and discovered the lack of gravitational pull. He and Vince had searched in Asia for such places, and out of the blue we find it here.

"There are two requirements for the tomb to be a weapon. One is energy to drive the beam and the other is to aim it. I was faced with the same problem scientists had. How do you aim the beam and still retain power to accelerate the electrons? I had to accept the limitations of the cavern just as the ancients had."

Veilkov said nothing and Medak felt the chill of the tomb. He was ready to leave, but Geigner wasn't finished.

"This way."

They followed him back into the mountain and turned down another long passage, this one carefully constructed by man. Inside another door was a room filled with computers and electronics and at the back wall an elevator.

"Not much to look at here, but at the top you will get the whole picture."

Geigner hit the up button in the elevator and a few seconds later, the door opened on a platform. To the right were solar collectors going up the side of the mountain. To the left the rocks and crevices blocked the view of the desert floor.

"Pretty heavy concealment," said Veilkov.

Geigner agreed.

"The natural rock formations were here when we found the chamber and are basic to the design of the laser."

They looked down at reflecting mirrors set inside the rocks.

"The reflexing mirrors are the prism. It took us some time to figure it out, but that rock formation isn't natural. The rocks have been arranged and cut to carefully fit. The work is by a master craftsman."

Geigner pointed to the mirrors.

"What they do is focus the beam, making it coherent when it arrives at a target out in space. Did you know the American government has spent billions on research on the concept of the size of the beam length? None of that is worth a dime. The beam only must be coherent when it arrives at the mirrors. Mirrors of the best optical quality create power which, like the ability to aim, is necessary to success."

"Impressive," said Veilkov.

Geigner said there was one more feature to see.

"The real breakthrough for us revolved around a phenomenon of nature that Leonardo da Vinci discovered. He called it *self-induced transparency*. Today, the name is nonlinear optical conjugation. Our beam in the chamber hits a prism and—no pun intended—the electron particles are spaced out. They reflect from the mirror to the prism at the back of the tomb and come back out. Then, they are sent to a point in space predetermined by the computer, which is tracking the satellite, missiles, and planes.

"Lleissle International makes the optics, and without them, we would be nowhere. We call them SIT, or self-induced transparency. Though modified, it is based on da Vinci's model."

He paused for them to think a moment about what he had said. "We don't have to knock down weapons. The computer, using the zero gravity of the tomb, targets the communications systems destroying the ability of the weapon to be aimed. Again, Lleissle International supplied the electronic parts, or I could never have put it together. The computer program to aim the laser at the weapon's communications system is the key to success. Simulators are great for running the computer programs, but how can we test the computer program in real life? The Alemien family thinks the testing we have done works, but it hasn't. They don't understand the system well enough to see the flaw."

"If it works, does that mean el Ben will tell the Russians and America to SIT on it?" asked Medak.

Geigner chuckled.

"Probably, but here's what's important. The Bedouin understand the need for energy to power the weapon, but don't realize the guidance system is critical. I've made programming the computer look easy, but you must be able to aim the laser.

"The laser is a single wavelength. When focused, it works best in the upper atmosphere. The missiles go into that atmosphere. Once there, energy is used to guide the weapons. In the simulation, I create energy through a computer program that energizes the heads and magnifies the force of the beam. The laser beam accelerates as the computer programs the distortion, then refocuses it.

As sophisticated as computer technology is, I am still not sure my computer program to guide the beam is correct."

He stopped for a moment, flushed with a feeling of pride in how much he had accomplished.

"Veilkov, I need you to verify the calculation to aim the laser. Benton was going to ask you, but then he died."

Veilkov understood. When Benton died, the fragility of human life became a reality for Geigner. To the monk, Geigner was an obsessed scientist. The truth was, all the Prowers he knew were obsessed, including Sonora and Benton. He wondered where Amy was in the spectrum.

"As you know, I studied laser technology until I entered the monastery. It's been a long time, but I'll take a look." He looked around at the dials and control room and realized the project at El Kanitaoui raised ethical questions about the use of science.

Geigner led them through a steel door to a control room built by technicians. Medak had a question.

"You talked about a power source. Where is it in your system?"

Geigner's explanation was a surprise.

"Below us is an electron chamber that the ancients used for power. The chamber is a free magnetic force field. As a weapon, it gives us a tremendous advantage. The superpowers are trying to build what they call Star Wars, but it already exists in this cavern on el Ben's real estate."

Walking down another passage, they were outside the chamber on top of the cliff. To the south were rough rock cliffs. They looked up, as out of the silence of the desert came the scream of silver and blue helicopter blades.

"The chopper is taking el Habed to join el Ben on the top of the mountain for evening prayers," said Geigner. "Now that you've seen the weapons, we can take the elevator down to the desert floor."

• • •

They arrived at the Jeep, and Geigner opened a cooler filled with German beer and slices of barbecued goat and loafs of fresh flatbread.

"This is the Arab version of a drive-in restaurant," said Geigner. "We will eat and drink, then drive back to the main oasis at El Kanitaoui before sundown. El Ben sends a plane to Cairo every day and I got you seats on it. I am not sure it is safe to drive back after you have seen the system. Accidents seem to happen in the desert."

They sat in comfortable camp chairs, listening to the silence of the desert air blowing from the cliffs across the sand as the last traces of the sun filled the sky with hues of red and orange. As the sun began to set, Veilkov spoke up. "Let's see the calculation."

Geigner took from his backpack the rendering of a small head of a man with a distinctive beard all in gold. He popped open the head and pulled out a piece of paper. Almost apologetically, he turned to Veilkov.

"I suppose I am paranoid, thinking someone would want this paper. I keep it in the head of Aaron's beard, the relic from the ruins. Confirm my calculation and prove the tomb is a land-based laser. I know it has been a while since you worked in Vienna on lasers, but God willing, you're my expert. You understand the guidance system and the need to accurately aim."

Veilkov agreed. Without a guidance system, the weapon was worthless.

"El Ben and his sons, understand the need for energy, about powering the weapon, but oddly enough, they think it aims itself. They don't understand the weapon will only work on one side of the world. It can't see the other side with China or Australia," said Geigner.

"Forget the other side of the world," Veilkov sounded like the expert he is. "A ground-based laser system isn't part of any peace agreement under negotiation that we know of. Whoever has it can rule the world."

He paused, thinking about the weapon. "I remember your Javanese expression, water from the moon. You want what you can never have. You created it, but you can't control it."

Geigner smiled.

"You're right, Veilkov. My last test was worthless. I think my calculation to aim the laser at the weapon was wrong. It might miss the target by thousands of miles. El Ben and his sons think it works because it works in a simulator. But I question whether it will work in the real world of space."

They both knew the calculation could allow any nation to reproduce the weapon. The force fields concept wouldn't matter. Veilkov knew there would be no distinction between using the weapons for peace and starting a war.

Geigner's knapsack seemed to be bottomless. He pulled out what looked like a small computer, but it was not an ordinary computer. As he turned it on, Veilkov knew it had to be something Sonora's Committee had procured for him.

Geigner turned on the screen and pointed to a shadowed pattern of lines.

"This is the ultimate in computer simulations. I call it windows to space. The computer on a preset program should direct the laser to the targets communication system. The mountains here form a natural prism and the force fields direct the laser in a beam. Vince, Benton, and I searched for years to find the so-called force fields. It is ironic Akhenaten's tomb is one of those fields."

"None of this is new," Veilkov murmured, almost sounding bored. "You have built a system and forgotten the point. This weapon could give Khadafy and el Ben the power to hold nations hostage."

"What can the scientist do?" asked Geigner.

Veilkov had no answer. He knew each man had to decide for himself what to do with his discovery.

Changing the subject, Geigner asked, "What do you think about the heads we called Aarons Beard?"

"They are icons of a different sort, a picture of the past and a symbol of the future," said Veilkov.

Medak, listening to their discussion, knew they needed to get back to today. It was time to speak up.

"The past is what people dwell on when there is no future. They cling to it to reinforce what might have been. Look up in the sky. The stars you see are where the future lies. The sands of time cover whatever past existed. In the Middle East, the Egyptian civilization, one of many, is gone. What do we have today?"

"This." Geigner held up a small flash drive.

"The drive holds all the programs and can be run on my laptop. Well, not just any laptop, but one like my super laptop. Like we have talked about, the real problem for any weapon system is aiming the laser and providing power to it. The aim is irrelevant if there isn't a power source."

Quickly he explained to Medak and Veilkov how he had developed a power source in the tomb by designing an alternating system run by a microcomputer using a series of energizing electronic heads to magnify the force of the beam. The computer on a preset program directed the level of energy out of the cavity to form a beam.

"These are Vince's windows to space. He spent his life searching for them and likely died trying to find one in central Asia."

The computer was running and as they watched the screen, an error message popped up. Geigner's program didn't work. Veilkov thought a moment, then punched a few keys, creating a revised calculation. Geigner ran the simulation again and it worked. He grinned at Veilkov and wrote the changes down, returning the paper into the gold head.

"Geigner, you did what makes sense when you have no gravity. You allowed for no distortion in the beam, only there is always the pull from gravity, no matter how slight. My research showed even in a low gravity field there is a slight distortion of the laser. Correcting the distortion corrects your calculation."

He gestured grandly to the sky. "If you don't correct, the laser will be aimed into the next galaxy. With the correction, you have the land-based laser."

Veilkov leaned across the table as though they were the only people in the world.

"All the research in the world, all the armies in the world, can't do what this tomb can."

Geigner sipped his drink. The force fields were real. The folklore of Asia that Vince, Benton, maybe even his mother, Jarra, had heard so long ago was true. Had Vince known before his death? What difference did it make now? The possibilities frightened him, as the weapon could be replicated anywhere.

One thing he knew more than any other. He could never allow el Ben to have the calculation.

• • •

The next step was to put the exit plan into operation. The correct calculation wouldn't be safe in the desert. He couldn't allow El Ben to control it. But he could trust Veilkov and Medak with the formula.

Geigner spoke thoughtfully.

"Can I trust you both to see my computer program survives? I want to give you a gold head; well, actually two gold heads. One will be a decoy, the other will contain the correct calculation. When you get to the Gracanica Monastery and Amy visits, give it to her. If anyone comes asking you about the calculation, you can give them the head with the decoy."

Veilkov was emphatic. "Medak should take them. I have the calculation in my head. It will be enough."

Medak agreed, but said he had no idea when he would see Amy. Geigner was confident he'd see her soon.

"She'll be back at the monastery. She's looking for the icon, the other part of el Ben's dream."

He picked up the heads and turned them upside down for Medak. The bottom of one head had scars from when it was dug out of the rocks, and he explained it held the original calculation. He took the other head—the one where he had put the correct calculation was smooth. He handed both to Medak.

"Geigner, I'm still confused. From what I have read, el Ben cares. He is a devout Muslim with none of the personal excesses of Khadafy. His dedication to the laws of Muhammad requires him to leave more in the world than was here when he came. This is his message from Allah."

"Medak," said Geigner, "El Ben's idealism is worse than Khadafy's excess."

There was a small pool of water between the rocks. Geigner pulled a coin out of his pocket. For good luck, he always dropped a coin into the pond. He looked at the coin and stopped. It was the so-called lucky coin given him by Marfkis. Instead he handed it over to Medak.

"Don't drop it in the pond like I almost did."

Medak looked at it.

"This is the so-called lucky coin. I knew the story and gave Veilkov's coin to Amy."

"Well, now you have mine which I got from Marfkis, unless Veilkov wants his back."

Veilkov laughed, "no way, keep it."

Geigner picked up a couple of pebbles and dropped them in the water. Concentric circles formed and radiated outward with symmetrical precision.

"Medak, I wanted to show you the circles. This is a concise picture of how the system works. Everyone is looking at the circles, or in the case of the laser, the beam, the light waves, but the rocks haven't moved from their location. This is the heart of the problem in strategic defense. It is to pick out the correct targets, the rocks. Discriminating systems is the technical term. Without it, the system fires at decoys."

They looked at the pond. Veilkov spoke.

"It is the Italian connection, Leonardo de Vinci, who was the first to say that the pebbles never leave their first location."

Medak put the coin in his pocket and said nothing. Geigner was tied to the past and was a part of the sands of this oasis. His mentor Veilkov lived in the past. Was he the only one with a future?

• • •

There wasn't much time if Medak and Veilkov were to catch the flight to Cairo, but Geigner needed to ask Veilkov about the icon, if only to help Amy. Quickly he explained to the monks how the Shroud of Turin was necessary to el Ben's dream of conquest.

Veilkov understood.

"He needs the Coptic support to rule and for that, he needs to give them a sign. The Shroud of Turin is the sign. There is nothing more powerful than a weapon and now, a symbol. It fits with el Ben's dream and the quote from Sun Tzu where you need power and a system. I quote, *all men can see these tactics whereby I conquer, but what none can see is the strategy out of which victory is evolved.*"

"Veilkov, you're right. But none of that is important unless we have the Shroud. Benton saw you more than anyone over the years when he visited the monastery. If he hid it there, you must know where."

Veilkov, holding up his hands as if in protest, said "All I know is that the artwork on the train was destroyed. I can still hear the explosion. My concern was for the baby who was raised and loved by my sister and the villagers."

Geigner didn't look convinced. He found it hard to believe Veilkov was there when the train blew up, and still stuck to the view the artwork was destroyed. Veilkov's insistence made him think the Shroud survived the crash. So where was it?

As he watched the two monks climb into the plane, Geigner thought *nothing ever ends.* He needed to put his back-up plan into action in case something happened to Medak. He would code the correct calculation in Vince's story on Strogatz and send it to Amy in Berlin. No way would el Ben's security bother with some trivial story called *Strogatz and The Legend of Escobar Cay.*

• • •

Veilkov looked out the window of the plane as the desert spread before them. He trusted no one and would keep the secret of the Shroud. How could any of them know so many years ago what the future would hold? Benton left Amy all those crazy clues, obviously confident she would figure them out. He had no reason to think she wouldn't.

When he met Benton Prowers during the war, he was never sure who was Benton's boss, or why Benton was with the two German women and the General to southern Egypt after the war. Supposedly they were hiding. Everyone was looking for Nazis in those days but not in Egypt. Today it seemed odd. At the time, it seemed normal because the Italian ports were the obvious escape route out of Europe not Albania.

Veilkov could still see the dirt swirling behind the Jeeps as they rushed across the southern tip of Egypt, trying to reach the cargo ship waiting for them at the south end of the Suez Canal. They could have saved themselves the trouble. Von Hagen would never have let the ship leave without them. The General risked his life to stay with them. Why, he never knew. Did the General not want to leave Eva, or was he waiting for more spoils of the war, artwork, gold, who could say, to show up?

Veilkov didn't believe in coincidences, but he knew what was happening today was because of those days in Egypt. Except for the Abbot, they were all there together, years after the war. He shook his head, attempting to shake the thoughts from his past. He was seeing innuendo in every statement, a Nazi behind every sand dune. He put thoughts of the past aside, knowing he was returning to the Gracanica Monastery for his annual retreat. Should he tell the Abbot where the Shroud was? There would be time for that discussion after his retreat.

He looked at the sky. The moon was out, and he could clearly see the desert below him. It wasn't flat, as so many believed, but rolled in what to him was a floral pattern. He would miss the sands of this oasis.

· · ·

Sonora looked up, glad to see Ace had dragged himself away from the computer.

"Your timing is perfect. The President is making a speech on the results of the summit conference with the Russians and the leaders of western Europe. Don't know about you, but I will need another drink to listen to his words. I doubt they will be filled with wisdom. Bourbon for you."

Ace agreed. "Right, I never drink wine. It is a taste I never have acquired—or I just don't like France or California."

Sonora laughed. "You could be a fascist for not drinking their wines. For me, just bourbon, and I don't care from what country."

They watched the TV screen. The President filled the screen as he walked down the red carpet from Air Force One to the row of microphones. His stride was youthful, and his smile a carbon copy of the man he had replaced. This man with the vacuous head—once the Vice-President—had taken over the seat of power for the Western world after the President, an avid jogger, suffered a stroke jogging and mercifully died. In Sonora's opinion, his death was a black day for the country and its political aims.

"My friends, this summit conference has changed the course of the world arms race. I am proud to announce that we anticipate signing a treaty with all UN members before the month is over. In the next few days, I will present the details to Congress and with my colleagues expect to take a step for peace that will last long into the next century. Living in a world with nuclear parity will be a new future for us, the entire world, and one all Americans desire. Star Wars is here, my friends."

He held up his hands.

"No questions, please. I'll have a detailed press conference in the morning."

Sonora turned the TV to mute.

"Thankfully, our business is more interesting than his speeches. The problem for the Committee in supporting Star Wars is politics. The President is playing political games, and no one knows what the rules are for a real arms strategy. Now the proposals are a public relations strategy. But if agreement comes, there will be another worry; the third world nations."

Ace knew she was thinking of El Kanitaoui and what such a weapon would give the Alemien family. He reminded her what Geigner had said on a visit a few years before. If the laser beam could not be aimed, there was no weapon.

Sonora for a moment was silent.

What irony, she thought, *if this was true*?

CHAPTER THIRTEEN

Vera Cruz

Her father told her it was important to know
the difference between truth and fiction.

As the plane began its descent to the Vera Cruz airport, Amy took
a last look at the white thunderheads rising above the dark Mexican
coastal mountains. She knew her future was tied to her parents' past.
Her parents were in World War II, but they never talked about it. And
until the plane crash that killed her father, she hadn't cared. Now their
past had everything to do with finding the Shroud.

Medak said what happened in a train crash in the rugged Serbian
mountains during the war was one more accident of nature or war. He
was wrong. The train wreck was her parents' past. Reliving that past
appeared to be her destiny.

She turned on the tape from the Committee's meeting, having
promised Sonora she would listen to all of it. The members shared
a common political interest. They were part Jeffersonian in human

rights, part Hamiltonian in economics, and part General Patton on defense. Over time they had simply become the Committee. She listened passively to the last few minutes of the tape. It ended with "We believe *el Ben may have a weapon system that will outdate the concept of global war.*" She flipped the switch to off.

Her cousin had spent years working on building the ultimate weapon using the tomb of the ancient Egyptian Pharaoh Akhenaten. If el Ben controlled the laser weapon, he had the world where he wanted it. And the world had no idea what was coming. Momentarily, she was glad her father and Vince wouldn't be around to see that end. They were the lucky ones.

I will likely be around, however, and the thought made her want to take some action—any action—to prevent el Ben from gaining control of the weapon. Geigner would be the one to stop him. He was always secretive and self-contained. Her father told her scientists had those traits, but she thought that was an excuse for being different.

Outside the plane window, she saw the blue waters of the Gulf of Mexico. Returning to Mexico was like coming home. She remembered the times she and her father spent at the hacienda. Today her family had sold most of their land but kept the oil leases. They were a reason to keep the hacienda where she could enjoy the sea and the Mexican culture. *I'm like Sonora. We both like big houses.*

She leaned back against the seat. *Why would my father take me to Serbia and then to Mexico? Why would he go to this trouble? He never trusted nor liked the General. They shared business deals and socialized together, but there was never trust.*

The plane bounced in the turbulence created by the mountains. Fortunately, she was holding her drink. She found the General charming, making it hard for her to imagine what his life was like in Nazi Germany. *We see the person the way they are today, the way we want them to be, not the way they are.*

Sonora had warned her, and her father had cautioned in his letter not to trust anyone with his clues. Her aunt believed he was killed for the Shroud, and whoever did it would not hesitate to kill her. Sonora worried she wasn't prepared for the type of danger she might encounter, but agreed the clues were meant for her to interpret. Her aunt called it her legacy. If there was a problem, she promised Sonora she'd get out of Mexico on one of the Prowers' company planes.

Both Sonora and Ace said she could handle the General, who trusted her because of the time they spent on joint business interests. Knowing she might be a target made her more determined to outwit her foes, whoever they were.

The plane hit the runway, forcing her out of her reverie. Right now, she needed a friend, and hoped the Prowers plantation manager, Jaime, could help.

• • •

Jaime was waiting for her at the airport. As they drove along the Gulf of Mexico to the hacienda, palm trees waved in the gentle breeze that blew in the port city. Ahead of them was the old fort, the San Juan de Ulua Castle with its' Spanish dungeons and ironically, the best view of the city. The setting sun silhouetted cargo ships in the harbor. In between were small fishing boats. The cobblestone streets ground on the car wheels as they circled around a statue in the square.

Within minutes, tires crunched on the white gravel roadway as the car slowed before the hacienda gates. The driveway ended at a multi-storied stucco house, with a ten-foot wooden door that Benton said belonged in a church, that opened into a cool foyer.

Jaimie's wife, Rosa, squeezed Amy in a bear hug, handing her a note. Amy opened it, not surprised to see it was from the General.

"Rosa, he wants me to come to lunch tomorrow afternoon before the reception. What do you think?"

"Isn't that why you came?"

Amy smiled. "Yes, I suppose so."

Then with more confidence than she felt, said, "Tell the General I'll be there."

• • •

Amy woke several times in the night. She kept seeing her father and hearing his voice. As the first traces of dawn crossed the sky, she found herself wandering down the staircase to his library. The leather-bound books stacked floor to ceiling in wooden cases were the equivalent of a small college library. Richly colored Oriental carpets gave the room a sense of tranquility.

She leaned back in the chair, the smooth leather cool on her back. She could feel her father's presence as her eyes focused on a row of World War II books. She recalled his reaction to her history assignment in high school on World War II and the death of Hitler. Her father began reading the textbook, and one passage seemed to upset him.

Listen to this, Amy he'd said.

In April of 1945, the world refused to believe Hitler and Eva Braun were dead in the Berlin bunker. Marshal Zhukov, head of the Russian Army, was the first to reach the Berlin bunker, but refused to issue a statement saying they were dead. General Eisenhower said he thought Hitler was dead until he talked to the Russians. Cremated human remains were found in the garden above the bunker. Hitler's bodyguard said it was Hitler and Eva Braun. No autopsy report was ever done.

When her father read that chapter, he said history books often missed the obvious. It was then she learned how her mother and Eva got out of Berlin.

When the Russians were advancing on Berlin, your mother landed at the air strip not far from the bunker. She flew Eva Braun out of Berlin.

Veilkov and I met the two women at the Serbian border to escort them to Mexico. The operation was known only to a few and was intended to end the war. I was never sure that was true, but it got the women to Mexico.

Amy understood his point. When the truth was hidden, history books like the one she was reading were worthless. He told her it was important to know the difference between truth and fiction. If you wanted the truth you had to do the research yourself.

That was the day she learned her mother knew Hitler. She should have asked more questions but was afraid of the answers. Knowing her mother was a Nazi—or worse, an unrepentant Nazi—was enough.

Now her past has become my problem.

On the carved oak table was a Bible and she remembered the clue from her father's letter concerning the book of Daniel, chapter seven. His letter warned of the fourth beast. The vision of the four beasts intrigued her. Even Daniel didn't understand the true meaning of the terrifying fourth beast. Was it a person or a nation?

She opened the book and read the short chapter, destroying her perception that Biblical chapters went on without end. *The fourth beast, the fourth kingdom, will appear on earth and be different from all other kingdoms and devour the whole earth, trampling it and crushing it down.*

What was on the note under the icon in the monastery? Medak said beware of the fourth beast. Amy closed the Bible and walked to the large glass windows. The pre-dawn color of the sky was now a vivid orange.

She had no idea what was on her father's mind in his last days. Between the General and Jaime, she hoped to solve the puzzle.

CHAPTER FOURTEEN

The General and el Ben

Benton's visits to the monastery
made him think the Shroud was not destroyed.

From his patio overlooking the port of Vera Cruz, General Georg von Hagen pushed aside the red snapper, el pargo, and thought, *damn the cook*. He twitched his thin nose. It hadn't tasted right; not enough of the famous Vera Cruz hot sauce. Had his doctor been talking to his cook to wean him off chilies? Life was difficult when the things he enjoyed— like green chilies—came in small doses.

He nodded to his staff to take the plate away, making a mental note to talk to the cook, and looked over the pool. In the distance were the shipping docks and oil tankers that he owned with the Prowers family.

The view of the city and gulf was the same as seen by the Spanish explorer Hernando Cortés in 1519, before he burned his ships, to prevent his men from leaving. Since then, over the centuries, the eastern coast of Mexico had developed into an international power exporting

Mexican produce all over the world. With the discovery of oil in 1938, the port became a hub for exploration, transporting, and refining of oil products. Today it was too small to accommodate super tankers, but one day it would, of that he was certain.

He watched locals stroll the tree-lined promenade along the coast of the Gulf of Mexico. On Sundays, they'd eat at little food stands, listen to local music and sip tequila. Large numbers of Germans had been immigrating to Mexico since the nineteenth century. They made Vera Cruz a safe destination for former Nazis escaping Europe after World War II.

Identity papers, he thought. No one got out without identity papers. His family had their friend Bishop Alois Hudal from Graz, Austria, to thank.

"*We must be careful,*" the bishop had said. "*The relief organizations don't know I am simpatico to the Nazis. Our families have known each other for generations. I will prepare a false background for you.*"

Pouring more tequila, the General pondered, as he often did, how ignorant the relief organizations were after the war. Naïve men and women had no idea the bishop was not only a Nazi, but an honorary member of the Nazi party. This group was more infamously known today as Odessa. The relief organizations never made the connection. The bishop provided references to the Red Cross, who issued new passports and identities. After all, who would question the word of a Catholic Bishop?

The General took a long sip of tequila. He enjoyed the taste, but wished it was vodka, still his favorite drink. The Bishop and the Catholic Church feared the Bolsheviks, the Communists. To them, class conflict and the communist worker movements in Europe were a threat to the Catholic Church and to the Vatican. The Nazis were secondary.

A dedicated Nazi, the bishop published a book in 1937 praising Hitler. Somehow that fact was lost at the end of the war. The bishop's brother was killed on the Eastern Front and after his death, the bishop became a Nazi. He was named the protector of the German national church in Rome and met SS Intelligence chief, Walter Rauff. The two set up the escape route for Nazis out of Germany, called the ratline.

The main escape route was planned from Innsbruck over the Brenner Pass to the Italian port of Bari. Nazi hunters focused on South American destinations and routes out of Italy. The General knew if he had used those routes, he would have been caught.

He owed his life to the bishop who used a different escape route for his friends. The Albanian port of Durres was where the General, Benton, Hanna, and Eva departed for southern Egypt. Looking back, he realized the timing couldn't have been better if they had planned it.

The two women, Hanna and Eva, believed that Hitler assigned the General to escort them out of Austria. The truth was, the General re-assigned the officer detailed to guard the women and personally took the duty. But he couldn't get rid of Benton or Veilkov. In the end, each needed the other.

"I don't remember the day I knew the war was lost," said the General to his peaceful view of the water, but he knew the Third Reich was finished long before the war ended. Eva and Hanna provided the opportunity to get out of Germany with his art and jewels. He had already moved the family's money to Swiss bank accounts.

He added another slice of lime to his tequila remembering, luck had a lot to do with getting out of Europe.

The timing had to be right, as Nazi hunters were everywhere. No one paid attention to an Albanian freighter heading to Alexandra. They waited over a year in Egypt, longer than anyone would have thought.

The Prowers family provided good cover. To an outsider, they appeared to be one group heading for Vera Cruz. If Benton reported the General, he would identify Eva and Hanna. He smiled to himself. Maybe he had blackmailed Prowers just a little.

Good fortune completed their cover when Sonora and her husband, a Swiss count, arrived to take the same freighter to Mexico. *Ironic*, he thought, *that during a war the couple continued to explore ruins in the Valley of the Kings.* He often wondered about the Count's connections. He seemed to know everyone. He and Sonora went through customs and official checks with no problems.

He looked up to see his butler hadn't forgotten him.

"Time for brandy, sir?"

"Please."

His doctor did not approve of brandy any more than the hot sauce, but the General didn't care. What did doctors know? What life did he have left? He didn't know, nor did his doctor. For all either of them knew, the tequila, vodka and brandy were keeping him alive.

His favorite German brandy was warm and refined. Mexican wines were tolerable and the tequila superb, but for brandy, there was nothing like the real thing. His thin hands raised his glass and savored the sips. It warmed his throat, a contrast to the cool sea breezes that blew against the mountain slopes above the city.

Now was the time to call el Ben. With Benton dead, the leader must be scrambling to know where the Shroud was. He could make a deal.

Lies and blackmail, he thought, *are my specialties.* No one seemed to know where the Shroud was, if it still existed. El Ben would never know he was lying.

Beneath the hacienda, the city lights flickered. One by one, the lights of Vera Cruz turned on, like a giant switch moving across the city. But so often today, his mind turned to memories of when World War II ended. These days he seemed to spend more time in the past than the future. His eyes saw images; his memories, moving in slow motion as if the past was a motion picture.

In the mountains, the partisans viciously attacked troops, but in the city of Belgrade, the ambiance was as if there was no war. Collaborators from across the Balkans flooded the city, trying to decide if Athens or Istanbul was a safer port to escape to South America. The restaurants and cabarets stayed open day and night.

He was young but had good reason to know the value of bribes— payments, as he called them. Early in 1940 while on a special mission, his ship was sunk in the Baltic. He was credited with a daring escape when he was in Rostock. He survived the incident with only a slight limp, the result of slipping off the step of the brothel in a hasty effort to leave before a raid. He paid the brothel owner a fortune to lie for him, but it was worth it. Unfit to serve on the front, he transferred to the SS, Hitler's elite protective service assigned to evaluate art works.

Assigned to Vienna, he used his knowledge to collect art for the Nazis. He traveled across the Balkans, collecting valuable pieces from every country. If the owner was Jewish, so much the better, as the price was cheap and often free. He never turned anyone, including Jews, into the authorities, because the war was an opportunity to pursue his interest in art. What good fortune, when so many were being sent to the front.

He studied and quickly became an expert in Renaissance and twentieth century art. His younger brother, now a monk, earned a reputation for his work with icons in Germany and Austria. The General still found it hard to believe his brother had spent his life in a religious order. He knew that when art was the issue, his brother's soul would always go to the highest bidder.

Before the war, as students returning from Graz, the two brothers visited the Austrian village of Lambach, between Linz and Salzburg. There, in a Benedictine monastery, were the best of the Byzantine frescoes painted by eleventh-century masters, unknown monks. Using family money, the brothers restored the monastery. They had no idea this was where the Fuhrer had attended elementary school. Hitler learned of von Hagen's work from those years so long ago and promoted him to the rank of general in the SS. Interesting, he had often thought, how art saved both brothers from the war.

He sipped his brandy. By the end of the war, smuggled artwork had made him wealthy. Nazi officers saw art as a source of funds to build a new Reich. The General was believed to be one of the leaders, when he could have cared less about the Reich.

The years in Mexico passed as he built a fortune but missed the adrenaline rush that came from war. Looking out on the lights of Vera Cruz, he wasn't happy, just resigned. The Shroud of Turin was an art object. He thought it was destroyed when the train blew up. But it wasn't. He mistakenly believed his brother would have told him if it was saved. *You can't trust the religious, even if you're related,* he thought.

There were two questions: was the Shroud destroyed, and if not, where had it been all these years? The mystery seemed absurd to him, but there was nothing he could do.

Impossible, he thought. *How could anyone trace a piece of cloth lost over fifty years ago? Lost, that is, only if it still exists.*

That was yesterday. Benton's visits over the years to the monastery made him think the Shroud wasn't destroyed.

If Benton told anyone, it would be Amy. He discounted Geigner, who had his head in the clouds. He also discounted Sonora and Ace, but less confidently. He tried to reason with Benton when he was alive, but never got anywhere. He continued to insist the Shroud was destroyed in the train crash. When Benton died, he was depressed, because he thought the Shroud might be gone forever. Anton and Olen rigged Benton's plane. The younger generation didn't understand. They were impatient. He blamed himself for not having taught them better. Or was it genetics? Anton was the son of a Serbian colonel. The General sighed; the colonel was psychotic, so what could he expect in Anton? Olen was his sister's son. It was comforting to know his nephew's genes were intelligent. And Olen and Amy Prowers were friends which pleased him. He needed to know the Prowers family, at least Amy and maybe even Sonora were on his side in his dealings with el Ben.

I don't have many more years, he said to himself. *But if I could spend them putting together a political regime to control the oil in North Africa, would I care about the character of the man behind the vision? Do I care if the Wiesenthal Foundation is looking into our past? No.*

He smiled. *Nothing can touch me. I am just like el Ben. Power is my life and opportunities come to me.*

Never would the General have thought some Christian artifact could become so important to an Arab dream of conquest. To him, the Coptics were a splinter quasi-Christian sect in Arab countries. But today, the Shroud of Turin was the Christian relic needed to cement the tribal factions in North Africa, specifically Egypt. El Ben could control North Africa from Morocco to the Red Sea. I will offer my services to find the Shroud. Trouble was, when dealing with el Ben, there was no certainty. But Amy, who'd been in the Balkans, was coming to Mexico. She was the key.

He paused to check his watch, then looked out at the gulf. Anton was due to call and update him on what was happening in Serbia. Almost as if on cue, the phone rang on the General's veranda.

"I'll take it in the study," said the General.

He listened and was silent. Anton hurried with his message, hearing disapproval in the General's silence.

"I'm near the monastery. They think I am Bulgarian, a good cover."

There was a pause. The General began to worry, and with reason.

"Anton, I think the Shroud is at the monastery. Looking for it in Mexico is just Benton's misdirection. I'm sure Amy will show up for the archeology meeting. Olen can handle what might happen in Mexico. My instinct is after the presentation Amy will return to the monastery. Eventually, she will figure out her father's clues. When I talk to her, I will get a better idea of what's going on."

Von Hagen placed the phone gently in its cradle.

When Anton rigged the engine in Benton's plane, none of them knew the implications of Benton's death. It wasn't until the General sent el Ben the so-called lucky coin, given him by Benton for supporting archeological causes, that he learned the importance of the Shroud. The Shroud still existed, or at least it existed in el Ben's mind.

His fingers massaged the glass of brandy. His eyes gleamed. He looked around the study and surveyed the fourteenth-century frescoes. He was annoyed. The icon of *Christ in Glory*, his favorite, was not in the collection, nor was the Shroud of Turin. What had Benton Prowers done with the Shroud? Too many questions and not enough answers.

There was no way to get around the question: if the Shroud had not been destroyed, who would know where it was? With Benton dead, the list was amazingly short. At the top of the short list was his brother, the Abbot, but the General didn't think he knew. Veilkov had to know.

He looked at the clock. Time to call el Ben and make a deal. The Arab didn't know he had no clue as to the location of the Shroud.

• • •

THE SAHARA

An ocean away, in the desert of North Africa, el Ben Alemien watched the sun fade into a dark orange horizon. Dropping to his knees, he felt the Sahara sands soft between his palms. From the desert came his strength, and the oil to fund his empire.

"Praise Allah, peace be unto him."

Slowly, piously, he uttered evening prayers, the *Maghrib*. Praying was for his image, not because he believed in Islam. The leaders of other tribes needed to see his devotion to Islam. When he meditated, he focused on how to attain his dream of ruling North Africa like Mohammed.

A new wave of leaders was sweeping the Middle East and the future was uncertain. No longer could he rely on the fact his father was a founding member of the Muslim Brotherhood. Today power was everything. For now, he controlled tribal leadership. Life was peaceful, but he didn't think it would last. There was tension in the tribes. One day it would explode.

If revolution spread to Arab countries, new leaders might think they didn't need this old tribal leader. No one would remember the years he funded local villages, building schools, and hospitals. With the Shroud, the Coptic would give him a wide power base in the region that no tribe could contest.

He rose to his feet, as prayers ended. The sun had set on the hot sand, and as the wind had picked up, he knew a sirocco was coming. Whether it was the Khamsin in Egypt or the Ghibli in Libya, there was no escaping the hot wind that swirled the dust into suffocating clouds. The Anglo saying, not fit for man or beast, he was sure, came from a desert sandstorm. He loved the desert most when there were sandstorms. Habid approached him.

"A message on the satellite phone. General von Hagen wants to talk. I say you at prayer and he ask you to call when done."

El Ben nodded yes. He gazed again at the desert that rejuvenated his energy and now he knew what he must do.

I've put too much faith in Geigner; if he knew where the Shroud was, he would have it by now. I must deal with the German.

He flipped the flap of the tent open and sat down. He picked up a string of fingers and admired them. The fingers were the small ones on the left hands of men he had executed. The large fingers were those of his enemies and those of his lovers. He believed it was a testimony to building his own destiny and a legend.

One of his aides passed him the communal pot. He leaned against the camel saddle and picked out pieces of lamb and a potato, setting them on the tin plate to cool. The women were making coffee, with the beans in the dallah, the roasting pan. He pulled a knife out of his boot, methodically sliced the pieces of lamb away from the leg bone. He enjoyed living like his ancestors had.

The sands of time shifted and now he needed the Shroud. He smiled. The good news was the old General's days were numbered. No one lived forever. There was some proverb Mohammed used about dealing with your enemies. Enemies became friends and friends became enemies.

Well, he thought as he digested the first bite of lamb, the Shroud of Turin was worth it, a means to an end. He motioned to an aide and gave him the message.

"Call von Hagen. Geigner's been a disappointment."

He leaned back on his haunches to finish the lamb. It always tasted better in the desert. Could the sand affect the taste of food? Ah, he thought, it was just a perception. Not unlike the Shroud, a perception in the minds of the Coptic Christian allies along the Nile.

The Shroud would tie the Coptic to him; give him their wealth, and more importantly, political power. With the help of Allah, praise be unto him, he would find the Shroud.

• • •

Von Hagen walked slowly to the phone, placing his long cigarette in the ashtray to concentrate on the call. He also adjusted his hearing aid. It wasn't that he was hard of hearing, it was just that sometimes the line had static. He wanted to be sure to hear not only the words, but the tone of el Ben's voice.

"General, my pleasure, and hope we may do some business. My

humble thanks are given to you again for your graciousness in sending me the silver coin. Few know I am an avid collector of Roman coins. They are my country's history, North Africa's history."

The General relaxed. El Ben was going to deal.

"I have something you need, and its good business for us both."

"So, tell me what?"

"The Shroud of Turin," replied von Hagen.

Praise Allah, thought el Ben, pleased that after all the years in Mexico, von Hagen had not acquired the tedious Anglo way of negotiation. He came directly to the point. Negotiating with other tribal leaders was tiresome enough. It was a relief not to have to talk around the subject.

"You have a plan, General?" asked el Ben.

"I have sources that can help recover the Shroud."

"Based on what?" El Ben was skeptical, with good reason. The Shroud had been missing for decades since Marfkis died.

The General had no qualms about lying to el Ben.

"During the war, I took the Shroud from the Cathedral in Turin and hid it at the monastery. Over the years I could have retrieved it for the right price, or the right reason."

El Ben didn't believe him. If the General knew where the Shroud was, he'd have used it for some purpose years ago, but with Benton dead, he needed to play along. The General was playing the game. Either he had the Shroud or knew where it was.

"What, General, may I offer to you in return?"

"My oil tankers ship from every country in the Middle East but yours. I would like to establish a reasonable price for your oil. Say twenty percent below the market rate."

"Twenty percent is a steep price to pay, General."

"But worth it for the Shroud." The General knew he was about to find out how much el Ben wanted the Shroud.

El Ben did not like to be put in a box, a box that contained his dreams versus his pocketbook. Today he had no choice. In the future, there would be more oil negotiations and he would even the score with the General. They bickered back and forth for a few more minutes, eventually settling on a percentage of eighteen percent. The price was good for both as long as oil prices continued to rise.

To el Ben, the deal was more satisfactory than having to negotiate with the Americans who were still organizing to explore for oil in the Maghreb. The Yanks were late to the party, whereas exploration in the area was not new to the Italians and Norwegians who had been there for years. He often wondered how America became such a powerful country when they made so many mistakes trying to find oil in the Sahara.

Ending the call, El Ben made his decision. He would send his own people to find the Shroud. There were too many players in this game, and he trusted none of them.

• • •

CHAPTER FIFTEEN

At the Villa

All those trips to the monastery wasn't for religious fervor.

General von Hagen's villa was at the end of the driveway that carved a path through thick jungle vegetation to the top of the ridge. The seacoast was spectacular in multiple blue tones and the Spanish-style hacienda basked in sunlight. A servant met the car. The butler opened the main door, an eight-foot tall carved edifice of a Mayan figure.

"The General is on the patio, Senorita Amy."

She walked thought the house, which she thought was more like a museum than a home. The General, a slender man, Amy's height, rose to greet her. He spoke English in a well-modulated voice without a trace of any accent.

"Amy, I hope the trip was pleasant." He continued, not waiting for her response. "I thought you might enjoy a glass of wine. It's too early for hard liquor, and wine will complement the light lunch Margo has prepared. It's your favorite, chicken salad with her special sauce."

He gestured at the staff moving furniture on the patio.

"Forgive the coming and going, as you know the reception is here tonight."

They seated themselves on the patio, and immediately wine was served in eight-inch-high crystal glasses. The General began to speak and sounded concerned.

"I heard about the death of your second husband, my condolences. He was an archeologist, right?"

"Thank you for thinking of me, General. He was an engineer and ran his father's international engineering company. My other two husbands were scientists, but always called themselves archeologists."

"The engineer, he had several children?"

"By his other wives. I was number three and we had no children. They're in college, and his parents are guardians. His father runs the company. I stay in touch with the kids on email."

Why the General brought up her stepchildren, she didn't know. He must be curious about any claim they could have on her estate. He knew that generations before she was born, land trusts were established in legal documents, as binding as a cement pillar.

The Prowers estate revenue was hers, but not the right to bequeath the land. Having no blood heirs, she, Ace, and Geigner discussed the possibility of breaking the trust, but never pursued it. They knew they wouldn't live forever, just lack of interest. Without heirs, the trust would go to charities, unknown until the will was read.

The three cousins had a pretty good idea that the beneficiary was the Catholic Church, as their grandparents were devout believers. Ace once said some bishop probably guaranteed them a place in the Promised Land. She and Geigner agreed.

"And tell me, dear, how is your aunt."

"She is well and in Berlin."

Sonora in Berlin was not good news to the General. She and her Committee were a thorn in his side and up to something, he was sure. The last decades he'd spent a lot of time trying to figure out how to deal with her and never figured it out. Managing Sonora would be a good test for his adopted sons, Olen and Anton, provided the old lady lived on.

"No plans to return to Vera Cruz?"

"I doubt it. She needs to be near a heart specialist and spends a lot of time going to doctors."

"Ahh, so sorry to hear." The General sounded concerned but hoped Sonora's death was near. He doubted it, though. Old broads like Sonora never died.

After Benton's funeral, Sonora let him know, using Olen, as a conduit, that she held him responsible for her brother's death and would prove it. Sonora was just like el Ben and himself, wanting to be in control. In some ways, she had protected Benton from reality. He ran around the world, looking at piles of rocks, while she and Amy ran the business.

What he had underestimated was that Benton's fantasy world enabled him to play politics. All those trips to the monastery wasn't for religious fervor. Those trips were the tipoff that the Shroud was still at the monastery.

Silently, he cursed Anton for tampering with Benton's plane. Olen should have stopped him. He must remember how impatient the young were. There was some advantage in being old; one learned to take one's time.

He glanced back toward the library. The eyes in the portrait of Frederick the Great seemed to follow him. Hanna had never forgiven him for outmaneuvering Eva for the painting. On such trivia, empires had fallen. How Eva managed to get it out of Germany and the Balkans, he would never know. He still thought she bought it from a refugee.

Amy brought him back to today. "I was at the monastery in the Balkans and met your brother, the Abbot. He helped me understand icons."

The General knew the details of her trip from Anton. He also was sure she didn't know where the Shroud was. His brother, the Abbot, was another matter. Did he know? As the years passed, he was sure he did, but wasn't telling.

"I collected icons for years with the help of my brother. We both believed someone had to save these works of art. In the past, they were often destroyed because no one realized their value."

The conversation continued on ranching and the oil markets. They discussed geological reports on a piece of land on the coast they jointly owned. Finally, they ended up on their favorite topics: North Africa, the Maghreb, oil tankers and leases.

He picked up his glass of wine.

"Sometimes, I think the world today has forgotten what a real war is." The General let out a long sigh.

"With the nuclear bomb, war will be over before we know it. Some men are meant for that type of life, Amy. I always thought your father was. He denied it, but the war was always with him."

"How do you know which type you are?" she asked, curious as to how the General made his assessments.

"You don't," he replied, "Not until you are there."

"My father was a hero in the war. Today I don't think it matters which side he was on."

Von Hagen laughed.

"I agree with the side not being an issue. But as for a hero, well, Amy heroes never talk."

The patio phone rang, and his houseman motioned to the General.

"I've been expecting a long-distance call. Why don't you look at the new paintings I've added to my collection in the library?"

There is nothing, he thought, *that would be embarrassing, and Amy loved his library.*

She crossed the marbled floor and entered a library lined with glimmering mahogany bookshelves separated by paintings. A huge eighteenth-century desk stared back at her. Skipping the paintings, she moved to the books on the shelves. The titles stared back at her.

As she walked behind the desk, she noticed an open book on a shelf. The worn title was almost unreadable: *A Modern History of the Coptic Church, Icons and Egyptology.* The book's cover looked as if it was a century old. She opened the cover page. The date of publication was 1902.

Amy smiled. In the world of iconology, this was modern history. She flipped through the book to the section on icons. Scanning the page, she read how icons in Egypt were taken to Istanbul at the height of Byzantine rule.

"What about icons in the Balkans?" she asked herself.

How were the books in this library filed? She walked over to the wall of books. There was history, then military history. Art history was in the first row. Following down the shelves, under the letter "I" was a row of books on icons. A worn, leather bound copy of *Icons of the Balkan Monasteries* was wedged in a row of books with titles on icons. This was the same book she had found in her father's desk.

Amy was amazed any of these books were read often enough to look used. Pulling the book out, it literally opened itself to a map of old Yugoslavia and northern Greece. A dull red pencil mark ran along the river to the monastery at Gracanica. She looked inside the cover and was shocked. The name *von Hagen* was written in pencil. Beside it was a hand-drawn soft swastika. Below in pencil was written the words *Christ in Glory,* followed by the year her father died. It was in her father's handwriting.

She remembered what the Abbot told her about the swastika. He said the book her father left in the safe was the wrong one.

Why was this book with her father's handwriting and a swastika inside the cover in von Hagen's library? Why did it focus on the same icon in the small book *Beyond the Face: A Commentary on Icons, Symbols, and Illusions* that was sent to Berlin after his death?

She put the book back on the shelf and sat down in one of the overstuffed chairs. If icons were the key, why had her father returned to Mexico? There were no icons here. What connection was he trying to show her?

Looking up, a tall blond-haired man—attractive if you liked the type—appeared in the doorway.

"The General is back on the patio." Olen always made the simplest requests sound like a command.

Amy followed him toward the patio, relieved to see the sun was still dipping in and out of the clouds. After the rain in the Balkans, blue sky was nice to see. Olen must have seen her looking at the book, but surely, he couldn't tell which one. The search for the Shroud was making her paranoid.

"I always admired the General's library. There are so many unique books."

"The General keeps me busy so I have little time to read. Maybe one day I will."

This was the first time Amy heard him refer to a future without the old General. Olen and Anton would inherit his estate. Olen was present on business deals and Anton was the expediter. Where, she wondered was Anton, and what was he expediting now?

The General was tasting the bouquet of a new bottle of wine as they walked on to the patio. Olen followed Amy. He had always preferred well-rounded bodies in women. Amy was too fit. *Still,* he thought, *you never know.*

"Amy, we learned from you," said the General, "All Argentina's wines are excellent, especially the red."

Amy waited while the butler poured each of them a glass. The glasses were so large they took the entire bottle.

"With your knowledge of icons, what did you think of my library?"

"The icon books are interesting and a nice collection. At the monastery I learned there is a message in the art of an icon. I suppose icons could serve as a letter before email."

She wondered again if Olen saw which book she selected. It was the only one on icons in the Balkans, but in a row of icon books on Russia, the Ukraine, and a Hungarian author's interpretation of the similarity of Tibetan thangkas with icons. Olen said nothing.

The General took a puff on his cigarette, coughing slightly.

"My doctors say these will kill me, but if not them, something else will. The Abbot is the real expert in our family, as well as one of the world's experts on iconology. My dear, I only dabble in icons. The structure is appealing in the classical sense. Everything is in its place. The icon painter was not assailed by doubt. Perhaps that is why I like them."

"You see," and von Hagen leaned toward her. "Historians blame certain individuals or ruling classes for the problems of our world. I've never agreed. In the days of my youth, I studied history and arts in Berlin and Paris where I came to realize the most dangerous man who ever lived was Saint Thomas Aquinas. He introduced rationality, the art of questioning. But the artists who drew the icons were not victims of his thinking, not assailed by doubts."

Amy held her glass tightly as if to capture some mystical message.

"I thought the icon held an abstract message."

Von Hagen smiled. "It's in the mind of the beholder. More wine?"

They continued chatting about the government of Mexico and, as always, oil. Amy noticed the general let Olen take the lead in discussions on oil, leases and regime change in North Africa. Like it or not, she could be in business with him when the General was gone.

Then it was time to prepare for the evening reception. Amy, almost reluctantly, returned to her hacienda.

• • •

Out the window, the Abbot watched monks trimming the lawn and planting the garden. Forget the monks and the gardens, he needed to think about why Benton came so often to visit Veilkov. The more he thought, the more certain he was that Benton had not taken the Shroud out of the Balkans. Benton would never risk moving it by plane. After Hanna's and Eva's plane crashed, he was a nervous flier. Especially nervous, remembered the Abbot, when piloting his own plane. Perhaps he foresaw his own death. *Where is the Shroud?* I have no idea, but it must be somewhere in his monastery.

If I cursed, he thought, *I would curse Benton and his love of symbols.*

He would curse himself for never getting a real answer from Benton *on what was at El Kanitaoui. Once he thought Benton and Geigner were* building a bomb. Now he knew Benton would never let el Ben have any weapon that worked.

He sat back down at his desk. The General had asked him to respond to a letter from the Simon Wiesenthal Foundation. For decades, the foundation had investigated the General's Nazi past as well as Nazi escape routes out of Europe. To date, they had no firm evidence of the general participating in atrocities. Now the Foundation's film company was focusing on how the German elite, not just Nazis, escaped from Europe.

The Abbot knew that keeping the filmmakers and historians focused on the Italian ports, known points of exit to most of the Nazi hunters, they would miss the Albanian ferry from the port of Durres to Alexandria,

Egypt. This was the ferry the General, Eva, Hanna, and Prowers had taken.

The past was history and served no purpose, in either his world or the world of his brother. If there were organizations obsessed with resurrecting the fourth Reich, where was the proof? Those organizations could exist in movies. There were no hard facts, everything was circumstantial. He and the General would keep it that way. They had buried the past so deep it would never be uncovered.

What couldn't be buried was his memory. He remembered the summer of 1941, when the terror started—only none of them realized what the terror meant.

In Belgrade, he watched Nazi soldiers post edicts and saw the shock as residents read them. For every German soldier killed, fifty to one hundred locals would be executed. Then he saw the truth. Unable to find Communists, who had hidden in the mountains, Jews and gypsies were murdered. Within a few months, the males in both groups were gone.

The old Abbot asked to meet with him. He spoke in a heavily accented German, knowing most of the brothers didn't speak the local dialects.

"I want you and Brother Veilkov to go to the camp at Semlin where I am told are only women and children. There is a new edict." He held up a brown edged paper in his weathered hands.

"Berlin is saying Serbia is *Juden frei*, free of Jews, but we know the women and children are still alive. That is, if you call their life living. You and Veilkov must take them food and we pray some of them will make it through this present trial."

"Of course," he told the old Abbot, thinking one trip wouldn't be a problem, never realizing they would make trips all winter. On one of the trips, even Brother Veilkov noticed how the sky was always clouded. "Never," he said, "Has the cold and snow been so penetrating. Nearly covered with ice, there was one open spot in the river where the current was clear, clean and seemed to offer to both men the hope of renewal. Now he wasn't so certain there was renewal.

Veilkov never discussed his life before entering the monastery. In the mountain villages, everyone knew his family hated and fought the Muslims. In the years both before the war and after it, they solicited German support, Italian support, the Communist and other ethnic minorities. Fights against the Muslims went on every year in every province.

The Abbot thought about the countries in old Yugoslavia, Croatia, Serbia, Montenegro, Macedonia, and Bosnia-Herzegovina. The wars of the past still swirled today. Veilkov's nephews and cousins were still fighting. The Abbot wasn't sure for what or for whom.

Only in the Balkans, he thought.

Outside the day was warm and clear. He walked out to the garden and looked over the low wall at the mountains above the river, remembering.

In the spring of 1945, the rain never stopped, and unnamed mountain streams were raging waterfalls. Then the partisans blew the bridge, destroying the train. The train was unusually short, only three boxcars, and there was no guard. How like the General to have shipped a fortune in artwork without any guards.

The contents of the train were still a question. Often, he wondered what treasures might have survived. He and Amy found some of the jewels in the Bank in Dubrovnik. But they had no idea how they got there. Benton and Veilkov would never be interested in jewels.

He sat down on a chair, thinking about the years he had been Abbot. Appointed in 1950, he vowed his allegiance to President Tito who ignored the Serbian Orthodox church and appointed the Catholic-German-anti-Communist von Hagen, as the leader of the monastery. Catholicism was a strike against him, but being German was a plus.

The villagers were Serbian and hated the Croatians more than they disliked him. Tito was a Communist. He became a friend during the fighting of the Ustasha, pro-Croatian fighters for a Greater Croatia.

In the Abbot's mind, not much had changed today. Each country was immersed in fighting wars, vindicating grudges and blood feuds from centuries past. The villagers would never escape their history. No one knew how many were killed in the latest wars. He thought about escaping to a monastery in the desert. But he had stayed.

For a moment, he could see the truth. El Ben killed Marfkis and the General likely killed Benton. His eyes narrowed, thinking that now it would be el Ben's turn to pay, and an eye for an eye.

Usually the silence brought back the memories he dreaded the most. The Abbot looked at the logs popping in the fireplace. After the war he visited the Prowers ranch. The marshlands along the lake and the river were full of waterfowl migrating from Canada. Benton said; *"These are the finest game reserves in the country and our family has owned them for a hundred years. Except a hundred years ago, my an-cestors didn't run it with computers. I'm a modern cowboy running my ranch with a calculator, a computer, and a pickup truck."*

When the war was over, Benton seemed to act as if all that existed was Colorado, Texas, and Mexico, where he had ranches. Had he forgotten the war? The Abbot doubted he had. The war was with you, even when it ended. But he had to admit Benton was comfortable with war and death. After Hanna and Eva died, he began to regularly visit the monastery. With Veilkov he drank beer and told each other tales about the past.

He thought about what Benton said during the war in Belgrade, telling him about faking the Shroud.

"It's not our mission to worry about where the true burial cloth of Christ is, or why we hid it. Our mission is to provide a suitable substitute.

We use a piece of linen, the oldest the Romanas had and a picture carved in wood that the old grandmother cherished. We warmed the wood, and while still hot, imprinted the image on the linen."

That night, according to Benton, they almost cooked themselves getting the right tone of brown on the linen. Then it didn't seem important, but he clearly remembered Benton saying there was a second copy—a back-up, he called it.

When Veilkov asked him to take one of the copies, he considered destroying it. He still wondered why he didn't. Perhaps even then, he thought it might be the real Shroud.

Benton had said, *"Who is going to really look at this thing? Nobody looked at the real one except Veilkov."* The Abbot had said nothing. He had seen the Shroud years ago and knew the truth. Then his old Abbot gave the bishop at the Cathedral in Turin the other copy.

Even during the war, Benton had a clear picture of the General and how he used people as if they were disposable. He made sure the General was in Belgrade and out of touch with the monastery when they were faking the Shroud. Today, it was easy to forget how poor communications were. Often, the phone lines didn't work.

The Abbot still remembered Benton's role in operations in the mountains, before the women came from Germany. One day he and Benton were on a train stopped by the local militia. Neither said a word, but they were worried. The train was supposed to be secure to the Albanian border. They both spoke German, but not the local dialects, and could be picked up in a minute by local militia.

"Let's go," said Benton, and they ran down the corridor to the end of the train car. The cold wind hit them as they opened the door. Benton looked out at the militia. He always saw quickly action was needed.

"We'll have to get rid of them. It's three to our two and we can handle those odds."

The door rumbled open and they turned. There was the conductor. "I'm sorry," and he shrugged his shoulders. He was a partisan.

"Don't worry," said Benton. "When you hear the first shot, hit the switch for the engineers to get the train moving. We won't have much time to make the border before they start looking for the militia and find the bodies."

The conductor nodded yes.

He and Benton headed down the outside of the railroad tracks. They stopped once or twice, and peered underneath, finally seeing shiny black boots. The Abbot followed Benton as they climbed underneath the cars and lay on the gravel between the tracks.

Slowly they both inched their way up to the front of the car, next to the junction box. After all the years and the subsequent killings, he remembered the moment vividly. Benton casually stepped out, glanced at the militia and said good morning.

He pulled a cigarette out of one of his pockets and asked for a light. One of the soldiers reached for a match, the others leaning, lounging casually against the brick stairwell. Benton pulled his revolver from behind his back and shot them one by one. Only the third man had a chance to reach for his gun, but that was all he had, a chance.

The Colorado rancher was an expert shot.

"Hurry," said Benton, picking up a body, hesitating a moment, looking over the brick wall into the river. Without a word, he and Benton rolled the bodies over the wall. He was a monk. He didn't kill, but never forgot the look on their faces.

Benton said, "You always remember the first ones."

Now, years later, he wondered who had been Benton's first. Why had it been so easy for him to kill? There was no real answer for any of this.

Stories he was told in the past haunted him. Benton and Veilkov were with Eva and Hanna when the train was blown up. The next time he saw them, the baby was gone. Somehow, the General made it to Egypt with most of his fortune, including artwork.

The Abbot believed Amy would find the Shroud. Benton used his fixation with symbolism, the icons, the Mayans, and the Bible to create clues to where he hid the Shroud. The symbols were confusing, but logical to Benton, who had to be hiding the Shroud from the General and el Ben.

The clues were for Amy to understand. *Or*, thought the Abbot, *me, because Benton knew who his daughter would ask for help.* Veilkov would be back soon. It was time to ask him to produce the Shroud.

The church bells rang, telling him it was time for evening prayer. Reluctantly, he left his past memories to join the other monks.

• • •

IN THE SERBIAN MOUNTAINS

It was another foggy morning with the tips of the mountains barely visible above the fog. Brother Veilkov, a thin, balding monk dressed in clashing shades of brown and gray, was following his retreat routine. He walked to a ledge, halfway down the mountain from the Gracanica Monastery.

The dirt trail ended at the bottom of the ravine, where large black rocks jutted out on a point into the river. To the north and south, tree-lined mountains bordered the river. With him was his worn leather-bound Bible and a small notebook. Comfortably seated, his back against the rock, he still could not concentrate.

Did he miss the monastery in Greece, the pale blue water? Maybe.

Over the years the monastic routine, reading and writing, allowed him to ignore the past, even forget it. Now, with Benton Prowers dead, his meditation was disrupted, and he kept reliving the past. He owed Benton much from their time in the war and what happened then was about to surface. Benton was dead, but others, like Amy, would come to the monastery searching for the Shroud. Amy was just the first.

Was the time of the fourth beast here, as Prowers said? If Benton was right a crowd of people would be seeking the Shroud of Turin. His years protecting the Shroud were good years. The legend was real. The ancient burial cloth of Christ brought those who were near it closer to the light of truth. This was his reward for leaving behind the struggles of nations and the men who ruled them. As long as men full of self-interest lived while other men were afraid to speak, nothing could be learned from history.

Was it his destiny to be drawn back into the web of the fourth beast, el Ben Alemien? If it was, he knew this time there would be no escape. His visit to El Kanitaoui showed him that fact.

Each soul had to confront God with his own life. He did not believe a man could judge another's moral values. Had he been blameless? Had he done all he could? Money and art treasures passed through his hands. Were those the funds Marfkis and el Ben used to build a private army in the North African desert?

General von Hagen was more interested in the preservation of Renaissance art figures than he ever was in der Fuhrer's grand dream. In this respect, the Abbot and his brother were just alike. The general saw before anyone else that the war was over, and the Germany they knew no longer existed. Hitler's and Eva Braun's suicide were history.

Only history had been fooled. Eva Braun had not died in the bunker, but left Berlin in a plane piloted by Hanna Reitch. Eva's life was in the history books. He was always amazed that someone hadn't spoken up to correct history. Neither he nor his brother, nor the Prowers family, had.

Why Benton was assigned to escort the women, he didn't know. Logically, someone in Germany, or the Catholic Church, got the American military to provide safe passage for the two women. Again, the why and how were missing.

Fluent in German, Benton needed a translator for local dialects in the Balkans. Veilkov met him at the Yugoslavian border with the two women and a baby. He thanked God when Benton swore it was not Hitler's, but a German Army captain killed on the Eastern Front. He translated the local dialects and became part of their world. At the time, he had no idea what his involvement would mean for his own life.

Partisan fighting delayed the trip as the train slowly moved from town to town. On the trip, Eva read papers from London, from Paris, from America. She realized the Third Reich was over and made a fateful decision asking Veilkov's sister to take her baby. She wanted the baby to have a life like she had known in the mountains of Bavaria before the war. That was the life his sister promised her. Raising Stephan Medak had been his sister's and his own greatest joy.

Veilkov could still see Eva's pale face as she handed the baby to his sister. With her and the rest of their family, the baby was raised as their own. One day, several years after the war, the past became too much. Eva and Hanna, on their way back to Gracanica to find the child, were killed in a plane crash. Their deaths took their secrets to the graveyard.

"Surely," thought Veilkov, "The hand of God was upon Medak."

At the village of Gracanica, Stephan Medak, as he was called, lived life on his own terms, without the burden of someone else's heritage. He was a man of strong character and, thanks to the monastery funds, well educated. For all who raised him and those who knew him, he was a blessing.

Today, the war continued in the Balkans and the world acted as if the war was new. Veilkov knew differently. It was a war born in past centuries. The provincial attitudes of his people, the Serbs, hadn't changed, nor had attitudes of the other ethnic minorities in the region. He thought about the Catholic Croatians and Muslims. All had the same prejudices, ethnic differences complicated by religion. The combination was unlikely to bring peace. The world had not seen the end of genocides.

Veilkov closed his eyes and leaned his head back against the rock. Memories of the dead were all he had left. He saw the rows of marching troops in their pressed uniforms. It was all in vain. No one learned from the past.

He saw himself enveloped in rays of super-terrestrial light, the same light he believed which was witness to the transfiguration of Jesus on Mt. Tabor. This was the method practiced by the Hesychast, the monks who lived a hermit life in holy solitude with the monastic spirit of past centuries. He focused on his favorite passage from the sixth book of Revelations.

And one of the four beasts was saying; behold a white horse: thee that sat on him had a bow, and a crown was given unto him; and he went forth conquering, and to conquer. And when he opened the second seal, I heard the second beast say, Come and see.

And voices kept saying, come and see, come and see. As the shot rang out, Veilkov never knew if it was the beast.

• • •

Standing across the river, Anton watched Brother Veilkov's body fall into the river. The body would decompose, making identification impossible. He watched the birds cross the sky in formation and aimed the gun. Then he stopped. His hunting for sport had been the monk.

Slowly he lowered the gun. It was the birds' lucky day.

• • •

CHAPTER SIXTEEN

Amy in Mexico

Symbolism was important to the rulers.
Money was important to the peasants.

At dusk, Amy arrived at the General's hacienda and looked out across the veranda at the lights of Vera Cruz. She loved the beauty of this bustling city. In the harbor were several cargo ships. The lights on their launches ran back and forth, ferrying passengers to the dock.

On the terrace surrounded by a horde of art patrons was the General, inviting the crowd down to the terrace level for more champagne and roast pig. Roast pig was not a favorite of Amy's; too much fat. She stayed on the terrace next to the open doors and quietly sipped the light, smooth champagne.

The General was serving his trademark French champagne. He guarded his secret stock like it was gold. The crowd slowly moved off the patio and onto the grounds.

Olen joined her; his nose arrogantly turned skyward. He spoke in a low voice.

"They always talk about this archeological bullshit, when the real issue is the gold that's been found in the bay."

"Gold in the form of black gold, meaning oil?" asked Amy.

He gestured toward the lights of Veracruz, pleased he knew something Amy didn't.

"No, real gold. They call it Cortés's conquests. They found over nine hundred pounds in the last year. Who cares about the ball courts, the temples, and what they were drinking in the central highlands in the fifth century?"

Amy agreed with Olen with surprising regularity. The two had much in common, but she never felt she could trust him.

The wind off the Gulf of Mexico had turned chilly and they moved off the patio inside.

"Olen, don't you think there's something of interest to be found in the tombs? The serpent is the symbol of death in the Mayan culture. My father said the burial tombs were full of symbolism using a serpent."

Olen understood.

"Symbolism was important only to the rulers. Money was what the peasants want. And money is what the elites—especially the ones who think they are cultural figures—want. But don't tell the General I said that."

Amy laughed agreeing.

"You don't really believe, Olen that these guests of the General are only into it for investment purposes. What are they going to discover —gold?"

"Yes." He spoke honestly. "All the ruins are covered with mango plants; why bother to dig them out if it wasn't for the gold? Remember, the culture was inferior, or so they thought."

The General entered the room and hearing the end of the conversation pointed to the portrait hanging over the fireplace. "That's the mark of a superior culture."

"Frederick the Great?" asked Amy.

"Yes, and did you know that painting hung over Hitler's desk in the days of the Third Reich?"

The General's voice was matter of fact, showing no sense of pride that Amy thought an old Nazi should have.

"What a legacy," replied Amy. "My legacy from my father is this necklace with the coin."

She turned her silver chain necklace and the face of a Roman coin gazed at him. Amy knew he was interested. It was just a Roman coin her father had set so beautifully for her. Why the interest? Then she realized he thought it might be one of the so-called lucky coins like the coin Medak had given her. Tired of the lucky aurora issue that she had heard about from her father and Medak, she explained the coin's meaning, knowing it was useless to try and convince the General the luck issue was an old wives' tale.

"The head is Gordian III who was a Roman Emperor killed in Persia in 225 A.D. when he was twenty-nine, leading his army in a battle near Circesium. Apparently, his claim to fame was defeating a rebellion in North Africa, but fame was short-lived, as he died young."

Her explanation fell on deaf ears. The General controlled himself, to not appear over-eager.

"The coin, may I see it? It could be very valuable."

He peered through his eyeglasses, needing it to see the coin clearly. It was a Roman coin, the same vintage he sent to el Ben, but the head was different.

"The head is not what I expected. Your father gave me a coin, one he called a lucky one that he acquired during the war. There were only three in existence and they date from the third century AD. I valued the coin your father gave me," said von Hagen. "But I gave it to el Ben to court his favor."

Possession and owning were part of his DNA and formed a major part of his character. Now, as an aging old man, he could admit it. He looked again at Amy. *What did Benton do with the other two coins?* He was sure these coins and the first icon, the Shroud of Turin, were connected. He now regretted giving el Ben the coin Benton called lucky. The luck he wasn't so sure of, but they were unique coins.

He glared at Amy.

"Did he ever give you a so-called lucky coin?"

The champagne made Amy stubborn. "No," she replied, her tone clipped.

She remembered her aunt's words to not trust anyone, especially the General. Medak gave her that so-called lucky coin, not her father. The coin wasn't with her; she had left it in her luggage. Besides Medak told her he got it from Veilkov.

Why was the General interested in a mystical coin whose powers were certainly suspect? Or were they? She remembered there were three coins. She had the one Medak gave her, which was Veilkov's. Her fathers had been given to the General who told her he'd given it to el Ben. She thought a moment. Whoever had a coin was alive, and those who'd given them up were dead. The General was trying to stay alive, but she knew, coin or no coin, he couldn't live forever. She wondered where Marfkis was.

"I promise you I'll look through my father's coins."

She was irritated at her acquiescence. Then the General was pulled away by members of the society as the party settled into a routine of drinking and eating. No one noticed Amy's early departure.

• • •

Hours later, the General watched the last car disappear down the driveway. He turned to Olen.

"Get el Ben on the phone now. And even if the son-of-a-bitch is in prayer, tell him to get on his knees. Allah has something he needs to start praying about. El Ben needs to know that I am close to finding the Shroud. Amy knows where it is. Otherwise, she wouldn't be here. We are going to keep an eye on her."

To himself, the General was remembering Ossery's influence on el Ben. He moaned softly.

Why do I get stuck with astrologers directing the normal evolution of power, influence, and greed? What rotten luck to again, as with Hitler and his astrologer, to have the abnormal personality drawn to the paranormal.

He knew Amy didn't go to the monastery for a love of icons. Her father sent her. For the moment, he was pleased Prowers and his self-effacing humility was gone.

Idly, he polished the head of a large black Mayan ceramic cat. For a moment, he saw Benton, Hanna, and Eva as they had been decades ago during their arrival in Mexico. He fiddled with a gold pen on the desk as Olen brought him the phone.

"You learned something tonight, General?" asked Olen.

"Tomorrow, go to Villahermosa. Try to find out what she knows about Benton's last visit. I want Amy followed, twenty-four hours a day."

"And the coin?" asked Olen.

"Who knows what happened to the other two? Maybe when we find the Shroud, we'll find them."

Olen nodded and silently slipped out the veranda doors. He knew the General well enough that once instructions had been given, von Hagen wanted to be alone. This evening was no different.

The General settled back in his leather chair and stared at the wall. He cursed Prowers in his grave. Benton had been a presumptuous idealist, but von Hagen conceded, a smart one. After all, he had tricked the General during the war into believing the icon *Christ in Glory* was destroyed along with the Shroud. The next thing he knew, it was hanging in the church and the monks were cloistered around it day and night praying.

His brother and Benton lied about the Shroud. Justice was due. Only von Hagen was not certain yet how to repay his brother. He slowly rose and walked to the framed map beside the etched brick wall. Pulling out a brick, he quickly opened a locked safe. Inside there was a single box and von Hagen reached for it gingerly. He returned to the desk and pushed the clasp.

There they were, he thought, *crown jewels from Italy, Greece, Romania, and Bulgaria.*

Instinctively, he plunged his hand into the box and let the rings and necklaces cascade off his forearm. Not all the jewels were on the train when it crashed. He had taken many with him to Belgrade and then to Mexico. Savoring the moment, he felt like the Balamob who, according to ancient Mayan ritual, was the guardian of the forest.

I am the Balamob, he thought. Now if he could just gain possession of the Shroud, who knows what might lie ahead in a liaison with el Ben for control of North Africa?

Power was an old man's dream.

• • •

Leaving the reception, Amy drove to the city square and walked across the cobblestone plaza. Behind her rose the tall glass office buildings of a bank and insurance company. Vera Cruz was, in many ways, a modern Latin American city, but the old Colonial city square overlooking the sea front was unchanged. White stucco buildings built by the Spanish formed a colonnade surrounding a park.

It was early evening, and amid the trees and flower gardens, a band played Mexican folk songs. Scattered about in no particular order were bronze statues of Mexican heroes dating back to the eighteenth century. Colored Christmas lights hung around the flagstone pavilion, giving the square the aura of a festival. Some stands sold beer, other venders were selling tacos and caramel apples. The locals stood in all the lines, as business was good.

Amy felt anything but festive. Jaime was waiting for her, seated next to the wooden bandstand, looking as if he had nothing else to do in the world. Amy wanted to ask him if there were any bodies lying around but didn't. Heads in the square were no joke with the gang violence over cocaine trafficking that was wracking the country.

They walked to a small café which had the most famous grilled squid on the east coast of Mexico. Amy did not feel like eating, but fresh grilled squid was an exception. Besides, she needed to talk to Jaime.

Jaime sensed her apprehension and put his arm around her shoulders to give her a hug.

"I know it is difficult for you, but please, you've known me all your life. Have I ever been anything but your friend?"

Amy patted his hand.

"No, Jaime. Just things have been so confused."

"Is it your father's death?"

"Yes. He left a letter with the lawyer asking me to go to the Gracanica Monastery, to find the Shroud of Turin. I doubted it really existed, but with all that's happened, I now think it's hidden somewhere. The trouble is, his clues take me back to what he did in World War II.

"I found another letter at a bank in Dubrovnik's safe deposit box with some jewels. The letter offered more clues, all rather obscure. All I really know is my father had a reason for returning here. Someone must know. We're not at square one, but about minus five, Jaime."

Jaime said nothing but looked at her knowing she was asking if he knew where her father had hidden it. As the manager of Prowers planation and shipping operations in Vera Cruz he would know if Benton had been here for business reason. He wasn't. The only place Benton could have hidden the Shroud in Mexico would be at the Mayan tomb near the coast.

"I think you go to Villahermosa. Bernardo will help. Go tonight. I stall the General if he come. No need he knows where you go. I tell him you go to Mexico City. Best you go on the train. Now we get you to train. Need anything at hacienda?"

She shook her head no. He reached down and picked up the black bag he was carrying.

"Rosa packed your bag. We thought you might leave unexpectedly."

"Out the back door of the restaurant?" asked Amy. "Isn't that the way they always do it in the movies?"

Jaime laughed; glad she had her sense of humor.

"Yes, not bad idea. Back of restaurant an alley. End of it is a back door to church. Front of church across from train station. We hurry."

Now he glanced down the narrow alley street filled with garbage cans and parked cars.

"I'll go to the cabaret up two doors. General's men will think that's why I'm here."

Amy turned to Jaime.

"Have you noticed anyone watching us?"

"Like the General's spies, no," he said. "But who can say are von Hagen's eyes. Whole city in his hand."

He glanced again at his watch and tapped his wallet pocket.

"Pesos, you have pesos?"

"Yes, I changed money at the airport," said Amy.

Jaime took Amy's hand.

"Be safe, promise?"

He squeezed her hand back.

"You are a dear friend."

"Bernardo will meet you in Villahermosa. You trust him, he is cousin and a good manager for the hacienda. Now go."

He watched her disappear down the alley and turned back to his table in the cabaret. The cabaret was crowded and noisy, but Jaime knew the waitress and got a table in the back corner. He continued to watch the door to see if they were followed.

The band began playing when Olen entered the room. Jaime would give him five minutes to get through the crowd and realize Amy wasn't there. Amy needed a little bit longer. *Ah, well,* he thought to himself. *It's all in a good cause.*

Marguerite, one of the ladies of the night who frequented the rooms above the cabaret, was an old acquaintance. He made sure Olen saw him trying to look as if he was following someone. He found the small back stairway and knocked on Marguerite's door.

• • •

Amy opened the splintered oak door and entered the damp adobe church. Rows of flickering vigil lights cast giant shadows on the walls. A piece of wax slipped onto the flame, sputtered, burned brightly and died.

Cautiously, she peered out the side door across the cobblestone street leading to the railroad station. Dominating the square was a stone statue surrounded with palm trees. It was another nameless military hero in one of the many nameless Mexican wars.

Quickly she crossed the street to the edge of the square and moved through the crowd to the ticket office. She had no way of knowing if she was being followed. With her bag over her shoulder, she didn't look out of place at the railroad station. Trying to look relaxed, she bought her ticket, thankful her Spanish sounded like the natives.

Being followed by anyone was no joke, as the road incident in Berlin showed. The harsh sound of the train whistle startled her. Jaime had been right. She was just in time. The conductor motioned her aboard the last coach, his thin voice shouting.

"Rapido, rapido."

As the train inched forward, she worked her way toward the first-class car. Second-class was Mexican life. There were straw baskets and bundles belonging to the Indians. Laden with corn, bananas, and coconuts, their baskets held everything from chickens to children. She thought about staying here with the locals, safety in numbers, and realized she would stand out like a neon light.

The first-class train car was almost empty as she seated herself on the wide cushioned seats, the one feature distinguishing it from the hard board seats in second class. Behind the train, the lights of Vera Cruz slowly faded as the mountains closed. This was no time for reverie. She had to figure out what her father was trying to tell her in the letters and Biblical quote.

All right, for the four hundredth time, she thought. *What is important?*

She couldn't stop thinking about the icon books in von Hagen's library. The confusing part was her father never mentioned icons. For him, symbolism was the Mayan culture. His letter talked about the Ceiba tree, a shield, and serpents, which were the main clues.

Pascal's tomb was one of the most impressive in Mesoamerican and serpents surrounded the carved entrance. Serpents could be the key; the clue her father wanted her to find. Pascal also had a shield, his sarcophagus. That left the Ceiba tree.

He used to tell her stories and even now, she could hear his voice.

"After the war, I bought the old French plantation west of Villahermosa. On its southern border was one of the most majestic settings of Mayan ruins, Palenque."

She gazed for a moment out the window. So, her father donated money to restore the ruins. In 1947, the crew from the Mexico National Institute of Anthropology and History, found the remains of Pascal and the famous Temple of Inscriptions were discovered. None of that seemed to matter now.

Von Hagen's book and the little book sent to her in Berlin had a soft swastika in the corner. Both featured the icon *Christ in Glory* with serpents surrounding the base. Was the serpent the symbol her father wanted her to follow? If so, *Christ in Glory* back at the monastery could be the key icon. She and Medak had looked at the wrong icon.

The little book that arrived, sender unknown, in Berlin, was about icons, including *Christ in Glory* and the icon of the *Seven Angels*. The sender must be Veilkov. She pulled the small thin book from her pocket and looked at the title, *Beyond the Face: A Commentary on Icons, Symbols, and Illusions*.

Slowly, carefully, she opened its fragile pages, each one full of tiny writing, and began to read. It was a complicated discussion on the meaning of signs and symbols. She stopped reading, feeling like she was getting nowhere. The Hakenkreuz inside the cover must be a clue, but to what?

She read several pages then turned to take another look at the first illustration in the book of *Christ in Glory*. It must be the icon she was supposed to find.

At the monastery, neither she nor Medak really looked at that icon, except to see the address of the bank. The icon required another look. She considered calling Medak, then realized she should go to the monastery herself. What made sense was her father was trying to keep the Shroud of Turin from falling into the wrong hands. Those hands likely belonged to el Ben.

Amy looked out the window at the dark mountain landscape. It was ironic how understanding the past gave meaning to the present.

All those years, her parents' past had been hiding in the shadows. On archeological excavations, a small clue could be a simple indicator or a sign to lead the team in a direction resulting in a significant finding. She had to find that clue.

Her father must have known he was in danger. The clues he left certainly looked like a back-up plan. He could have made it easy by telling her about the past but didn't want anyone else to find the clues. Now she was surrounded by danger, as the shooting incidents at the monastery, and in Berlin, showed. As long as el Ben and the General needed her to find the Shroud and looked like she knew where it was, she was safe.

The night was clear, and the train seemed to be following the stars as it wound through the jungle villages. The only lights were the stars. Electricity still hadn't come to many of the small rural villages. She reached for her bag and took out her father's letter from the vault in Dubrovnik. She read it again, looking for other clues beside the serpent.

She read the quote from the book of Proverbs; *Keep your heart with all diligence, for out of it are the issues of life?* Why would her father— who didn't read the Bible—quote from the book of Proverbs? This letter was his voice.

She slept for a time, and when she woke, the red morning sun was rising above the haze in the eastern sky. It was another hour to the train station at Villahermosa, but Amy couldn't go back to sleep. There was still something missing.

She pulled out the book sent to her in Berlin, *Beyond the Face: A Commentary on Icons, Symbols, and Illusions* and looked at the title page.

She had never paid attention to the title of chapter one, *Icon and Illusion*. Today she realized the title said it all. Illusion could be another clue. She turned to the page number written inside the cover.

The chapter was on the colors in the icon and their symbolic unconscious associations. This made sense. She finally saw another connection her father made to icons and Mayans. Gold was a symbol of divine energy and magnificence. Gold was her father's message and gold were the symbol of the Mayans.

This was a clue, but what was the meaning? Right now, she knew less than when she started.

• • •

In Berlin, the butler signed for the air freight package. It was addressed to Amy from Geigner. Still he took it to the secure closet to be opened. Every letter and package to Sonora's houses was opened as if it was a bomb. After being cleared, Sonora, looked at it with more than a little skepticism.

"I hope this is not more jewels."

They both laughed.

"I'm going to open it. He never sends anything from the desert so it must be important, and I'm not sure where Amy is."

Sonora opened the package to see a worn leather book staring up at her. Opening it, she saw the title: *Strogatz and The Legend of Escobar Cay*. She knew this was the notebook with the short story Amy found with Vince's luggage after he died in the Hindu Kush. Amy gave it to Geigner as a gift, since he and Vince searched together for the magic points on earth.

Sonora never understood the significance of the title, and even though she asked, never got a straight answer to the identity of Strogatz. Sending the notebook to Amy was an odd thing even for Geigner to do; odd but important. It must have some type of message.

She opened the thin notebook, and on the top of the first page, saw Geigner's faded handwriting. She could barely make out the words.

"We are close. Akhenaten is here. We felt his spirit. Sometimes I think I can see him in the wind as it blows down the Desert Mountains."

Sonora was not sure what Geigner meant, but the words had to be a coded message which was why he sent it. But coded for what?

The book, a story of lost gold, was once Benton and Vince's obsession. She didn't see that it was relevant today, but by sending it, Geigner made it relevant. She'd ask Ace to look at the book. Maybe he could make out why Geigner sent it. One thing she did know. The el Alemien family had no idea the notebook was important, or Geigner would never have gotten it out of the desert.

Flipping the pages, she noticed there was writing—no, those were calculations—in the margins. They were faded like the handwriting. She almost missed them. Turning to the last page, she saw one short sentence.

"I knew you would get it."

And she did. *I'd bet my fortune these calculations in the margin have something to do with the weapon.*

Why send it to Amy in the old book of Vince's? Of course—it was so obvious. Geigner got it out from under el Ben's nose by putting it in a book he was sending to Amy. El Ben's men would search anything, but a book would be ignored.

Where was Ace? If anyone could interpret the calculation, he could.

She looked out the window, feeling the undertow of currents that had taken down so many people, so many countries across the centuries. The excavation at El Kanitaoui looked to be taking down her nephew as it had her brother Benton.

Sonora knew Geigner believed the secrets in the dry mountains in the southern Saharan desert belonged to the desert. He was like an Arab committed to returning to the desert what the desert had given generations ago.

Geigner's second obsession was his own death. In that way, he was like his mother. He was in the desert; she was likely dead in the jungle. They would come to the same end. Geigner would die in the desert.

Had it been a quarter of a century since Benton returned from seeing their sister Jarra in Asia? She had chosen to live in Southeast Asia when it was still like the Asia of pre-World War II. On a plantation with two small sons, her husband dead, Jarra lived then and now as an Asian with Asians.

"I've gone on to a new life," was all she would say. Benton honored her wish to remain in Asia and took her two small sons back to the States to be raised. With no word from her for decades, and expensive searches that produced nothing, the family believed she died as an unknown during one of the little wars in Southeast Asia.

Geigner become a man much like his father, who had been a leading scientist obsessed by wars he never fought. Now he was acting like his mother, secretive and preoccupied with his own agenda, regardless of the costs. She recalled Jarra's favorite Javanese expression that said *your desire was like water from the moon.* That was Jarra, wanting always what she couldn't have. Today that expression fit Geigner and his life.

She felt a sense of relief. Fortunately, Amy and Ace were down to earth and practical members of the Prowers family.

What was important now was their commitment to the Committee. With the Count, she shared a belief that having heirs were no guarantee they'd be productive individuals. They only had to look at the lives of the rich occupied with endless consuming. Geigner she feared was lost, but Ace and Amy were, in a spiritual and practical sense, the Prowers heirs. Somehow, she had to persuade her niece to assume an active role in her inheritance.

Now, decrypting notes in the margins of the legend of Escobar Cay was a priority for Ace. She would query her Committee members to see if they had any information for sources in the desert. El Ben wasn't the only one to see the tactics but not the strategy, as Sun Tzu would say.

Her favorite quote of the Chinese general was *"Of all those in the army close to the commander, none is more intimate than the secret* agent; of all rewards, none more liberal than those given to secret agents; of all matters, none is more confidential than those relating to secret operations."

There were many secrets and she knew how to find them.

• • •

Sonora never spent much time reflecting on World War II. Tonight, was different. She poured a glass of sipping tequila and looked across her Berlin lawn, seeing all the players as they looked in the year after the war.

Was it only yesterday they traveled on the freighter, the *Meridian*, from the Red Sea to Vera Cruz? At the time, it seemed coincidence that they were all together, but now she wondered. Everyone had a secret. World War II was over, but the secrecy lingered on.

She saw her husband, the Count. "We have this opportunity to participate on a scientific team excavating the southern Sahara west of the Nile River."

"Darling, it's in Egypt. There is a war over there."

"Don't worry, it will be all right." And he had been right, until the end of the war. Then he was insistent they return to Mexico with their findings.

"Without publication, all will be for nothing."

To their surprise, on the freighter heading home was her half-brother Benton Prowers, his new wife Hanna, their German friend Eva, and the General who knew Benton and Hanna in Germany. Her sister, Jarra, had flown back to New York, avoiding, as they said, all that water. The world was unsettled, and old man Prowers wanted his daughters back in the states. He had given them the opportunity to experience life, live adventures. He didn't know they would become addicts, adventure junkies, but approved when he found out his son was on the ship.

The *Meridian* headed down the Red Sea and around the horn of
Africa across the Atlantic to Mexico. Hanna and Eva looked forward
to a new life in America on the Prowers ranch. The fresh sea air made
them confident in the future. To Sonora, they were optimistic about
their life in America. She wondered again about coincidences.

How quickly the days and years had passed. She heard the clock in
the library sound the hour of the day, reminding her that although the
years may have been kind, there had been many. The thought of the ship,
the *Meridian*, made her feel the rush of time passing.

As if it was yesterday, she could see everything clearly, even the
Captain's cat. There were chairs on the outside deck where she enjoyed
the sea breeze. The breeze was only a problem if the wind was blowing
the wrong direction. Then the soot from the engine covered the upper
deck. The yellow eyes of the black cat flicked at her as it walked along the
rail, undisturbed at the thought that it was walking over water.

Relief was what she felt in having to leave that part of the world,
though their research had been beneficial, and the subsequent publication
of their findings recognized worldwide. As the ship passed through the
southern end of the Suez Canal, the desert road beside the canal was
filled with tanks and trucks going both north and south. It didn't look
like the war was over.

At first, she had little contact with the German women. Eva, the
blonde-haired woman, rarely rose before two or three in the afternoon.
The other woman, Hanna, a dark-haired, rather stiff beauty, walked
around the deck with her new husband, Benton Prowers. Even then
Sonora sensed Hanna's strength, but never felt any emotion toward her.
What she knew without acknowledging it was Benton and Hanna had a
strange relationship.

Her husband, the Count, though born in Switzerland, was raised
in Mexico where he knew Prowers' grandfather. The Prowers property

included a large ranch outside of Vera Cruz. Benton was not a scholar but was knowledgeable on the Mayan culture. Discussions with the Count and Sonora fueled his enthusiasm to be a part of a future team looking for the lost civilizations in the central Mexican jungle. They spent hours discussing philosophy or in poker games, drinking with the Captain and mates. So much rum and tequila were poured, she wondered how the crew ever located the port of Vera Cruz.

The General followed Eva around the deck like the proverbial puppy dog. To her, the old Nazi seemed to be a hypocrite. Today she knew she was wrong. He was a deadly viper.

One day, three fat anti-sub airplanes buzzed low over the ship.

"Your friends, Benton," joked the Count. "They are out here, eh?"

Benton shook his head. "No, the war is over, at least for now."

"Ah, then," replied the Count. "Another disposable life, another disposable civilization. We create nothing permanent, although when I think of some of the things that have been done in Hitler's Germany; it is a good thing the Nazis disappeared."

"True," said Benton. "What is fascinating, at least for me about the Mayan culture and the sun gods they worshipped, is they were just as disposable. They may have lasted centuries, but now they are gone. It is really a commentary to live for the moment, a hedonistic philosophy."

"That is the destiny of all civilization."

They turned to see von Hagen beside them on the deck. Sonora remembered even the cat turned and without a backward glance, slowly stalked off to the Captain's cabin.

"It is," continued von Hagen arrogantly. "One of the ironies of our fragile lives is to think we can carry on from one generation to the next. Instead we must take what we can in this one and use it for all it is worth. But one failure does not a philosophy make, and I think we shall see again in all our lifetime similar attempts."

"I hope you are wrong." Prowers' voice was quiet, but Sonora remembered the intensity she heard in her half-brother's voice.

They cruised across the Atlantic in near-perfect weather. The Captain said if they were sailing, they would have been stalled in the middle of the ocean.

The ocean seemed to go on forever. Benton Prowers and her husband pored over manuscripts and old maps, talking about excavations. From her deck chair, she watched the blue sky along the African coast.

The excavation in Egypt had been exciting; if one liked digging in dirt. She worried the war wasn't over. Yes, the Germans had surrendered, but it was hard to believe the war just stopped.

Sonora poured more tequila, from the perpetually open bottle in her indoor solarium, so necessary because of Berlin's weather. Her memory took her back to the long oak table where passengers ate dinner and argued over icons and ancient ruins in Egypt. The General, an expert on icons, knew little of the Mayan culture, but learned quickly.

One day when she could no longer stand the tedious conversation, she climbed the steps to the bridge. There she found Benton, casually watching the waves stretch into the horizon.

"Don't tell me you are tired of chatting?" he asked in a voice that bordered between understanding and sarcasm.

"I have no interest in icons," she had replied.

He laughed. "Yet we hide among the lost civilizations of the past."

One night there was a storm. In the middle of the southern Atlantic Ocean, the ship caught a front coming off the African coast. Rough weather was not unusual, but this storm was one to remember. The old freighter rolled sideways and pitched forward, its bow breaking through the huge waves. Dinner around the captain's table developed into nightly drinking bouts for the men.

As the seas became rougher, one by one, the drinkers returned to their cabins. Sonora remembered being wide awake, listening to the roar of the ocean. She left her cabin and climbed the rail stairway to the bridge, wet from the blowing spray. The bridge was dark except for a small night light and the glow of the radar. The first mate spoke no English or Spanish, and pointed to the screen. He mumbled something and his words in any language were prophetic of the storm that followed. The pitching increased violently.

Every now and then, the old freighter would emit a huge shudder. She was glad she couldn't see the size of many of the waves. They appeared as a shadow and seemed taller than the ship. The freighter plunged into each wave and rose on the next, repeating the process over and over.

Then out of the violent night, a small figure appeared on the outside deck as the horizon rolled back and forth. Thinking it must be a crew member, she gestured to the mate. He shook his head and muttered what sounded to her like a curse. Before she realized it, he was out on the deck, returning with the figure.

Removing the rain cape, Sonora was surprised to see frail Eva. It crossed her mind how odd a woman who never walked the deck on a clear day without holding someone's arm was out alone on the deck on a night like this. Eva took a cup of hot coffee which the mate handed her and raised her mug in a salute to Sonora.

"Is a bad night." Her English, though halting, was remarkably clear of any accent.

Sonora agreed.

"I could not sleep," continued Eva. "I thought, why not be out to watch the storm. Is much more exciting than the same old sea every day."

For the first time, it occurred to Sonora that Eva was bored.

"All the men," Eva asked. "They have gone to bed?"

Sonora smiled. "Yes, they drink too much."

Eva laughed. "Well, if they are not too sick, then they are missing the finest night of the voyage."

They both remained on the bridge throughout the storm. Occasionally a member of the crew acting as lookout entered for a hot cup of coffee, bringing with him the driving rain. Otherwise the bridge was warm and the coffee hot. Only the howling wind and the pounding of the sea could be heard as the ship rose and fell into the waves. In the hours before dawn, the wind and rain stopped. The skies brightened as the sun began to appear over the eastern horizon.

Eva yawned, appearing tired.

"I shall return to the cabin. A good night's sleep and soon to Mexico. Vera Cruz—I understand it is beautiful and warm weather."

"It is very nice. I think you will like it."

That was the last time she saw Eva until they had docked at Vera Cruz. According to the General, she had the flu.

To Sonora, Eva seemed a picture of health that stormy night. Eva's fate was to be a person of rumor and innuendo, and of mystery, since the world believed she died in the bunker with Hitler. There was no point in the truth being told. Yet Sonora felt a bond with her because of that night on the sea.

All that had happened so long ago. Today what was important was what she and Ace, and Geigner, and Amy did in the present. *We are the future,* she thought.

• • •

CHAPTER SEVENTEEN

Amy and Bernardo

I can't see how my father's death, icons,
and serpents relate to each other.

From the elevated train platform, Amy looked over the tile roof tops
of Villahermosa, a city of over 600,000. In time, all things change and
this city in central Mexico once a primitive farming community, was
now a thriving metropolis, complete with congestion and pollution.

Picking up her knapsack, she walked out of the station and into
a crowd of natives selling fruit, fish and colorful clothing out of tall
wicker baskets. She looked around, hearing her name and saw Bernardo,
the hacienda manager.

"Bernardo, hola, como esta?"

"Senorita Amy, *bien*," said the Prowers family's plantation foreman.
"I come to find you. Jaime called, so we know you come. We'll have
lunch at the hacienda."

She climbed into the Mercedes, edged with rust from the jungle humidity, and listened to Bernardo as he practiced his English. According to him, workers on the plantation reported seeing not one, but two jaguars. She knew jaguars came out at night, stayed away from people, and yet made their presence felt. As the largest cats in the Americas, and eaters of meat including man, the plantations descendants of the Mayans identified with the big cat's power.

Amy thought the domestic cats born in Colorado but now living in Berlin had mystical powers, so it was easy to believe the powers of a jaguar. When locals were fixated on the jaguar, little else would be on their minds.

Then Bernardo shifted to his favorite topic, the disappearance of the Mayan. Everyone who lived in the area was well versed on this topic. To him, disease was what caused the end of the Mayan civilization. As the population died, the size of cities decreased, priests and nobles died or moved on, and the rigid social structure disappeared. By the end of the ninth century, the Mayan culture was gone.

"Descendants of the Mayans still live here, speaking fifteen different languages. Their bodies are tattooed, their hair braided. While they worship maize, there are many other crops like avocadoes, sweet potatoes, guavas, tomatoes, and chocolate made from the cacao bean. The Spaniards were impressed by the Mayans' use of herbs and roots for medicinal purposes. Today Mayans use plants for any disease."

He sighed, not the sigh of one who has given up, but of one who realizes as the years pass, he will never know.

"Sometimes I think they just tired of their leaders, paying homage, and sacrifice. The jungle gave them their life, and they forgot that it was what created their society. We are all alike. We forget where we began."

Amy totally agreed with that philosophy.

The road was bordered by high trees and low jungle grass. Tops of ruins peeked in and out between the jungle greenery. Multicolored orchids filled in the gaps between green palms and mangroves. Along the road were houses on stilts and cattle grazing in an occasional cleared meadow with neatly planted rows of sugar cane. Then the car melted into the jungle and they arrived at a gate opening to a driveway that curved toward the red tile roof of the old Prowers's hacienda.

"Come," said Bernardo, leading her to the veranda. "I knew you'd like a large cup of tea. A night on the train is tiring."

The villa's veranda looked out at the jungle surrounding the estate. Behind them were the ruins of Palenque. The top of the Tower of Inscription was visible above the jungle floor. The air was heavy with humidity. Thick green vegetation hid the birds, but their sounds mingled with other gentle noises of the jungle, common, yet unidentified. Amy knew somewhere there was a birder who could identify each of these species.

She listened again to the jungle sounds. Was the jaguar out there living on the ground of the hacienda and the ruins? She'd like to see that cat, but it would never happen. No one finds a jaguar unless the jaguar lets them. Beyond the foliage, in the soft jungle soil under the thick walls of Palenque, was the final home for generations of Mayan rulers and the souls of their ancestors. Those souls she was sure were watching over her, just as she was sure the jaguar was.

Bernardo poured tea and looked at Amy. Only in the high forehead and wide mouth did he see any resemblance to Benton. She had his quiet strength, not Hanna's ruthless approach to life.

"I haven't been able to express my sympathy on the death of your second husband. I know you were divorced. Still must be a shock."

Amy shrugged. "Thank you, I feel for his children. He died of a rare blood disease, which I'm sure was because of his drinking, but who knows. He was one person who was married more times than me, with five wives. Sonora misses him very much."

Amy's voice sounded strained and tense as she focused on the purpose of her visit.

"I'm here because my father's death, icons, and serpents relate to each other. I know he visited here before his plane crash. In the Balkans, I found a note he left in a bank vault in Dubrovnik talking about the Ceiba Tree and finding a treasure. I don't know enough about the Mayan traditions to know how the tree, the serpent, and the icons would be connected. Can you help me?"

"Of course," replied Bernardo. "Legend says there is a seductress, Xtabai, who lived in the Ceiba Tree, trapping everything within her reach. The Ceiba Tree is a common Mayan symbol and the center of the cosmos. Its roots reach to the underworld, while its branches reach to the heavens. The beginning of the Mayan civilization, some say was 2500 BC, is often obscure and tied to the fall of northern cities such as Teotihuacán, now a ruin visited by tourists outside Mexico City. You've seen the Ceiba tree many times on the Yucatan peninsula."

"I was afraid it would be something like that. When Father said the Ceiba tree, what was he thinking?" Amy asked.

"Do you have his letter?"

She handed him the letter, and he quickly read it. What had been Benton's purpose in writing it? He remembered how Benton asked him to always help Amy, protect her when she was in Mexico.

"My dear, Pascal means 'shield.' But this other reference to the foot where the serpents are is Biblical."

"My father wasn't into the Bible, or its prophecies, so why these references?"

He considered Amy's question, as he lit a long thin panatela cigar. It was time Amy knew the truth, but Bernardo didn't want to endanger her life. But then it was likely in danger. The General and el Ben would do whatever was necessary to find the Shroud.

"Amy, before his death, your father saw the Shroud as a symbolic way of unifying North Africa. One time, he talked about a dream he had before Marfkis died. He trusted Marfkis, but not el Ben. There is an astrologer who advises el Ben and sees el Ben as the man who can save the Muslim Empire. To your father, el Ben was the fourth beast, and nothing would prevent Benton from stopping such a person. Benton said he was the same type of leader as Hitler. Your father was afraid that in the wrong hands, the Shroud would provide the beast—that is what he called el Ben—with power to control the world. Artifacts are symbols that we see in past civilizations. The burial cloth of Christ, a symbol, would give el Ben his dream of uniting North Africa."

Bernardo took a drag on his cigar. Amy didn't need to smell the smoke to know it was a Cuban cigar.

"I know this. Your father risked his life to keep the Shroud hidden."

A servant entered with a fresh pot of tea. The distraction gave him time to consider what had been on his mind for some time. This charade must stop. Is that what Benton had meant when he said, help Amy.

"The Temple here in Villahermosa is so huge, we let everyone think this is where Pascal was buried. He lived during the height of the classical Mayan era, so a temple of this size makes sense. The truth is, his grave is in a small tomb on Playa Del Carmen known only to the few of us who excavated it. The tomb is of very intricate design and the public would destroy it.

"One day, on the island, not far from the Temple of Inscriptions, but a significant distance if you're hauling a body on a donkey to the tomb, a local looking for a natural spring found the entrance to another tomb. Your father and I excavated and found the mummy of Pascal. How did we know it was Pascal? The funeral mask of jade with his features was inside the sarcophagus. We donated the mask to the Museum of Archeology in Mexico City."

He paused. "You know where it is, Amy, because you visited us when we were working on the site. But there is more. You deal with today and forget the past; only the past is always with you. On your summer visits to Isle of Carmen, you remember it, no?"

"Is that where the twenty-foot scrolled engraving of the Ceiba tree is outside the temple?"

"Yes, at each end, the jaws of the earth monster are holding up the tree. The foot of the tree, or the root of the tree sits in the monster's mouth. On a moonlit night, you see that. The people who live near the temple claim they hear singing. Many nights your father, other archaeologists, and I spent on the isle, waiting to see if the mystical ghost, a seductress, was real. We saw nothing, but we heard the singing."

Amy remembered that tomb and her father telling her about the singing. She often visited him on the island, which also was the headquarters for oil exploration in the gulf. Slowly she had watched as oil took over and the local fishing industry collapsed; the price of progress her father called it.

"Go, my dear, and search the tomb. Your father, flying his private plane, could have stopped on Carmen before going to Vera Cruz. I would go with you but have a presentation to make in Mexico City for the archeology society. I cannot miss it."

"Bernardo, did Father mention anything about a book on icons? This book arrived for me" and she pulled it out and handed it to him. "In Berlin after his death. Could it be a real clue or a decoy?"

He quickly opened the thin cover and saw nothing written inside.

"You expected something?" Amy asked, thinking of the Hakenkreuz.

"The book I am thinking of may have been destroyed in Benton's plane crash. Don't remember its name, but an icon book he was reading had a name written inside the cover. I paged through looking at the pictures of icons and saw it."

"The Hakenkreuz, the soft-sided swastika?" asked Amy.

"Amy, yes!"

"I saw the swastika at the General's. It was penciled inside the cover of a book titled *Icons of the Balkan Monasteries*. My father left the same book for me in his desk at the ranch, but no swastika."

Bernardo's head filled with questions. The two books were the same except for the swastika inside the cover. *How did von Hagen get Benton's book?*

"Amy, it's important you go to the Isle of Carmen. Take one of our cars. You know the road. Our hacienda staff makes regular trips to the island, so we'll pick it up later. Remember, Doco Petroleum will get you off the island. They fly in and out almost every day."

As a servant brought the car around, Bernardo felt like a surrogate parent.

"Please, my dear, be careful and Godspeed."

"Thank you for everything," said Amy, "Especially loaning me the car. I know the road to the island. Thank you, Bernardo, and *adios*."

"*Hasta luego*. Please, let me know how it goes."

As he watched the BMW curve its way down the mountain road, he wondered if he had overlooked something. He tried to remember conversations with Benton, but for the moment his mind was blank. Benton had spent so many years on excavations and keeping the Shroud a secret. Was it all for nothing?

The phone was ringing as he went inside the villa. His houseman took the call and reminded him Olen was flying to Villahermosa in the afternoon. Bernardo sat down and poured another shot of tequila.

He hadn't been completely honest with Amy. True, the books and their symbolism made little sense to her. What he hadn't told Amy was that her father on his last visit was distant, self-absorbed, which was not like him. Since Benton's death, he'd thought more of his own life. How quickly the days and years had passed.

He poured another glass of tequila. The real issue wasn't the Shroud or the Mayan legacies. It was the excavation in the desert that was

Benton's obsession. What were they doing at that so-called archeology excavation at El Kanitaoui? What had Benton and Geigner found?

It is ironic, he thought, *that the excavation and the Shroud of Turin were tied together as one.*

· · ·

Jutting out on the Rio Grijalva were worn wooden docks and an occasional shack with a dilapidated Coca-Cola sign, none of which interrupted the river on its journey to the Gulf of Mexico. Clusters of sea gulls congregated on tiny sand bars, oblivious to the tide coming in and out of the mouth of the river.

She drove along the bumpy paved road and thought about the Ceiba tree. The tree of life was its name, because the tree roots reached into the underworld, at the same time its foliage brushed the heavens. It was a sacred tree, the dominated center of the cosmos, tall with a bottle-shaped trunk, a fan of foliage above.

Then there was the tomb. Her father always told her stories about investigating the different tombs. When they first found Pascal and opened the sarcophagus, there was a mask with over two hundred pieces of jade covering Pascal's face. That mask and Pascal's body were now in the National Museum of Anthropology in Mexico City.

She looked ahead on the road, feeling like somebody was watching her. Short palms blew in the wind warning of a coming storm. The land was flat as she drove toward the coast. She crossed another small wooden bridge. There were few rivers or streams in this part of the Yucatan. Underground, huge caverns of water lay trapped in a limestone base. When the bedrock collapsed, it formed what was called a cenote, or a well, the peninsulas only source of water.

On a day like today it was easy to wonder what happened to the Mayans. Was it smallpox, brought by the Spaniards, which wiped out the entire civilization? Whatever—the Balamob, the guardians of the jungle remained, and so did the Mayans.

She forced herself to concentrate on driving. She passed through another village town with huts elevated on high stakes to keep them off the marshlands. Several mangy dogs lounged in what passed as a front yard. She didn't see any people sitting outside. Usually, descendants of the Mayans worked hard and took a break only on Sundays, socializing in the small village plazas built by the Spaniards.

The sun was shining brightly, but ahead on the road to the east a black cloudbank was rising above the horizon. The narrow blacktop road enclosed by the jungle broke into an open marsh, with a wide panoramic view of the Usumacinta River flowing toward the Bay of Campeche and the Gulf of Mexico. The tide was coming in as the river ran against itself in rivulets.

Here and there, she saw a whitecap crashing across sandbars formed as the river flowed into the Gulf of Mexico. Then, the road was sucked back into the dense jungle foliage. By the time she reached the ferry crossing, the cloudbank overhead was dumping what felt like a bucket of rain on top of the car. The ferry churned across the Bay of Campeche to the Isle of Carmen, the Ciudad Del Carmen.

With the rain, it was impossible to see any oil rigs. Since its discovery in 1976, the Gulf of Mexico had been one of the largest oil fields in the world. The Cantarell complex, as it was called, was now aging and was being explored for ways to obtain more oil. The field itself was unique. It was created by an asteroid strike, called the extinction strike because scientists believe it also was the climate-changing event that took out the dinosaurs.

In the distance, Amy could see the oil exploration ships in the port, side by side with a few fishing boats with the ruins of ancient Mayans buried in the vegetation of the island.

Chatting in Spanish to the crew running the ferry, she learned there were only a few rooms left in the Hotel de Drina. The boatman said it was his last trip until the storm ended. A storm like this one could stop the ferry service for several days, so they said.

• • •

Humidity hung like an invisible veil as Amy walked into the blue-green ceramic tile-lined hotel lobby. The island was already taking a severe beating from the storm, but she got one of the last rooms. The clerk repeated what the boatman said. It could be several days before the ferry was running.

Listening to him, she felt trapped. *How could she get off the island once she checked out the tomb? Of course, Doco Petroleum.*

She'd almost forgotten the private airline owned in part by her family. She'd be able to get a flight off the island and back to the monastery in Europe. Maybe by the time she got there, Ace would have deciphered her father's clues.

The room was sparse; most occupants spent their time on the beach. She headed for the patio restaurant where the rain had washed away the dust and diesel fumes of the boats. The waiter looked at her expectantly. She and her father had always ordered a local drink called a Mamacita. Cranberry and orange juice were a cover for a lethal mixture of brandy, and rum. No way could she handle any alcohol, so she ordered iced tea.

It was still early, and the storm appeared to have let up. She ought to be able to get to the tomb this afternoon. Storms on the island came in waves, and this was a break she needed.

She pulled out the books and notes to try again to figure out what her father was telling her. There was the letter from the bank in Dubrovnik.

Keep thy heart with all diligence for out of it come the issues of life, and then remove thy foot from evil.

Her father's letter referenced the sun and guardians, Mayan symbols. The fourth beast and the other quotes in the letter referred to the monastery and the icons. Why confuse the issue? Her father had to be paranoid; his clues would be interpreted by someone besides her. He was tricking her, while he was busy tricking them."

Then Amy realized the obvious; the book on icons he left for her, *Icons of the Balkan Monasteries,* and the book sent to Berlin, *Beyond the Face: A Commentary on Icons, Symbols, and Illusions,* talked about the same icons. There were no clues; just his paranoia trying to confuse everyone. He knew she would go to the monastery, and using the icon book, figure out where the Shroud could be. It didn't matter that the General had the same book on icons, and she knew it didn't matter if there was a Hakenkreuz in it or not. Most likely he had used the Hakenkreuz as misdirection.

Amy looked at the introduction page of the book sent to Berlin by the mystery person she was sure was Veilkov, and read:

The icon is a concept of writing and once the artist has mastered the preconceived patterns, he can develop his own.

The book he left for her, *Icons of the Balkan Monasteries,* was to direct her to the monastery. Between Veilkov and the Abbot, he figured she would find where the Shroud was hidden. The note to go to the bank to find the jewels was another decoy. The jewels were to show some treasure from the train crash had survived, so the Shroud must have survived.

For the first time, she felt as if she was going to find it.

Likely Veilkov sent the book that arrived in Berlin: *Beyond the Face: A Commentary on Icons, Symbols, and Illusions.* That book was Veilkov's decoy. The Shroud had something to do with the icon in that book. It had to be the icon *Christ in Glory.*

Was Pascal's tomb an illusion, a decoy, while he hid the icon at Gracanica? Something had bothered her about the Gracanica Monastery and the Icon. She couldn't quite visualize it because she wasn't an expert on iconology, not yet.

Since she was here, she might as well check out Pascal's real grave. The tomb likely was only an illusion in her search. Reality was, she hoped to find it again.

• • •

Where was the turn?

Her eyes were riveted on the jungle beside the road, searching for a dirt trail that once was an old Mayan road. It had been years since she'd come to the tomb during her father's excavation. How exciting it had been to be a part of that excavation, even if only for a few days. She remembered a Ceiba tree was at the turnoff. Haze from the storm made the late afternoon light dim, but she saw it ahead. The shadow of the tree emerged, and she turned to the left down a rutted road.

Immediately the road was swallowed by the jungle then opened out into a clearing. Beyond the low jungle grass, she could see the heavy gray foaming gulf. She kept driving, knowing the crumbling stone ruins, and edifices used as altars for human sacrifice, were impossible to see from the road.

Those alters were important as Mayans were absorbed in blood and death. Their history said the human heart, still warm and pumping, was given as a gift to the gods.

Her father told her this tomb was Pascal's. His body was buried centuries ago. When his team opened the tomb in the Temple of Inscriptions in Palenque, Pascal's body wasn't there. They were stymied until a farmer on one of the estates having drinks with Bernardo said he'd seen a sarcophagus, on this island. Her father and Bernardo were the first to excavate and find the sarcophagus. It was their secret.

Ahead of her, the road wound into the jungle, ending in front of a crumbling gray vine-covered stone pyramid, rising nearly four stories. The pyramid looked to her like part of the jungle. For a thousand years, this was Pascal's real tomb, not the Temple of Inscriptions. The structure might show up on infrared radar, but no one would ever find it unless they were looking for it along the jungle floor.

Amy remembered her father telling her about a duct that went directly into the crypt. It was an air passage and came out on one of these crumbling heads. Through these heads, the dead heard the chants of their priests leading them to the afterlife. She wished she could just call down and ask the priests if the Shroud was there.

Thankfully, the car had a battery-powered lantern and a flashlight in the car's glove compartment. Braving the wind squalls, she followed the dirt path to the tomb and came face to face with the head of the giant stone monster on the gray stone wall. Remembering when she visited years ago, she reached up and pushed hard at the jaws on the face as her father had. Slowly, the stone slab in front slid to the side. Amy felt as if she was being watched, but she couldn't turn back. No one was around to help her.

This is the last thing in the world I want to be doing, she thought. The tomb fit the definition of creepy.

Forcing herself to ignore feelings of claustrophobia, she started down the steps. They were surprisingly dry and free of mildew though she could hear water dripping from somewhere below.

"There are twenty-one steps, and then another door."

The sound of her voice was reassuring in the darkened corridor. She would be worried about bats except the tomb was sealed, or she hoped it still was.

The next door was also guarded by two stone heads with jaws. Again, she pushed the jaw and the door opened.

She entered a small room completely enclosed with smooth slabs of stone. In the center were three skulls and bones. It wasn't Pascal, but the bones of young children sacrificed when the ruler was sealed in his grave. Their sacrifice was necessary to protect him from any evil spirits on his journey into the long night. Bones of iguanas, jaguars, and dogs were scattered in the corner, but humans were the ultimate sacrifice. Benton insisted all those years ago, the bones remain untouched. No one wanted to disturb the spirits.

And neither do I, thought Amy.

Carefully, she walked between bones of small skeletons lying as they were found in the tomb. Her light flickered on the floor's stone slabs. Near the bottom of the wall was the stone head of a serpent. Reaching down, she pushed hard. Another edge of stone slowly slid flush with the floor. There was a slight grating noise and she looked up.

The wall had moved backward opening a triangle door. Before her was a spectacular crystal grotto crypt. In the reflected light, it looked like a diamond jewel. The center held another carved stone slab, etched with the face of man. At the top was an ornate cross, its arms the heads of serpents.

Amy turned the spotlight on the stone sarcophagus, Pascal's coffin, and nearly jumped. The stone face carved on the top looked as if it was alive and looking at her.

She had been in the crypt several times, yet the lifelike qualities of the stone face always took her by surprise. Her father told her Pascal's face was lifelike because it was carved in stone before death to please the spirits of the tomb. She put her hands on the top of the stone sarcophagus, glad her father had let her open it so many years ago and pulled the top of the coffin open.

The light caught glimmers of green and red inside the sarcophagus, flickering on a smaller funeral mask, a jade shell which once covered his skull. There was the stone in the mouth of the mask, symbolizing the immortal spirit. The real funeral mask and Pascal's mummy were in the Archeological Museum in Mexico City. Benton gave one of the Mayans a piece of land to make this replica of the funeral mask.

Both the Mayans and Benton were superstitious about Pascal's grave. His mummy might be in Mexico City, but the funeral mask honoring Pascal was keeping the spirits quiet. The spirits were still in the tomb, said Benton. She didn't want them coming after her. Then, as now, she hoped they were friendly.

Holding the light above the sarcophagus, she slowly moved the beam around inside. The light flickered on the stone sides of the tomb. She spotted a piece of plastic resting against the side of the sarcophagus. It was the same plastic as the package in the vault at Dubrovnik.

Quickly, she reached for it and put it in her knapsack. From the weight, the packet felt like the jewels in the packet at the vault in Dubrovnik.

Not more jewels, she thought.

There was a rumbling noise, almost a roar. Having been in several earthquakes in the Mexican mountains, she knew that sound.

She took a deep breath, flicked the flashlight around the sarcophagus, but there was only his funeral mask. The tremor was real, and she had to get above-ground. For a moment, she gazed again at the unearthly stone mask covering the sarcophagus, showing the human features of someone who had lived so long ago. She wondered how long it would be before Pascal was disturbed again. Maybe the answer was never.

Quickly she slid the stone cover closed, sealing the coffin.

The claustrophobic feelings of the Mayans grabbed her psyche. Local Mayans, the natives, say the Balamob—the guardians—are here keeping watch, keeping the evil spirits away. She hoped their magic worked a few more minutes as she quickly walked back through the winding passage.

How could someone tell the difference between the good and evil spirits? How did you know? Spirits were like people; you couldn't tell by looking.

Her footsteps startled a small lizard. It ran crazily from side to side down the passage, attempting to get out of her way. Amy followed it, glad to share the passage with something alive.

• • •

CHAPTER EIGHTEEN

El Kanitaoui—The End

El Ben and Khadafy were determined to prove
their heritage was linked to the Egyptian pharaohs,
making them legitimate heirs to most of North Africa.

Geigner walked to the edge of the oasis, watching the sun drop in
the western sky. He looked up at the dry, desert Mountains he loved
so much. For him, it was easier to reflect on the past than to believe in
the future. A decade ago, when he first arrived, it was just sand.

He recalled getting used to the searing heat. The first summer in
the desert was brutal, as the soaring temperatures sapped his endurance.
He had no idea then it really might be in Akhenaten's tomb, but today
his laser weapon would light up the Maghreb for the next century.

El Habid rarely left him alone. He was always asking questions. At
least he was a realist. While his father prayed, he made sure the family
dream would be a reality. El Ben believed it was the will of Allah that
one day the Alemien family would rule from the Atlantic Ocean to the

Red Sea. It was written in the sands of the Bedouin destiny. His son knew their family needed his skills.

How could he forget the bar in the Hotel Ibis, on the Nile River south of Cairo, where it all began? With his aunt Sonora they excavated tombs in the Valley of the Kings finding nothing. The pharaohs' tombs were picked over. They were a century too late.

The bartender overheard their conversation and asked if they knew the legend about the old Berber burial grounds. They said no, and looked at each other, trying not to laugh. They had listened to many so-called legends.

The tale the bartender told was about the Bedouin who lived in the southern mountains near an oasis called El Kanitaoui. Besides water the oasis had a burial ground. From their research, both knew that area of the Sahara had not been explored. The tribes were hostile to outsiders, not to mention the difficulty of surviving deep in the desert. The bartender said they should find the Alemien family and talk to the oldest son, el Habid.

If it had been up to me, we'd never have believed his story, thought Geigner. He remembered how Sonora pulled out of her bag a map of the entire Sahara sent to her by a French map dealer in Paris.

"How did you get that?" he asked.

Sonora looked bored. "I always travel with a set of maps from Pierre, especially in North Africa. Look at this."

She pointed to the Nile River. Her map, a detailed ecological map suitable for a geologist, showed where the Nile flood plane had been over the centuries. With her finger, she traced the river.

"The Nile has tributaries traveling from the mountain range that borders Chad. The entire area could have more tombs, maybe more than in the Valley of the Kings. Lack of humidity means they likely are preserved, and the isolation assures protection from grave robbers who destroyed many of the Egyptian tombs. The one Pharaoh we haven't found is Akhenaten. This could be the place."

Egyptologists didn't agree, but the Prowers, using their family fortune, followed their own conclusions. With Geigner's computer skills, they focused on the thirteenth century before Christ, the reign of Amenhotep IV, as Akhenaten, the Sun King, was called.

Today looking out at the El Kanitaoui Valley today, he thought what a coincidence that a bartender and a Berber legend took them to what he now knew was Akhenaten's tomb. One day flying over the desert, after a rare rainstorm that rearranged many of the dunes, they spotted the huge stones—the talatat—along a worn camel trail, their first real lead.

The talatat that they found told the story of the Valley of the Kings and the Nile River. The stones used to anchor the pharaohs' temples were pillaged and scattered across the western world's museums in Paris, London, New York, and Berlin.

Geigner visited the museums in Paris, London, and Berlin, to reconstruct the stories the stones told. He and el Habid used the research to convince, not only his father el Ben, but the Libyan leader, Khadafy to support the excavation at El Kanitaoui in the southern Sahara.

El Ben and Khadafy, both Bedouins, were determined to prove their heritage was linked to the Egyptian pharaohs. That link would give them a legitimate claim as heirs to the kingdom on the Nile, and most of North Africa. Over the years, el Ben came to trust Geigner and his Uncle Benton, who aided in the excavation.

Geigner knew another reason that was important. As followers of the prophet Mohammed, the el Alemien family knew the one god was Allah, but to legitimize their rule, the tribe needed to be descended from the Pharaohs. Akhenaten and his single god were the perfect ancestor.

Thirteen centuries before Christ lived, Akhenaten, the Sun King, believed in one God. He was King Tutankhamen's father and a progressive ruler. The concept of only one God incurred the hatred of military leaders' priests who forced his abdication. They kept his death and burial site a mystery to keep archeologists and tomb raiders out.

Looking out at the desert valley, Geigner knew he had proven the el Alemien family's lineage. He had found Akhenaten's grave.

• • •

Years ago, when he arrived, it all looked so different. He took a sip of water from his flask and remembered the first time he saw the edge of the oasis of El Kanitaoui. From the glare of the desert sun, it appeared as if it was an arm's length away.

El Habid, his guide, explained.

"If it was winter, there would be less haze. We could see the Jebal, the range of mountains where we will begin the search for the tomb. Now we are standing on the edge of the Nile flood plain. Historians say this is where the city of Thebes originally was, west of the Nile. Today they forget where the water ran centuries ago."

Geigner looked west at the desert burning in the heat of the day and took another drink of water. The Bedouin were waiting under the thick palm trees for the leader. He heard a helicopter bringing in the leader.

Through the glare of the sun and blowing sand, a dark-haired man in a crisp uniform walked toward the trees. It was Khadafy. An aide handed him one of the flowing Bedouin robes. Two other choppers landed and a contingent of men in robes and uniforms walked to the clumps of trees.

El Habid motioned to Geigner.

"There is a memorial under the trees. It's for battles during World War II with the Italians. The memory makes my father very emotional."

The group formed a half circle around the stone memorial. It was then Geigner noticed through the dusty haze that the oasis wasn't on a flat desert plain, but in a wadi backing up to the desert mountains. Next to the nomadic Bedouin tents were a few white stone houses and a dirt road. The sound of high-pitched wailing caused him to quickly turn. The size of the group had nearly doubled with the arrival of women wearing bright blue robes and veils.

He remembered looking at Colonel Khadafy, his thick curly head thrown backward, and his gleaming white teeth smiled above trembling vocal cords as he spoke. Khadafy raised both hands.

"The hawk has gone to heaven and one other sits in his place." He spoke in a dialect impossible for Geigner to follow. El Habid translated.

"He is making some reference to the occupation by the Italians. It was at Kufra that the Italians massacred the Bedouin during one of the bloodiest battles of World War II. He speaks too rapidly for me, as he uses a little-spoken dialect of the desert tribesmen."

Geigner was beginning to feel the desert heat, as it was nearly mid-day. Surely even Bedouins need a break. As if to read his mind, Khadafy turned and walked toward the palm trees, the crowd following him. Geigner knew he needed to stay in the shade of the palm trees and drink fresh water from the oasis.

An older man walked over to them. El Habid introduced them.

"My father, Sheik Muhammad el Ben Akhenaten-Alemien."

El Ben was shorter than Geigner, but taller than most Bedouin. His tanned face and thin beard gave his face an intelligent look. His eyes told Geigner he was a leader. From his English accent, Geigner guessed he was the product of an English University, likely Oxford.

"It is a pleasure for you to join us. I have been told about the matter of your visa. Please consider it to be renewed indefinitely. I look forward to speaking with you soon at my desert home at El Kanitaoui."

With a short bow he was gone, heading down the road toward the village. He never thought Khadafy would last so many years, but he had. Now he was gone. Only the desert and el Ben remained.

• • •

Today, Geigner was looking at the tall windows of the hotel, which had all the modern features oil money could buy for visiting family and friends. None of that mattered to him. The more he researched the past, the more dissatisfied he was with life today.

"It is my choice," he thought, then and now. The gusty wind blew the sand in spirals. This was his home and he loved it. Now he would leave forever. Somehow, he didn't feel as if he was leaving.

Looking to the south, through the dust, he could see the outline of a high ridge of mountains. The ridge to the east was Akhenaten's tomb and the weapon. He needed to concentrate on the job at hand. For the first time in his life, he was doing something for the Prowers family and the world.

The roar of a jet banking against the horizon interrupted his thinking. He stared up at the fighter. At least in Khadafy's day, you knew who the good guys and the bad guys were. The thrill of working on a dig was the discovery. Today in the oasis he felt like a prisoner.

Veilkov had corrected his computer program. *My mistake*, he thought, *was simple. I forgot how gravity distorted the beam, even in the tomb.* Years ago, Vince convinced him there were places on earth free of gravity. If true, his original calculation would be correct, but the laser in the chamber at El Kanitaoui was affected slightly by gravity.

The weapon worked because the tomb reduced the pull of gravity, not because there was no gravity. The computer program had to adjust the aim for the small pull of gravity that remained. Veilkov saw the error and made the correction. The laser could be aimed and more importantly, now the calculation could produce a laser anywhere.

He smiled. There really was irony in science. The calculation had become the weapon.

What was necessary, he had done. Medak took the correct calculation back to the monastery in the gold head of Aaron's Beard. Being a good scientist, he had a backup plan. In the book, *Strogatz and The Legend of Escobar Cay* that he sent to Amy at the villa in Berlin, he had scribbled the calculation in the margin.

Knowing his family, Amy, Sonora, and Ace would figure it out. He hoped to be there with them but had been in the desert long enough to know there was no certainty in life.

The sun had set and Geigner could see the silhouette of the mountains framed against the darkened sky. He wished he had the faith of Benton Prowers and the Abbot, or even Veilkov. The world was too complex for one man to make a difference. He looked at the ridge to the south, seeing a cloud of dust. El Ben was almost to the top.

Looking at him on the mountain, Geigner thought it might be the last time he would see the old man. He would run a simulation for el Habid using the wrong calculation, and at sunrise, leave the oasis, which had been so much of his life, forever.

• • •

Silently el Habid stood and stared through the glass window, watching Geigner move wires attached to a small red box. With the simulation still in progress, Geigner left.

El Habid thought nothing of it, since Geigner had left simulations before. His half-brothers were self-proclaimed experts on the weapon. After all he watched Geigner run simulations on the computer. He had relied on them to have gotten the calculation. They were confident they knew how to run it, but el Habid had doubts they were sophisticated enough to understand everything Geigner did. He trusted none of them and realized he should have gotten the calculation himself.

During the ideological discussions between his father and Geigner, he never believed in collective identity, especially when it related to his relatives. His idea of an elite ruling class included himself alone.

He saw Geigner pick up some papers and head down the stairs. Much as he wanted to, he couldn't talk to him. His father, finishing prayers at the top of the ridge, was waiting for him.

Smiling slightly, he turned to two of his half-brothers.

"We have the right to rule the world, and now possess a weapon to do so. The tomb of Akhenaten is our heritage. There was a city and a man in it who saved the city, but no one remembers the man. It is a prophetic statement about Geigner, because no one will remember him. Do we need Geigner? Our father thinks so. But we are the next generation. Let us try a simulation ourselves."

His half-brothers agreed, happy they no longer needed Geigner. El Habid was their father's favorite, but after they ran the weapon system, their father might look at them differently. Now they could run the simulator.

• • •

El Habid arrived at the top of the ridge, with his father still in prayer. The sun had set, and he was never sure if his father was up here for the view or to get away from his wives. Nonetheless, this was when the old man was most dangerous. This was where his father planned his future moves.

Above the desert floor on the rocky ruins of Amarna, el Ben's face shone beneath the light of the early stars. His father enthusiastically supported the excavation. Why not? The excavation would prove the Sun King, Akhenaten, who had been the first to believe in one god, was in the direct line of kingship from the days of Egyptian rulers through the Prophet Mohammed to el Ben's desert tribe.

Who could have predicted that out of a search for lineage to Egyptian pharaohs would come a laser weapon to dominate the world? Geigner's calculation was just as important as proving the lineage of el Ben to the Prophet.

El Habid sat with his father, reveling in lineage dating to the ancient pharaohs. Had some ancient king, maybe even Akhenaten, known of this phenomenon that the tomb created? It didn't matter to el Habid. What did matter was the feud with his half-brothers. In-fighting provided opportunities for increasing power. He was waiting to see if they could run the simulation without Geigner. Nothing seemed to be happening, and el Habid realized that if they didn't have the correct calculation, he would have to get it from Geigner.

• • •

El Ben looked across the desert valley and thanked Allah for the linkage to the pharaohs that Geigner found. He envisioned the days when the dried riverbeds ran with water from the mountain springs. The life blood, water, was today only in the oasis, but in its place, Allah had provided black gold. Oil brought the cash to develop the desert valleys. And Allah had given him something else, the tomb of Akhenaten, the natural cavity that was the laser weapon. To him, space was the new age of reason.

Here in the African desert he intended to use the laser to build the prophet's dream. He looked at el Habid, wishing his son was as adept at running a nation as he was at flying planes or shooting guns. His own time was almost over and the leadership of the country would be in el Habid's hands, *inshallah*, as Allah wills.

"My son, our safety is in the laser Geigner has designed. For it to work, we needed his computer program with the calculation. Now we have it all."

• • •

El Habid said nothing. Obviously, his brothers had been talking to his father. He wished he could be as confident. One thing his father did know was a sense of when a person was going to die. El Habid was never sure if it was internal or was told by his holy men.

It was Geigner's time to die, thought el Habid. His informants in Egyptian customs told him a paper was hidden in the gold head of Aaron's Beard given by Geigner to Medak. The head was in Medak's luggage when he flew to the monastery. El Habid was sure the calculation was in the head and was Geigner's backup plan.

The sun had already set, but the old man was wound up on the past.

"I remember the days when the Germans occupied our country. They sat in the cafés in Benghazi, in Tripoli, listening to the discussions of what I consider to be the only positive side of German history. Friedrich Schiller wrote in a discussion of the philosopher Nicholas of Cusa that with education comes freedom. The development of sovereign nations is the role of the state in assisting technological progress. The colonization of space and the technology of outer space put us today into a new age of reason. If the superpowers were truly as enlightened as the world press would have us believe, then the peaceful settlement of space should be our goal. Allah be praised.

"Our leadership is needed for the world to move forward. We are necessary to build a world as Allah created it. To do so, we must apply force. It is up to us. We will be the nation to sound the global blitzkrieg. Here in the desert we have a political, social, and economic philosophy that transcends the need for any other escapist ideology."

"Father." El Habid was relieved to get a word in. "It is time to finish prayers."

They turned to the Persian carpet laying on top of the hard rocks. Together they knelt and faced the darkened sky to the east, toward

Mecca. What his father was praying to was of no concern to el Habid. Over the years he had developed an ability—he thought of it as acting —to create a look on his face that appeared to onlookers as surrealistic; proof to them of his spiritual integrity.

Today the ritual was a relief. The laser weapon was his first priority. His father was getting old and it was time for his succession. His brothers and Geigner could test the laser weapon. With or without Allah's help, he would have the weapon and the Shroud very soon. He alone would go to Mexico, find Amy and follow her until she found the Shroud. As for the calculation, if Geigner wouldn't give it to him, Amy or the monks would know where to find it.

He believed blood was important. Geigner would have told his cousin Amy where to find the calculation.

• • •

STURGEON ONE

The desert was dark with only a thin red line beginning to show the crimson sun rising in the east. Bedouin were conducting prayers on their small rugs on the cold desert sand. In slow motion as each bent over to pray, the desert seemed to be a swell of blowing robes. For Geigner, the time spent at prayer was his interior reflection. His belief in the god of Mohammed was as nonexistent as the day he had first arrived. Now he was a part of the desert. There was no way he could praise Allah, because he didn't believe in Allah.

It was nearly time for him to do what he had known since the first day he had arrived. He realized he had never felt more alive. *Was that the result of living on the edge?*

Life had not turned out as he intended. He was like his mother, who fought and died for a cause she couldn't win. Here he was, after a lifetime of escaping now involved in a problem with greater ramifications than the little Asian wars his mother lived. He supposed she was proud of him. Since he wasn't sure there was an afterlife, what difference did it make?

Geigner watched the red dawn spreading like a scarlet river above the desert.

It is my destiny, he thought, as images from his past flowed by like a kaleidoscope. A *life that never leaves the past.*

Leaning back on the prayer rug, he knew he had found something worthy of a fight; the tomb. The rock formation inside the mountain formed a natural accelerator for the electrons that created the laser beam. The ancient Egyptians had given him this gift. El Ben's philosophy was everything man had was provided by the prophet Mohammed. He wondered how the Prophet felt about el Ben's use of the tomb as a weapon system.

"Your work will enable el Ben to hold hostage the weapons of both superpowers. They thought Khadafy was bad: el Ben with the system could be worse."

Those were Veilkov's words. As he listened to Veilkov, he realized the legacy Akhenaten's grave had given him. Benton told him you leave nothing behind. It always goes with you. He was living the present through the past. Nothing had changed. He still had a decision to make.

El Ben had been right about his ancestors being Egyptian pharaohs. What did it matter? The only future that existed was today. What happened tomorrow was not a reality for Geigner. He took comfort in this philosophy without addressing how selfish it was. The old leader was obsessed in proving that El Kanitaoui had once been the site of a great civilization.

The sun was rising slowly into the sky. The tribesmen were rolling up their carpets and with their herds of goats and camels, began to move across the sand to the next oasis. He thought about his dreams, seeing the irony. It was time to go. He quickly drank a cup of tea and headed for the helicopter pad.

On the pad, the helicopter was loaded with two rockets. El Ben's planes, if they could carry a weapon, did. Geigner hoped they worked. The attendant knew him and didn't object when he got into the pilot's seat.

Carefully, he placed his computer bag on the seat beside him. To destroy the weapon would take more firepower than the rockets.

There was no doubt in his mind he had set the charges in the tomb correctly, a talent he learned from his uncle Benton. The technology was from World War II, but the skill to detonate explosives hadn't changed.

He pulled up vertically and looked back at the oasis, the tents and a few stucco houses. The explosion in the mountain wouldn't touch them. He wanted to take out the operations center with el Ben's sons as well as the weapon, but the chopper didn't have the fire power. The target must be the weapon in the mountain above the tomb.

Inshallah, next time I will get the operations center.

Looking back at the desert, he pulled the helicopter to the top of the ridge. Remnants of campfires flickered to his left, where the tribe of nomads were breaking camp. No electric lights for them.

The oasis was the jewel in a desert that stretched from the Nile River to the Atlantic Ocean. He remembered reading a desert legend that an oasis was the most dangerous spot to be. Everyone could see you. Looking toward the remains of a dried-out riverbed, he saw it stretched across to the edge of the mountains.

Lining up the coordinates, he opened his briefcase, taking out a small steel box, and casually flipped the switches. Pulling the helicopter sharply up and over the top of the ridge, he hit the button to fire the rockets.

He waited, listening for the sound of the explosion. All he heard was the wind. He turned the chopper around crossing the ridge back to the valley. Then, as if in slow motion, he saw the side of the mountain slowly collapse on the desert floor.

Enough, he said out loud. *Get out of here.*

Heading back across the ridge, he couldn't resist turning in a large circle to view a series of secondary explosions. Half of the mountain ledge had collapsed. None of the systems inside would ever be usable.

At this early hour, no staff were inside; at least he hoped not. He turned the chopper on a new course, south-southeast. A thousand miles of desert and he would be in Khartoum.

• • •

On a ridge above the tomb in the rising sun, his father was saying his morning prayers. El Habid understood his father's lust for power, but not his obsession with the religion of the prophet Mohammed. Didn't the old man realize religion caused the collapse of nations?

Their prayer time was interrupted by the sound of the explosion, then a rumble. They turned and saw the mountain housing the weapon collapse, crushing the tomb. Dirt, dust, and rocks filled the air in a brown cloud where once had been the tomb. Slowly the sky filled with dust.

As he watched the dust, el Habid thought that after so many centuries, about three thousand years, Akhenaten was at last buried.

Then he heard the helicopter. He focused the binoculars on it, suspecting it was Geigner who blew up the tomb. El Habid knew how obsessed Geigner was with proving the tomb was the Pharaoh's grave and how it must hurt him to destroy it.

The helicopter turned south, leaving no doubt the explosion was no accident.

No, Geigner, he thought, *you are not getting away.*

Taking his cell phone, el Habid called the oasis operations center. How stupid for Geigner to leave it intact. He used his code name

Sturgeon, after the great fish in the Caspian Sea whose eggs produced the finest caviar in the world.

El Habid could taste the salt as he pushed the button on the phone.

"Operator, this Sturgeon I, come in Sturgeon II."

He heard the operator pick up the phone.

"Surgeon II, the fish are out tonight. Set the nets. Knock the chopper out of the sky."

He turned the phone off and looked back down the valley where the dust from the collapsed mountain was coating everything. Above the dust, in the clear morning air, Geigner would meet his destiny.

His father was silent, watching the dust and haze reach into the sky. El Habid told his father he was heading to the operations center. The moment of truth was here. Would his brothers have the calculation needed to aim the laser?

• • •

On the ridge to the southeast, Geigner pulled the helicopter level and intently studied the computer map. The GPS told him he was almost on the tops of the mountains heading southeast to avoid the radar of El Kanitaoui. But there was no reduction in the clutter. He picked up several blips on the tuner.

They are monitoring me, he thought.

Using the computer, he had simulated his escape route to minimize the effectiveness of the navigation system el Ben had installed at the oasis. He flew over the next ridge and dropped down between the ridges. Why hadn't his route worked? He was still being tracked.

At the oasis control center, the operators looked at each other. Sturgeon One had given orders. One reached over and pulled the lever firing the rockets.

Geigner never heard the whistle of the rockets when they hit the chopper. In slow motion, the helicopter burst into flames and disappeared in the sand.

• • •

In Berlin, the sun was not yet up. Ace woke up to the sound of a phone ringing in the hallway. The computer room phones were only used by The Committee members.

Sonora got to the phone before he did, almost as if she was expecting it. In fact, it was a call she had imagined receiving for years. She was remarkably calm.

Their contact in the desert, a reliable Bedouin and friend of Benton's, told her there had been two explosions, one in the tomb at El Kanitaoui and the other believed to be a helicopter crash. The source was told el Ben's family said Geigner was on the helicopter.

The source said this must be true because as the sons prepared to test the weapon, they realized they didn't have the correct computer calculation. Geigner had it, but he was killed in the helicopter crash. The sons frantically searched for the gold heads with Aaron's beard believing that was where Geigner hid the calculation. Nothing was found.

Sonora went back to Ace with the news. She knew in time she would even the score for her nephew's death and that thought made her able handle his death without much emotion. The emotion would come when one day they put up his tomb.

She knew Ace would be calm. For a moment he was silent, then asked.

"Did he see the body?" The answer was no body, just the crash site, that no one could survive.

"The tomb and the weapon were destroyed," said Sonora calmly.

They were both silent for a moment, neither surprised by the news. To those who knew him best, Geigner lived on the edge, always ready to die. Death must have been a relief.

"We knew this might happen. Ace, we can hope he is at peace. For once, I am glad you're just driving the computers. We have to make Geigner's death count."

"I am not so sure. With the weapon gone, the Shroud is more important than ever, and I may need to get into the game. Or maybe I feel the need to avenge my brother's death."

Sonora didn't disagree. For Benton, and now for Geigner, they had to find the Shroud.

It was late night in Mexico, when Ace texted Amy the news. This was not the way he wanted to deliver it, but she had to know. For all he knew, she could be on her way back to Gracanica.

Ace knew the Shroud was the last piece needed by el Ben to fulfill his dream. His uncle and brother were killed trying to keep el Ben from his dream. The least he could do was follow in their footsteps.

On the desk, Ace looked at his analysis of the clues his uncle had left for Amy. He believed Mexico was a decoy and the Shroud was at the monastery. The question was where. Monasteries centuries old had many places to hide icons, and not all would be obvious. Regrettably, he realized he had to leave his comfortable seat behind the computer and go to Gracanica himself.

• • •

South of Belgrade, a local fisherman began pulling in his nets. In the light of the full moon, he saw a piece of shirt on his oar. The water-logged fabric was heavy, and he shook the oar. As he did, in front of the boat a bloated body rolled over, facing the moonlight.

A small group of locals congregated on the bank to listen as he told the police how he found the body. The Abbot walked over to the police contact.

His voice was low. "Are there any real clues?"

The official shook his head.

"Shot at close range, up the river below the monastery."

He made a forward motion with his hands. "Then the monk Veilkov went into the river."

The Abbot slowly walked through the darkened streets of Belgrade. Why had Veilkov's life ended like this, why was he killed? The Abbot had no answer.

The bar was still open at the Duke of Novi Hotel. He doubted it ever closed and ordered a double scotch. He needed something stronger than the local plum wine, slivovitz, and ordered scotch. The band lead by a tall blonde girl began to play the same old songs. The tune, "Somebody Loves Me," made him groan inwardly. Even the music was from the past.

So many years had passed and now he was living with the ghosts. The Abbot blamed himself. When you leave loose ends hanging, you never can tell when they will come back to haunt you.

He could still see Veilkov dressed in various shades of vague brown. His hair was the same, scraggly and brown, only his eyes told anyone who looked into them that he was different. Few knew Veilkov had shared so much of the past with him, and he felt a symbiotic bond with the old monk.

What secrets had died with Veilkov and Benton? What did they talk about on all of Prowers' visits? Or was there another reason he came to the monastery? If the Abbot guessed, he knew it had to be connected to the train blowing up outside the village of Gracanica in 1945. A man's character didn't change because he was a monk. Either

Veilkov or Benton could have salvaged the Shroud from the train when it was delayed in the village before the crash that destroyed it.

He sipped the warm scotch. He needed to find the clue to locating the Shroud. What had Benton and Veilkov told him in the past?

Over the years Veilkov talked about how he and Benton picked up the two women and a baby and took them as far as the village of Gracanica. Eva, with the sick baby, indirectly saved their lives. Because of her, they were delayed in the village and not on the train when the bridge blew up.

That must be the answer. They took the Shroud of Turin off the train before the crash. That would explain how Benton knew where it was. He and Veilkov hid it from the Nazis and the Communists, and kept it hidden all these years.

The Abbot never imagined Benton would die as he did. Little was known about the mountain storm that forced Prowers' plane down. It took days to locate it, even with an emergency beeper. Was Benton watching the altimeter or the air speed? The air currents must have pushed the plane up and down like a yo-yo.

Yes, thought the Abbot.

The mountain must have pulled Benton right into it. Otherwise he would have returned to the safety of the airport. Or had something happened to the plane, something his brother and his staff did in Mexico, before Benton left? He knew the General and anything was possible.

The more the Abbot thought about it, the less mystery there was to Benton's death. Veilkov's death was different because it made no sense, unless the killer thought he knew where the Shroud was. Had Veilkov told someone before he died? There was no way to know.

The Abbot looked down at his glass of scotch. It was the best.

• • •

CHAPTER NINETEEN

Isle of Carmen

Amy hesitated,
but seeing the gun changed her mind.

The General watched the storm clouds slowly move across the Isle of Carmen toward the mainland. The storm had passed, and he knew the company Gulfstream jet would soon land. He knew el Habid would be pissed with the delays, even ones for weather.

His favorite restaurant overlooked one of the few white-sand beaches in a harbor cluttered with fishing boats, mango trees and the crumbling remains of an old Spanish fort. In the middle of the large bay, he could see was one fishing boat. The other boats were for oil exploration. Behind the fort, the blue gulf water, sprinkled with patches of light red coral, formed circles reaching up to touch the surface. A sailing ship tacked with the outgoing tide. The oil company staff was enjoying an outing. Far out to sea, he could see a ridge of thunderheads moving toward the bay. Fortunately, they were too far north to delay the incoming plane any longer.

But, thought the General, *the delay pleases me.* He disliked el Ben's son el Habid, for no particular reason.

He listened to the heavy-set waitress jabbered in Spanish to customers, mixing in a word or two of French. The language was a legacy from rubber and banana plantations owned by French colonists in Central Mexico. Their history was lost. He vowed such obscurity would never come to him.

The air was wet and heavy as the storm passed. The air was laden with moisture and the humidity was exhausting. He was forced to admit he wasn't as young as he used to be. The waitress brought him a glass of iced tea, the fresh lime adding a refreshing tang. He was satisfied with his life.

I've outlasted them all. And I have made a fortune. During World War II, North Africa's desert was called a sandbox. Who knew there was a fortune in sweet crude below the sand?

Today, he was near his goal, to find the Shroud and give el Ben control of North Africa. *With the leaders' concessions for oil drilling, I will make another fortune.*

He might not live to see the end, but he had been in the game and that was what life was all about. Olen and Anton knew his business philosophy. What they would do after his death was another story. He realized his dream might not be theirs. They would run his company which he positioned to benefit from oil leasing and transport. He often wished Amy was his ward. She had so much potential, but then again, she was Hanna's daughter.

We will leave our mark, he thought. *Not a new Reich, but quietly, from behind the scenes. It would happen so subtly, and the start will be North African oil.*

His thin mouth formed a smile. Who could say what other minerals were in the desert sands?

He glanced around the restaurant, seeing old fishermen, Americans, and Europeans. Once fishing had dominated, but now every oil company was exploring for oil. Jogging shorts, a revealing T-shirt, and a good tan were mandatory attire.

A man held his little girl's hand as, barely able to walk, she toddled across the sand. Her little white sun suit, edged in red, was a match for her laughing face. Joy to her was sand and securely holding Daddy's hand. He knew he'd made the world fit for children like this little girl to live in. Or had he? Where were the old values? And how soon would it be before this little girl was wearing jogging shoes and a T-shirt?

He felt a sense of peace that his time in the world was nearly over. He looked at his watch to check on the plane's arrival. Turning, he saw the small toddler staring at the ancient Roman coin he'd pulled from his pocket with the watch. Her parents called to her, but with the innocence of a child, she sensed no harm.

Von Hagen reached across the table to give her the coin. She smiled and took it from him. He nodded his approval to her parents and accepted their *gracias*.

"Take it to your parents, until you're a big girl," he said in Spanish.

She knew his words meant the coin was hers. A sweet smile filled her face and she proudly carried it back to her parents. The coin, though old, was not one of the three so-called lucky coins given to Benton by a peasant during World War II.

Years ago, Benton gave him one of the lucky coins to seal a business deal. What made the three coins Benton received lucky? He didn't believe in such stories until a coin dealer pointed out the letter M on the so-called lucky coin. That initial wasn't present on other silver drachmas and had to be what made the coin unique, or to the superstitious, lucky.

He loved the coin and cursed himself forgiving his to el Ben. The gesture achieved the result he wanted; not friendship, but a partnership of sorts. Even though Islam did not believe objects were lucky or had religious significance, he was sure el Ben would keep the coin. He wondered where the other two lucky coins were.

The gift of the coin to el Ben gave him a gift, to search for the Shroud. For years he thought it was destroyed in the train crash. His brother, the Abbot, never told him the Shroud had been saved from the train. He knew finding the Shroud had given his life purpose and now saw it was his destiny.

Now he and el Ben were partners in the search. The General had forgotten how clever Benton was and regretted underestimating him. His death was costly, as Benton may have been the only one who knew where the Shroud was. He was counting on Benton's ego to have told someone where the Shroud was, and his bet was on Amy.

Now she was on the island. He expected a call from one of his employees. The island was too small for someone not to know where she was.

• • •

"Escobar's a cozy place where locals drop by," said the pudgy bartender.

"Where are your mates?"

"Not with me this visit, but I'll have a tequila for both of them," replied Amy, remembering how her father and Vince loved this bar. They would drink tequila, eat seafood and talk forever about where on the earth were places without gravity. To her, their search was like looking for a needle in a haystack. Now they were both dead. She held up the shot glass and said a silent toast to their spirits.

Nodding to the bartender to pour another shot, she thought about Geigner. Her father, her husband and now her cousin, all three were dead over the Shroud. She felt a loss of her cousin, but they were never close. He spent more time with her father than anyone. She always thought Geigner was the son her father never had.

Maybe it wasn't over the Shroud, but he died because of his involvement with el Ben. Like her cousin she was also involved, indirectly, with the Arab ruler. Somehow, she felt a need to make the deaths count. Only how? She didn't know.

Her phone call to Ace, after his text to her, told her Geigner's so-called accident was no accident. First her father's death, now Geigner. She hoped paranoia wasn't setting in. No, there was too much at stake. The time to mourn would be at his memorial which Ace said Sonora would hold in Berlin, once things were settled with the Shroud.

Ace had questions.

"I'm still trying to make sense of the notes in the margins of the book. What is the background on the name of the book and who wrote the story, *Strogatz and the Legend of Escobar Cay?* Who is Strogatz?"

She had asked the same question so many years ago when Geigner gave Vince the book.

"I always thought the story was something the two made up sitting around the campfire in the Desert Mountains. No TV, no phone, I think Geigner sent me the book for one reason, to get his calculation out of the desert."

Ace agreed. They both knew the el Alemien family wouldn't bother themselves with an old notebook.

Now she was in Escobar's, drinking tequila and looking at the quay. There were no coincidences, and she realized how important the book could be. Geigner, like her father, was hooked on decoys. The calculations in the book might be the real thing or a decoy.

She had confidence Ace would figure out what the notes mean. She had enough problems dealing with her father's clues on the Shroud. Where was the Doco Petroleum representative? He should have picked her up by now.

• • •

CHAPTER TWENTY

In Berlin

Ace, like his aunt, believed the
Shroud was still in the Balkans.

The meeting of her Committee was a welcome relief for both she and
Ace, giving them something to focus on besides Geigner's death. A
television screen the size of a wall filled one wall of Sonora's offices in
the villa. Ace was on a computer screen, following the same information.
The Committee members were scattered around the world, and met
via telecommunications, a method they started using in the last year.
No one missed the long plane flights. Sonora was still adjusting to the
technology. She liked personal contact, yet had to admit, she was getting
used to talking to the screen. They had more frequent meetings and they
were safer.

The meeting ended with no decision. The Committee supported
Middle East regime changes yet were savvy enough to know change was
not always good news. There wasn't enough information to decide the

role the Committee should play in the Middle East. They agreed Sonora should review the alternatives and advise them if they should be a player or watch from the sidelines. The screen turned to black, meeting over.

Now she and Ace could focus on Geigner's death and what the loss of the tomb meant to el Ben.

Not quite, she thought, *where was Amy?*

She looked at her nephew sitting in an oversized leather chair needed to hold his weight. In front of him were three computers and another that resembled a phone. He was a wizard on what Sonora called the electronic world. His home was the family ranch in Texas, where he said were the best telecommunications services. Interruptions were rare, and all he had to put up with was the wind and blowing sagebrush.

To Sonora, the Texas connection was an excuse for her nephew to wear cowboy boots in Berlin where he spent most of the year drinking German beer. Big-boned and overweight, in no way did he look like Jarra, his mother, dead more decades ago than she cared to remember. At least the family thought she was dead. Without a body, there was no proof. Today the proof was in the passing years.

She turned to Ace, who'd looked good on the telecom conference in a dark blue suit that fit. A girlfriend must have taken him to a tailor, since nothing on the rack fit him. Usually this wasn't a problem, because his idea of dressed up was a clean T-shirt.

Ace was looking at his aunt.

"Okay, I can track Amy by trying to locate her satellite phone. She may be out looking at oil leases with the General, or am I being optimistic?"

They both knew Amy was focused on Benton's clues, not on oil leases. But they were worried. Since Amy called Ace, after he texted her on Geigner's death, they'd heard nothing.

A few minutes passed while Ace accessed a computer program. A moment later, then a light blinked.

"Her phone is at the Isle of Carmen. God, Sonora, that's Doco Petroleum's headquarters in central Mexico. I'll put in a call to her."

Several attempts later Ace, who rarely showed emotion, sounded frustrated.

"I can't get her to answer."

"The point of having a cell phone is for it to be on." Sonora was also frustrated.

"Amy's phone is on, but there is no response. It goes to a voice recording."

Sonora looked at the world time clock on the desk. She thought about calling the Abbot, whom she never completely trusted. Ace was right. He should go to the monastery where they believed Benton hid the Shroud. She was tired of Benton's opaque clues and annoyed her brother just didn't tell her, or someone.

There was a possibility, however slight, that the Shroud was in Mexico. She knew, what few did, that the Isle of Carmen was the actual site of Pascal's tomb. If Amy's phone's location was correct—and who could doubt today's technology, though she did—Amy was on the Isle of Carmen. What she was doing was anyone's guess, but Pascal's real tomb was on the island. If Benton hid anything on that island it would be in the tomb. Still she was convinced the Shroud never left the monastery.

"Ace, where are the copies of the letters Benton left?"

"Right here." He pulled them up on the computer. "I put them online and am still running programs to see if patterns can be identified."

Even before he read his uncle's letters, Ace, like his aunt, believed the Shroud was still in the Balkans. He thought the Mexican trip was pandering to the General and wished he had asked more questions when she was in Berlin.

"He talks about a shield. When Benton found Pascal's grave, there was a carved shield covering the sarcophagus. I think that is the clue Amy is following."

She watched Ace find the phone number and thought again about the Abbot. Would the old monk have told Amy?

The monastery was the logical hiding place for the Shroud. The Mayan clues and Benton's trip to Mexico was simple misdirection to lead the General and el Ben away from where it was hidden. Benton might mix and match symbolism between cultures, but in life he kept them separate, and that meant the Shroud never left the monastery.

• • •

CHAPTER TWENTY-ONE

Leaving the Island

The Gulfstream was on the
long sandbar used as a runway

Amy could no longer hear the wind, and without looking, knew the water of the gulf would be gray with white caps. The storm had passed, and the Doco Petroleum plane should be able to land and take off for the Balkans. She knew they'd have to refuel and hoped it would be in Atlanta, or Bermuda; the farther east the better.

While she was sipping coffee in the hotel lobby, a chubby Mexican approached.

"Amy Prowers?" he asked, with an accent that sounded to Amy German or Austrian. "I am the Doco representative."

Klaus, as he was called, said the fastest route to the airport, which was on a peninsula on the gulf, was across the Bay of Campeche in a motorboat, even with the rough seas.

The water was rough, but worth the ride when Amy saw the Gulf-stream on the long sandbar used as a runway.

"They are waiting for you," said Klaus, "None of the three pilots are Mexican. I thought that strange but called the General and he said okay."

"Do they know the flight plan to Serbia?" asked Amy.

Klaus said yes. "They told me no one will be asleep."

Amy laughed, but was wary. "It's not a Doco Petroleum plane?"

"Yes and no. Two pilots are Doco and the other is a stranger. But not to worry, the General said okay."

The more he said not to worry, the more Amy found herself worried. True, the General was partners with the Prowers family in Doco Petroleum, but that didn't require him to monitor the company plane's flight plans or the pilots that flew them.

The boat was approaching the dock on the sand bar. The plane's insignia read Doco Petroleum. Amy got out of the boat and said good-bye to Klaus, who headed back across the bay.

She climbed up the ramp and settled into a seat, thinking they should be airborne and off the island any minute. The cockpit door opened, and she could see two pilots in the cockpit. The dark-haired pilot, introduced himself as el Habid, approached her and spoke in a soft voice, with little accent.

"We have, ah, a change in destination."

Amy stared at him and suddenly felt cold. Her family and the General owned the airline. What was the problem?

"I need the parcel that you are carrying."

He pulled his jacket back, letting her see the heavy black handle of a pistol strapped to his side.

Amy froze, but seeing the gun changed her mind. She knew he couldn't risk firing the gun inside the plane, and the package felt like more jewels. They weren't worth being shot or dying over. Where was the General, the usual Doco pilots? She had to buy time.

"What's the point?" asked Amy, knowing he would open the package. She fumbled for a moment, then reached into her backpack and handed him the wrapped parcel from Pascal's tomb.

She didn't believe they would harm her, but how could she be sure? A bargaining chip was needed. What did she have that they needed? There was nothing. *I'm a hostage,* she thought, *I've been one before in Saud Arabia, but why now?*

But the why wasn't important. What was important was she had to figure out a way to survive, like she had before.

She watched el Habid, handling the package as if it was a viral disease, walk

quickly back to the cockpit. He locked the door behind him and turned to the copilot.

"Call the General at the hotel on his personal radio. Tell him we've got the package."

"Wouldn't it be a good idea to check the parcel?" asked the copilot.

El Habid shook his head.

"Can you tell real Shroud of Turin from a tablecloth with stains?"

Then he turned on the cockpit light and looked at the map to plan the flight back to North Africa. His father would be waiting, but not patiently.

His phone blinked, highlighting the phone number of el Ben's compound. Only his family and a few tribesmen knew Geigner was dead, so the call had to be about the calculation. What he heard was not good news. His half-brothers had not been able to locate it in any of Geigner's possessions. None of this was a surprise. He faulted himself for not making a copy of the calculation.

El Ben was not happy but stated the obvious to his son.

"You must find the Shroud of Turin. With the calculation gone, it's all we have for the Coptic. I supported the excavation to prove the lineage of our tribe to the Egyptian pharaohs. Who could have predicted a search for lineage would produce a laser weapon system to dominate the world? Now the weapon is gone, I have only the symbol to unite us."

El Habid understood. His half-brothers, using foreign contractors, might be able to reconstruct the calculation in time. While they did this, he could consolidate his power. With the Shroud, he had it all. His half-brothers had stupidly underestimated the American.

But I have not, thought el Habid. Geigner was always lost in his world. As a scientist, he was consumed with details, and would have left a copy, but where? The logical place was to give it to Medak when he visited in the desert.

Akhenaten's tomb and the weapon were buried under the jabal, the mountain, but the calculation would allow the weapon to be built anywhere. Nothing was lost if the calculation was with Medak. Now he needed to find the Shroud, then he would rule.

• • •

CHAPTER TWENTY-TWO

The Isle of Carmen

No one realized the importance of the shroud.

Amy sat on the plane for what seemed an eternity. She found herself thinking about her mother, her father, Ace, and most of all, her aunt Sonora. If this was a kidnapping, and it felt like one, someone was sure to be called for a ransom. As she calculated what the ransom might be, the door to the plane rattled, then opened.

General von Hagen stepped into the jet. Amy gasped out loud.

"General, what are you doing here?" Her voice trailed off.

"I figured out what your father was doing in Mexico on his last trip. I think you did, too, and found something I have wanted, the Shroud. El Ben needed help to find it, and I told him I could find it."

He paused and pulled out a thin Cuban cigarette.

"Do you mind?"

Amy shook her head. She never said no to anyone smoking, and since she was a prisoner, what difference did it make? The plane was a trap. There was no way she could get down the aisle of the plane and out the open door. Besides, where would she go?

"You really don't know the importance of the Shroud, do you?" The general asked the question, but it was a statement of fact.

"The world is about to explode. North Africa is a tinder box. The Middle East could blow up anytime. And Amy, it will. Maybe not in this century, but the next century is only a decade from today. I may not be here for it, but remember, my dear, my words."

Amy listened to him, as she always had in their business dealings.

"Your father was an idealist. El Ben and I are, too. Benton never realized that. The only possibility for peace in the region is what el Ben can do with the Shroud."

For a moment, the old man looked sad. Amy knew it was because he would miss it. The General had lived most of the twentieth century; for him, life was over. He looked at her intensely.

"The Shroud of Turin is an ancient relic and if the truth was known, that might be all it is. But two thousand years of history give it a special aura. For El Ben, that's fortunate. With it, he may be able to maintain peace in North Africa. Why? Because he wants to rule as Mohammed did from the Atlantic to Arabia."

"And the oil fields," said Amy. "They would be consolidated and that would be good for business."

"Of course, dear."

Now Amy knew if the package held more jewels, the General would be infuriated. The Shroud must be at the monastery. It had to be. She didn't think she'd be harmed but couldn't be sure. She had to convince them she knew where it was and wait for a chance to escape.

"Forgive me," said el Habid, stepping from the cockpit into the lounge. "Maybe I was too direct. You see, it is very important for the future of my country that we have the Shroud."

"General, this man took the package from me."

"No harm done, I'm sure," said the General patronizingly.

"Now for the package." But his eyes turned to el Habid, who was idly flipping a worn coin. Could it be one of the lucky coins the old man had given Benton so many years ago? Amy was watching him, thinking of her options. Would the General harm her? She didn't think so, but feeling the pressure of the moment, wasn't sure.

"Where did you find the package?" he asked.

"In Pascal's sarcophagus, his original grave that my father found on the island."

She explained how her father concealed the actual burial site on the island.

"The local Mayans allowed the deception, not wanting to disturb the leader's spirit."

The General smiled, thinking about the superstitions of the Mayans, the lucky coins, el Ben and his astrologer. He was surrounded by superstition. He had been right about Benton knowing other ruins existed on the Yucatan Peninsula. Unexplored ruins were everywhere, overrun by the jungle, but he never thought Benton hid the Shroud on the Isle of Carmen.

"Let's look at what you found and see what's so important to el Habid's father."

He gestured to Amy.

"This is your opportunity, my dear, to unveil the artifact."

"General, you have the honor."

He didn't hesitate and opening it, saw the plastic. Before he could catch it, a small cloth purse dropped to the floor. He reached for it, cursing under his breath.

Slowly, he untied the string and lifted out a gold chain. Dangling beneath it, encased in sculptured gold and diamonds, was a huge ruby the size of a silver dollar.

"Oh, no," groaned Amy, trying to look surprised.

"What is this?"

Von Hagen pulled the medallion out. His face showed the annoyance he and Amy both felt. She had seen one almost exactly like it in the bank vault in Dubrovnik.

"It's the king's medallion from the House of Savoy, sixteenth-century Italy." He let it dangle, its aura creating a hypnotic effect in the lounge of the plane. Then with a quick motion, he flipped it up and grabbed the ruby in his hand.

"The Shroud," shouted el Habid, his face flushed. "You said it would be the Shroud."

The General glared at him.

"El Habid, we are locked in the mysticism of centuries past. The Shroud of Turin may have been uprooted in modern times, but if I know Benton, he cloaked his clues in terms of the mystics. He left this medallion in Pascal's tomb, but not the Shroud. What's obvious is if the Shroud exists today, it is at the monastery."

• • •

Amy saw her opportunity, thanks to the General. Her knowledge of where the Shroud might be could ensure her safety. The knowledge of icons she'd learned in the past few days would make her sound like an expert.

If she could just get to the monastery, Medak, and even the Abbot, could help. The flight was long, and Sonora and Ace should be looking for her. At least that was her hope. Now was the time to show some bluffing skills and convince el Habid and the General the clues were meant for her to interpret.

"I know where the Shroud is. My father believed deeply in Mayan symbolism. Icon symbolism was new to me. I have been interpreting his clues that he left for me to understand."

"What clues?" asked the General, looking as if he needed some convincing.

"You know, General, icons are symbols. And though my father never mentioned them when he was alive, he left me a book with the icon of the *Seven Angels*. The monastery has so many icons. One is *Christ in Glory*. Both are in the church at the monastery. We must return to Gracanica and see what that icon tells us. Don't you agree, General?"

"Of course," replied the General, sounding reluctant. He clutched the king's medallion and realized he had no desire to return to Europe, especially the Balkans.

"I am an old man, and the journey is long. You, el Habid, can find the Shroud for your father. But I wish you'd do me a favor."

"O.K.," said el Habid, finally reaching for the gold coin.

"The coin you were flipping. It looked very old. Might I take it to study?"

"It is done," replied el Habid. He wanted the Shroud and didn't have time to argue.

His father shared with him the story of the coin the General sent to him. So, he understood why the General wanted his coin back, or what he thought was the coin Benton gave him. Only el Habid knew it wasn't Benton's coin. The old General's eyes weren't what they used to be. El Ben kept Benton's coin. If the coin was lucky, the luck was with el Ben, Allah be praised.

• • •

Ace picked up the ringing phone and immediately motioned to Sonora to pick up.

"Que pasa," said Guzman, the manager of Doco Petroleum on the Island of Carmen, and one of the few who had Sonora's private number.

"The General told me to let this plane land, and now it is leaving with Amy on it. The flight plan said first it was going to Tripoli, and now it is going to Dubrovnik. And there are three pilots on board, not our company men. The flight plan includes a stop for fuel in Bermuda. The General is staying in Mexico."

Why would the General stay; certainly not because of a lack of interest? thought Sonora.

Amy wasn't answering her phone, nor had she tried to call. A text to Ace asking about the analysis of the Strogatz book Geigner sent was their only contact. The plane was going to the Balkans. The Shroud had to be at the monastery.

"I'll call the Abbot," said Sonora. "He needs to know what is going on, if he is to be of any help."

Sonora believed the General's adopted sons were not as committed to his dreams as they ought to be. Olen was more likely to know what was going on and to tell her.

"Try Anton and Olen. Someone has to be acting in the General's interests."

• • •

CHAPTER TWENTY-THREE

At the Monastery

He could do nothing about the man and a gun,
but maybe he could understand the two icons
so important to Amy Prowers.

Winter often arrived early in the Serbian mountains. Stephan Medak
watched the leaves run in erratic races down the mountain ravine. The
passing seasons gave him cause to reflect.

Brother Veilkov was dead. The Abbot called it an assassin's bullet,
not an accident. He said the monks must forgive. Veilkov was at peace,
but Medak could not accept a death that was intentional. He had no
idea who killed Veilkov; all he knew was that very soon his friend,
fellow brother, would be buried.

Pulling the calfskin wine pouch out of his knapsack, he poured a
glass. Sipping the wine, he raised his glass to the sun and toasted his
beloved teacher. He lifted the wine pouch again and toasted his own
life, different than the one he envisioned a week ago.

Adopted by Veilkov's sister, he always felt like he was part of their family. Today, except for a few cousins in Vienna and Istanbul, most of Veilkov's family was dead, including his adopted mother. With the family gone, he felt alone, something he wasn't used to.

He looked up into the blue-gray sky looking for a sign from the Creator, but the sky was empty. Inside he felt like the sky, empty, though outwardly, he appeared the same. *The bullet that killed Veilkov had also ended my vocation as a monk beyond repair.* He never had a desire to be a priest, but the quiet solitude of a humble monk was his vocation.

Now, that vocation was superseded by another emotion; revenge. Why had God called Brother Veilkov? God was accountable. God owed him the opportunity for revenge.

"Dear God," He prayed his first prayer since Veilkov's death. "Grant me the opportunity to avenge Veilkov."

From where he sat, he could see both directions of the road leading in and out of Gracanica Monastery. In the distance was the village of Gracanica. He could almost smell the wafts of smoke rising from the kebab stands. The Abbot had instructed him to keep an eye out for unusual activity on the trails, the road, and in the parking lot. Something was about to happen.

A flight of small birds filled the sky. What startled them? Just out of his sight was a mountain lake. He focused his eyes on a trail leading from the lake. He wasn't disappointed. A man emerged and then disappeared into the woods. What made the man interesting was that he carried a rifle.

Medak couldn't tell in which direction the man went. He felt as if he was living an illusion. He could do nothing about the man and a gun, but maybe he could do something about understanding why the two icons were so important to Amy Prowers.

The Abbot had ignored his concerns, but he was sure something wasn't right about the icon *Christ in Glory*. Something was hanging behind the icon *Christ in Glory*. What the icon was hiding was not an illusion in his mind, but a shadow, a silhouette.

To look behind it, he had to pull the icon off the wall. Monks were always praying in that niche of the church. He could not disturb them while they prayed. Taking it down would defy the Abbot, but the Abbot would get over it.

As for the gold head with the calculation, he'd have to see who came for it. In his pocket was the supposedly lucky coin Geigner had given him at el Kanitaoui. Did it have magic? Was it lucky? Maybe.

He was still alive but Veilkov and Geigner were dead. Amy was still alive, and she had the coin he gave her.

I'm surrounded by symbols, he thought.

The corner of his eye caught a movement on the road below. He pulled out his binoculars, used for sighting birds, out of his knapsack, and focused on the road below. There were no birds, but a tour bus. The monastery was closed for the winter. He looked again. The bus was clearly on its way to the church parking lot. Unannounced tourists were becoming commonplace. There was something to be said about the structured tours during Tito's reign.

Taking a short cut through the woods, he arrived too late. Some twenty people with a guide were walking up the path to the church.

"Don't they know we're closed?" Medak asked the driver in German, guessing at the groups' nationality.

The bus driver shrugged.

"They're pilgrims going to Medjugorje. A rockslide closed the road and they are staying in the village for the night. Someone suggested they come up here and look at the icons."

Medak thanked him, grateful he knew German, and headed after the pilgrims. There was no way to stop them from entering the church, so he offered to conduct a brief tour. He searched his memory for what he knew about the apparition at Medjugorje so that he could relate to the spirit that brought this group.

The Medjugorje village had many claims, almost monthly, that the Virgin Mary had appeared. The Catholic Church considered the vision bogus and hired scientists to investigate. What they found was that all five of the faithful followers looked at the same spot, one fifth of a second from each other. No one, including the representatives of the Church, knew what that meant. Over a million pilgrims visited the village every year. Believers were waiting for the Vatican to validate the vision.

The Church continued to believe the visions were political, not religious, and therefore, they weren't real. At the time, Medak found their reasoning ridiculous since how could Mary's messages be political? The countries of the Balkans were so intermixed with religion and politics that to him, her message of peace made sense.

When he reached the group, to his surprise, the guide was preaching politics, not religion.

"This monastery was once the heart of Croatian Nationalism. The family of the leader of the nationalistic movement lived in the valley and some of his relatives were monks at this monastery."

Oh no, thought Medak. *He's talking about Veilkov's family.*

The Abbot strived to keep the monastery out of politics. Politics and religion were one and the same in this region but rarely discussed openly, especially with pilgrims. The monastery guards, local police, didn't understand German, so they showed no reaction to the conversation.

Medak stepped up beside the guide looking back at the elderly pilgrims.

"The monastery is officially closed, but I would be pleased to show you the important icons in the church."

Surprisingly, the guide willingly agreed and repeated what the driver said about the road closure. For his part, Medak was relieved they were from Austria and spoke German, one of his languages.

They trouped into the church. Medak was grateful he had researched icons and their history when he was trying to find where Prowers might have hidden the Shroud. The facts were still fresh in his mind. The pilgrims were going to Medjugorje to see an apparition of Mary. He needed to relate how Mary fit into icons. The first words were the easy ones.

"The Gracanica Monastery was founded in 1321 and has been in the foreground of icon history for centuries."

He stopped in front of the wooden doors.

"Tomorrow you will travel to Medjugorje and see the site of today's apparitions. I hope you will find the tour of icons and their history useful to your pilgrimage. The emphasis on Mary and icons are part of the dogma of the Orthodox Church showing the Incarnation and her indispensable role in the life of Christ. A second part of the philosophy of icon veneration is that mankind and the world are restored to the image of God that was lost because of sin. Finally, man is saved when he himself becomes an Icon of Christ by the way he lives."

He held the door as the group entered the church. Looking back at the mountains, he saw a man crossing the field behind one of the monastery's outer buildings. Even at a distance Medak could see he was carrying a rifle. He couldn't tell if it was the man he had seen on the mountain or someone else. Then the man disappeared down the path. He considered pointing the man out to the guards but didn't. What was the point?

Something was wrong, thought Medak. Could someone want the gold heads Geigner had given him? Who would know he had them? It wasn't the heads the el Alemien family wanted, it was the calculation. Anyone who knew he visited the desert would realize Geigner could have given him the calculation. Inside the church confessional, under the seat, the Abbot kept a gun. He needed to get that gun.

Then there was the Shroud.

This morning as he prayed and the sun came through the monastery windows, he clearly saw a shadow or some type of border on the icon *Christ in Glory*. He was certain of that.

The Shroud could be in the monastery, hidden in plain sight. He knew in his heart the el Alemien family would do anything to find the calculation and the Shroud. Why, he didn't know.

But now he needed to get this tour group out of the church and out of danger.

• • •

CHAPTER TWENTY-FOUR

The Gracanica Monastery—Again

Where the Shroud was, she didn't know,
but her life depended upon it being in the monastery.

The air turbulence woke Amy and, looking out the window between thin clouds, she recognized the train station. They were landing in the valley next to the monastery. She took a deep breath. Her life depended upon staying a step ahead of el Habid.

What came next, she wasn't sure. As long as she could convince el Habid he needed her, she was safe. Where the Shroud was, she didn't know, but her life depended upon it being in the monastery. Her father had to have hidden it there. His clues seemed like a locked box, leading nowhere. He didn't want anyone else to follow them; the trouble was, neither could she.

She opened the book Veilkov sent her in Berlin, *Beyond the Face: A Commentary on Icons, Symbols, and Illusions,* and looked at a swastika inside the cover. She was surprised the first time she saw it and wondered at the meaning. There was some reason Veilkov sent it to her. She flipped to a back chapter on how Orthodox churches hid their treasures during wars. The discussion centered on bank vaults, false bottomed drawers and duplicate keys in safe-deposit boxes. The book credited Serbian royalty with coming up with that illusion. She'd seen that at the bank in Dubrovnik.

The next illusion in the book originated with the Orthodox Church. Icons were hung on cement walls, but there was a recess behind the hanging where valuables could be hidden. They also could hang another icon on the back of the icon. Stained glassed windows in churches and cathedrals allowed the sun to shine on the icon. When an icon was attached to the back, the hanging icon looked as if it had a shadow.

Another illusion, she thought.

Then the obvious occurred to her. She and the Abbot found the false-bottomed deposit box in the bank. Looking behind the icons would be worth a try. At this point, she had to try something.

She couldn't guess what was going on with el Habid, but this was as good a plan as any. The help of the Abbot or Medak might not be enough. She looked again at the swastika. The book she was sent in Berlin had it, but the book in the safe didn't.

The symbol was also in the General's book. Could the swastika be the key?

Across the aisle, el Habid also woke up with the landing. He slept through the refueling stop in Bermuda, as the two other pilots, one from Doco Petroleum, the other one of el Ben's staff, flew across the Atlantic Ocean. Now he started giving orders.

El Ben's pilot exited the plane and went to the customs office in the station.

Amy watched through the window and saw the pilot return with a key. She knew then that el Habid's staff had done some planning.

Getting in the BMW with el Habid, she looked at the mountains, wishing she was hiking to the monastery.

El Habid confidently turned off the main road to the monastery. He tried to make a call on his cell phone but was not successful. He must have a contact somewhere in the area. Moments later her suspicions were confirmed as he pulled off the road and turned off the motor.

"We wait for contact. Call me Habid. Akhenaten is my family's ancestral name, but we use the common tribal name el Alemien, adopted during the occupation by the Italians and French."

Amy wanted to ask why the el Alemien family killed her cousin Geigner but didn't. She controlled her anger. Showing emotion wasn't going to keep her alive. El Habid was still lecturing her on last names. She was silent, listening to see if she learned anything.

"Akhenaten was the dominant ruler of Egypt and his tomb is at El Kanitaoui. What everyone remembers is that Akhenaten was the famous King Tut's father. People think my father is mad to want the desert land of the southern Sahara. They do not realize it is our birthright. Our ancestors from the time of Akhenaten ruled from Sudan to Tunisia."

He finally stopped the history lesson and got to the point.

"At this monastery, we look for a monk called Medak. He visited Geigner in the desert. In fact, your cousin was most insistent the monk visit the tomb at El Kanitaoui."

He did not mention Geigner was dead, believing only his family knew. Not mentioning her cousin's death confirmed for Amy that Ace and Sonora were right. The el Alemien family was responsible for killing Geigner. She had to be careful, or she would be the next Prowers executed. Somehow it still seemed like a game, a game of secrets.

El Habid had no way of knowing she knew Medak.

"I met the Abbot once," she said, trying to appear helpful.

El Habid wasn't satisfied.

"You know where your father hid the Shroud?"

"Of course," she said with a confidence she didn't feel. "It will take a bit of searching."

A bit of searching was her only hope. The Shroud was in the monastery—of that she was sure—but she didn't have a clue where. The concept of illusions was a beginning. If the book was her guide, the Shroud might be behind the icons. Veilkov sent her the icon book on illusions for some reason. She had better be right, or she was dead.

"Ah, at last," shouted el Habid. She looked toward the forest, and from behind the trees came a man with a rifle, Anton.

Good God, she thought, *Anton was the contact?* He looked at Amy as if he had never seen her. She followed his lead, acting as if she didn't know him.

As the two men talked, Amy realized they had never met. El Habid kept calling Anton the Bulgarian. Amy found herself looking around for the real Bulgarian.

• • •

Ace stepped off the local bus from Belgrade dressed in a brown monk's robe and carrying a knapsack. Looking around, he thought how the gray limestone mountains of the Balkans all looked the same. He knew enough of the language to fit in like a local, as long as no one wanted a deep discussion on the economy or politics. He reminded himself to look at the ground and try to appear humble. *Who,* he thought, *would be interested in an aging monk with a limp?*

He was right. No one paid any attention. His monk's robe was good camouflage.

Local buses did not use metal detectors. He concealed the sniper rifle, procured from an old contact in Belgrade, by hanging it on his side under the robe. He had to adjust it on the bus seat which reminded him the last time he carried a gun; he was a lot thinner and in better shape.

Interesting, he thought, *how his sniper training continued to be useful*. When he was selected for the elite team of Rangers, he had no idea years later that these skills would be important. He smiled, recalling how much he had practiced on the firing ranges.

The pilgrims were the perfect cover. He followed them off the bus and into the church. One told him there was a funeral today for a monk. It had to be Veilkov's. The Abbot had called Sonora and told her the monk had been killed. No one knew by whom. His death finally convinced Sonora that he should go to the monastery. Whatever was going on Amy needed protection.

With the group, he was easily able to pass by the guards. There were no metal detectors, but if there had been, he was prepared to crawl on the ground, knowing that should work. It wasn't uncommon, as pilgrims often crawled along the ground to one icon or another. No one would stop a monk humbling himself by crawling on the floor up to the icons.

An aerial view of the monastery complex was what he needed. It would be difficult to climb up the tower with his bad leg, but he would make it. Amy and who was on the plane with her should be here soon; at least that was his hope.

Now he needed to find the stairs to the church tower.

• • •

The Abbot walked through the monastery garden, finding the exterior peace in the gardens inconsistent with his inner turmoil. The turmoil was real, and in monastic life, you did not ignore it.

The Abbot's inner struggle was over the way Brother Veilkov had died. He was killed, executed like a criminal.

After talking to Sonora, his anxiety increased. She seemed to think Amy had been kidnapped and was on her way to the monastery. She told him Ace called Olen, who confirmed Amy was on a plane going to the monastery. Sonora's claim that Amy was kidnapped seemed credible.

What surprised the Abbot was that Olen also said he was concerned for Amy's safety. The Abbot was impressed. Olen was thinking for himself, not just following the General. Maybe the future held some hope for him, or it was the smart move. Olen might have no desire to be a part of the past. He and Anton would inherit the General's estate. With his future in front of him, he would not want the baggage of the von Hagen legacy.

The question was, who else was on the plane with Amy? Otherwise, as Sonora correctly pointed out, her niece would be answering her satellite phone. He had asked Medak to keep an eye out for strangers, which was all he could do.

In the past, he had delayed investigations into the past on his family to protect the General and himself. Olen and Anton were never part of that past. The two might inherit, but the Abbot was sure his brother, even from the grave, would have strings attached to his estate.

Today none of that mattered; the question was still where the real Shroud was, and could they keep it from el Ben.

Veilkov often spoke to him about the robes of Christ shimmering with gold lines like delicate shafts of light from the center of the icon *Christ in Glory*, to the corners of the icon representing the world. Icon painters, like the Impressionists, were concerned with light. The Byzantines see light as radiating from a source behind the painting and illuminating it in the way the rays of the sun glow through stained glass.

At the end of the war, Benton and Veilkov gave him what they said was a copy of the Shroud, asking him to protect it. That seemed odd, but he hid the so-called copy in the monastery library. Even then, he wondered if it might be the real Shroud. Why did Benton have to be so clever? Or was Veilkov the clever one? Lying never seemed to be a problem for either man.

For the past months, Veilkov seemed obsessed with the icon *Christ in Glory*. That wasn't the icon Amy believed was her father's clue. She thought it was the icon of the *Seven Angels*. Amy and Medak interpreted the clue but picked the wrong icon. Medak tried to tell him there was something odd about the icon *Christ in Glory* and he dismissed him.

I need to look at the icon myself, he thought.

He walked to the church, closed for seasonal repairs. To his surprise, there was a tour bus parked in front. Two monks were coming out of the church.

"A tour group is inside the church?" he asked.

"Yes, Medak's with them. They are pilgrims going to Medjugorje, only the road was closed because of a landslide. They were forced to stay in the village and decided to come and view the icons."

The pilgrims had to get out of here. There was no telling what might happen to them when Amy and whoever was on the plane arrived. With relief, he saw the group coming out the side door as the bus moved to the door. He saw why. Many could barely walk. Thankfully, Medak was with them.

The engine of a car caused him to turn. A gray BMW was pulling into the parking lot. As the Abbot spotted the rental sticker, Amy Prowers stepped out of the car and walked toward him.

"I am glad to see you again." And she was. With the Abbot, she might have a chance.

"And I, you," replied the Abbot, who kept his face blank as Amy introduced el Habid and Anton as the Bulgarian.

Sonora told him Amy was kidnapped, but it looked to him like she and el Habid were together. Something was wrong, but what?

Anton wasn't correcting his identity, so he had to be hiding it. He was willing to bet el Habid had a gun. They were just going along, waiting for a moment to take him out. Right now, he saw no way to assist, but would be alert.

He looked over their heads, saw the tour bus pulling out of the parking lot, and Medak walking toward him.

Amy was frustrated. The Abbot seemed distracted but plunged ahead. He had to pick up the thread of what was going on, or she was dead and likely he was too.

"We need your help to find the Shroud of Turin. When I was here before, Medak and I thought my father's clues were directed at the icon of the *Seventh Angel*. Under that icon was the address of the bank in Dubrovnik, which had jewels. Medak and I saw the icon of *Christ in Glory*, but never paid any attention to the angels and serpents that were in it. In Berlin, a book was sent to me. When I read it, many of the references were the same, but the focus was on *Christ in Glory*. The description of each icon is similar and both icons are side by side in the monastery. So, they are easily confused."

Amy paused. Now was not the time to lose her nerve. Thank God, the Abbot was following her words so intensely she was sure something was wrong. She kept talking, hoping the words would confuse el Habid.

"He used a Hakenkreuz drawn inside the books, which appeared to be the clue telling us which books were important. Only it was an illusion, a fake. The quote from scripture in Father's letter said, *keep thy heart with all diligence, and remove thy foot from evil.* That quote is the key. In the heart of Pascal's sarcophagus, in his coffin, Father hid more jewels. Only the second part of the quote refers not to Pascal, but to the icon, *Christ in Glory,* removing the foot from evil. That icon is here in the monastery."

She paused, thinking *this better be right.* She couldn't let herself think of the consequences.

"If the book's picture is accurate, at the bottom of the icon are the serpents, the evil ones. And with them will be another clue."

Except, thought Amy, *to her it looked like the real evil was here in the parking lot with these men.*

"So," said the Abbot. "The Shroud is hidden where?"

"We won't know until we look at the icon," Amy hurriedly replied, knowing el Habid would be impatient.

"The icon *Christ in Glory* should give us the final clue."

The Abbot could tell Amy was tense, while el Habid was relaxed. Then he realized why. El Habid believed he was in control.

The Abbot was glad he had the copy of the Shroud in the library. He doubted el Habid or anyone, even himself, could tell the copy from the real one. The copy could be useful, as he doubted el Habid knew what the Shroud should look like. He wondered again, as he had of late, if it was really a fake. Right now, he was silent.

Amy had taken over and was speaking to everyone. The way she handled the situation would have made her parents proud.

"I looked at the book from my father's safe, another sent to me in Berlin by someone unknown, likely Veilkov, and the books at the General's. Now I believe the icon *Christ in Glory* holds the answer and not the icon where Father carved the address of the bank."

"Come," said the Abbot, and motioned for them to follow.

Anton said no, remaining at the doorway with the guard.

The others followed the Abbot into the church and down the aisle to the icons. Both Veilkov and Medak had spent long hours in prayer before the icon *Christ in Glory* in a small alcove on the west side of the church. After five hundred years, the icon had acquired its own aura. A handwritten page was nailed to the wall.

Occasionally Veilkov replaced the quote tacked to the wall with a new one, but the practice stopped with his death. Why it was important to Veilkov, no one knew.

The inscription read from the seventh chapter of Daniel: *The fourth beast is the fourth kingdom.*

Amy looked at the note, and then at the icon. The feet of Christ were crushing the head of the serpent.

"My father feared the fourth beast could rise to world power and dominate the world. I know my father wanted everyone to think all the clues meant something. That was the real deception, right, Abbot?"

He was glad the church was dark. No one could see his face. He might be the only one left alive that knew there were two copies, one in Turin and the other—given to him by Benton and Veilkov so many decades ago—in the library.

Again, it occurred to him they might have given him the real one. The two men knew he would guard the copy as if it was the one and only Shroud. What better way to hide the real Shroud then to give it to him as a copy?

Piously, he looked at the icon thinking of his options with a fake Shroud in the library. He could give it to el Habid only if he was sure it was a fake.

"Yes, after they faked it, Veilkov told me they brought the Shroud to the chapel. Over the years, it is my belief that they hid the Shroud in many places."

"Abbot," said Amy, "Everything returns us to this icon. I think the Shroud is right in front of us."

"I am confused." El Habid spoke for the first time with a voice heavy with sarcasm. "How does the icon help us find Shroud?"

"It may be easier than we think," said Amy, wondering where she was getting her voice. Up to this point, she had followed her instincts as if telling a story. The ending was now. There was no use stalling, she had to produce the Shroud. Once they found it, she would worry about how to stop el Habid.

"Besides the focus on this icon, the term *gold* was used in finding Pascal."

"And the jewels in Dubrovnik?" asked the Abbot.

"Another dead end, that's the pattern." Amy looked intently at the icon.

"Symbols no longer matter because the icon is concealing the Shroud. That I think is the illusion."

They turned abruptly at the sound of the voice. It was Medak.

"Forgive me, what you're looking for is behind the icon."

He paused a moment to give them time to think about what he had said.

"All my life it seems I prayed before this icon as if it was the apparition. The icon inspired me. The children who saw the apparition at Medjugorje said Mary stepped out. I couldn't get that image out of my mind."

He looked at Amy.

"Do you know what that means?"

"That she was speaking to you through the icon?"

"Something like that. Shortly before Veilkov died, Benton Prowers came to visit him. The two men prayed for hours before the icon. One day, after his last visit, I was here in the chapel praying, always searching for the message beyond the face of the icon. The sun came through the light of the stained-glass window and I noticed a change in the face, as if I could see a silhouette that seemed to reach out to me.

"At first I thought it was a sign from God of life. Then as the sun set, it disappeared. I couldn't contain my curiosity. I walked toward the picture searching for an answer. Then I saw it. The pattern of gold that illuminated the face had been changed. Where once it glowed, now it was darkened."

They were all staring in silence at the icon. Amy saw what Medak meant and remembered in her icon book the references to illusions.

Medak looked at the Abbot.

"Remember, Abbot, when I told you about it? The Shroud is hidden like a silhouette, a shadow, beyond the face disrupting the pattern of gold. I came back days later and still saw the shadow."

"Yes," said the Abbot, "I remember you told me the sunlight can do tricks to images in a normally darkened monastery. I lecture on how the Byzantine sees light as radiating from a source behind the painting and illuminating it in the way the rays of the sun glow through stained glass."

Then the Abbot, a tall man, walked over to the icon and reached up. His arm disappeared. There had to be a space behind the Icon.

"Here it is."

They heard a rip.

"It's only the tape."

Out came a packet wrapped, as the jewels were, in a waterproof packet.

Before the Abbot could speak, el Habid spoke in a low, intense voice.

"Hand me the packet." Turning, they saw the revolver in el Habid's hand.

Amy's mind searched for alternatives and saw none. Rationally, she thought the Shroud belonged to whoever had the power to keep it. Now, it was el Habid with his revolver. There had been so many packets, she wondered if this one really was the Shroud. The reality of how fragile they were was clear to her. He could kill them all and there was nothing else they could do.

"Religious monks do not see much. And villagers, they busy with funeral of Veilkov. The Bulgarian told me. The plane is fueled, waiting, and el Ben waits for me. You see, don't you?"

Momentarily, el Habid sounded almost apologetic. He looked at Medak.

"Time to give me the gold head I know you got when you visited Geigner. Now, if you want to live."

Medak reached into the pocket of his robe and handed el Habid a gold head. He saw Amy look confused, she didn't know about the head, but she said nothing.

"Walk ahead slowly. Church too public place. Go slowly, out to woods at end parking lot. Take maybe little longer to find bodies."

• • •

El Habid pointed toward the empty parking lot with his gun, when the same black nondescript dog Amy saw on her last visit ran around the wall of the monastery, wagging its tail. Amy kept on walking as the dog did a dance of greeting. The dog stopped, puzzled at being ignored. The Abbot called the dog and as he did, Amy stumbled as if she tripped on the dog. She had no idea why she faked the fall but thought any distraction might help.

El Habid raised the revolver. Medak turned and pulled his arm down. The shot echoed into the sky. Medak kicked sideways, his legs knocking el Habid down. The gun slid to Amy's feet. She picked it up and pointed it at el Habid, who was crawling behind an ancient brick well.

The mountains echoed with the sound of a gunshot—a different sound than the shot from el Habid's revolver. El Habid staggered and turned, struggling to hold the package, and, unable to grip it, dropped the gold head into the well.

Medak looked at Amy. "We are safe!"

He pulled a coin out of his pocket. "Geigner gave me this coin after I gave you the one Veilkov gave me. Maybe it does have powers."

Amy took hers out of her pocket. She was sure it was an ordinary ancient coin, but who was to say.

• • •

Trying to ignore his aching leg, Ace looked down from the church tower, at the group around the well and the funeral party by the cemetery. The old Prowers luck held. He was still a sharpshooter. Now he had to get down the tower steps.

He unscrewed the bolt of the rifle, concealing the pieces under his robe. There was one more kill, and then he would be on time for the funeral of Brother Veilkov. These mountains were cold, unforgiving, but he'd always managed to survive. The hit on el Habid was a good one and justified. He'd been responsible for his brother's death. The next kill was to take out Anton, who had some part in the death of his uncle. He'd waited for this opportunity.

He stopped on the stairs to rest halfway down at an alcove with a window. There was movement on the mountainside. Using the telescopic sight on his rifle, he saw Anton on a path to the river. He was too far away to take the shot. His eye caught something moving further up the mountain. He turned his telescopic rifle lens to the spot.

Anton was being followed. Judging by their clothes, two local men were on a trail to intercept him. He focused the lens on the spot where the two trails met. Anton looked like he was alone. Then he heard another shot, as Anton fell to the ground.

He swung the rifle to look above the trail. Another local man with a telescopic lens not designed for hunting deer was starting to dismantle a rifle.

Veilkov's family had avenged their brother.

• • •

Outside the monastery, they stood over the well, as if there was some way to retrieve the head. The sound of another shot echoed above them in the mountains.

Amy looked at Medak's face and saw satisfaction.

"I didn't kill him, but I would have," said Medak, holding the rifle the Abbot kept in the church.

Amy handed the Abbot el Habid's gun. Several monks, who heard the shots, appeared from the entry to the church. One bent over el Habid and said he was dead.

"Brother," spoke the Abbot. "Please attend to his body. I will notify the authorities in morning."

He turned to Medak. "Brother Veilkov's funeral is about to start."

Medak appeared unaffected by the incident. "Whoever shot him, Abbot, avenged our Brother Veilkov."

The Abbot looked at the mountains above them, and thought, *or for himself*. He took the packet from el Habid's hand and walked toward the monastery.

"I have duties at the graveside service for Veilkov."

Medak turned to go with the Abbot down the path toward the cemetery where Brother Veilkov was to be buried. The black dog followed him.

He thought about the other head, the one with the correct calculation that he had hidden in plain sight. Only he knew the real calculation was not at the bottom of an aging cistern. Geigner trusted him to protect it, and he had. Sometime there would be a right time to reveal its existence.

• • •

Silently they climbed the cement stairs that wound slowly up to the Abbot's private office. The monks might be used to silence, but to Amy, the silence roared. Coals from a small fireplace warmed the room in preparation against the approaching mountain storm. A small kettle was sitting on a hot plate beside the fireplace, and the Abbot prepared a pot of coffee.

As he did, Ace appeared at his door out of nowhere, wearing the brown robes of a monk. Planning was what her father said he did. Obviously, her cousin had some other talents. Had he killed el Habid?

Ace looked at her and she was certain he had. At least, she wouldn't have to ask.

Amy wondered if Ace had figured out the calculation from the Strogatz book. She hoped so, since the real calculation was at the bottom of the well in the gold head. Then it hit her, and she felt silly. Geigner had found several gold heads.

Only one was in the well. There must be other heads with the correct calculation. Who but Medak would have them? Forget the heads; now they had to see if this was the Shroud.

"The packet." She pointed to where it sat on the table. "Let's see if it's the Shroud or another piece of jewelry."

"I think it is the real thing," said the Abbot. Slowly he stirred his coffee and gazed out the glass window, wondering why, after all this time, what was the rush.

A dilapidated brick barn, with the roof caved in, was to his left and beyond that the cemetery. Several brothers were busily walking back and forth between the monastery and the church. Opening the packet could wait. There would be time enough after the service.

He glanced out the window again. A line of monks was heading toward the cemetery. In front of the church he could see Veilkov's family preparing to carry the coffin. The villagers wearing black and the women with their heads covered were heading up the path to the cemetery. Veilkov was related to almost all the villagers.

Ace stood up to go with him, and he turned to see if Amy was coming.

Amy looked away and then at the Abbot. "I'd rather not. It isn't as if I knew him."

"Right, when you see the group break up, come back, and we will open the packet. I think it is the Shroud."

The truth was, he had no idea which of the Shrouds was the real Shroud of Turin, the one in the packet or the one in his library. Knowing the two men as he did, anything was possible. Thank God for carbon testing, which would identify the real one.

The Abbot picked up the packet to lock it in his desk, and as he did, it came apart. A small envelope attached in the fold. He handed it to Amy.

"It has your name on it. Why aren't we surprised?"

• • •

Amy walked outside the monastery with the envelope in her hand. Ace came with her and sat on a small wooden bench. He pulled what looked like a cigarette case out from under his robe and lit one.

"I am starting to like wearing this robe."

Amy looked at him, knowing and waiting to smell the smoke. He was always smoking a joint, he said, for medicinal purposes due to his bad leg. She sniffed the air. It was a cigarette. Maybe his monk's role was a good one for him. "I gotta go." And he joined the group heading to the cemetery.

She walked on over to the edge of the mountain trail and leaned against a large rock. To her right was what had once been an old mill pond. The decrepit, crumbling, red brick barn and storage houses were once an active industry for the monks. A family of ducks was swimming on the small pond.

Below on the hillside, she could see the crowd of people at the cemetery standing quietly as the Abbot conducted a graveside service. Maybe she should have gone; he was her father's friend. Below them, the leaves in the canyon ravine were beginning to fall. Winter was coming. She thought a moment about all that had happened. Surely this was the last letter to be opened. What could it say that hadn't been said already?

The handwriting was the same as the address of the book sent to Sonora's villa in Berlin. It must be Veilkov's. As she opened the envelope, she wondered if all the subterfuge was necessary. She made a promise to herself never, ever, indulge in games, and just speak the truth.

I know you will find this note, Miss Prowers. I sent you the book after Benton's death, trying to help you. In my heart, I never wanted the Shroud to leave the monastery. It has been a protector for all these years, even as we have protected it. But time ends all things and that time is past. Please see it is returned at last to the cathedral at Turin. If you are reading this note, I must be dead, and you have the Shroud of Turin. God be with you in your life. Veilkov.

Finally, she thought, *it's over*. The bells of the monastery began to ring. She looked over at the small crowd of people on the edge of the cemetery. The funeral was over. Groups of monks and Veilkov's family were beginning to head down the mountain to the village.

Amy knew returning the Shroud to the Cathedral at Turin was only the beginning. She saw it as the first chapter in a very long story and knew the ending went beyond finding the Shroud.

Sonora's public responsibility agenda had won out. She would join her aunt's Committee. She had become what her aunt said; an individual citizen with a family fortune used for the public good. At least Ace had made the meetings teleconferences. She found herself smiling.

• • •

At the monastery, daylight was beginning to fade. It wasn't cold enough for the snow, but soon it would come, thought the Abbot. He was remembering the past. The Abbot did not believe life was pre-destined, but neither could he explain the past completely. Benton, Geigner,

Marfkis, and Veilkov were all dead.

He took the packet out of the desk. They had delayed long enough. Slowly, he removed the wrapper, then the thick plastic piece that encased the linen. The wrappings showed no signs of age. Someone had opened it since the war.

Today he would see the Shroud as he had seen so many years ago. The transfiguration of Christ, the resurrection, had taken place with a burst of energy. Gently, he lifted the ancient piece of linen from the packet. He unfolded it edge by edge, spreading it out across the wood table until the cloth was entirely open.

Amy, Ace, Medak and the Abbot stared in silence at the cloth. There was a definable image of a head and around the head appeared a crown of thorns. One hand in the center of the palm had some type of mark, the type of mark a nail could make. If this wasn't the real Shroud, then the Abbot silently complimented Benton and Veilkov on their reproduction.

There was a rumble of thunder. Medak hurried to close the window. He glanced up at the sky, which had turned a peculiar shade of yellow. As far as his eye could see, a cap of thin clouds looking like a veil for the accompanying storm covered the sky.

• • •

Epilogue

From his veranda, the General heard the clap, not of thunder, but the eruption of one of the central Mexican volcanic peaks. He watched the mushroom cloud to the north and knew the jet stream would blow the dust away from the central highlands. The Mayan ruins at Palenque would miss the fallout.

When will we control nature? And as he was thinking a pain cut across his throat. The pain moved to his chest and as he reached up, he slowly collapsed on the stone veranda. His head looked up at the dust-filled gray sky.

Death couldn't happen to him, only to others. The lucky coin, he should have kept it. His eyes watched the clouds above and he vaguely heard a servant call for the doctor. Could death come so easily? He vowed it would not. There was still too much to do.

• • •

The desert sky was clear as el Ben walked from his tent to the masjid, his place of prayer in the desert camp. He stood and turned east to Mecca. It was past sunset, and the twinkling stars were his staircase to Allah. He meditated and considered his options to find the calculation and the Shroud. His son was dead, but he was blessed with other sons. Allah, be praised.

Then, from the east, moving across the desert in a preplanned pattern, there was a cascade of falling stars like raindrops on the desert.

He recalled from the stories of ancient tribesmen who said Allah would come when the sky fell. He raised his hands. Was this a sign from Allah, or a sign his ambition was delayed? He bowed down and covered his head with the hood from his cloth robe.

"There is no God, but God and Muhammad are his Prophet." Allah was good.

• • •

Time seemed to be suspended across the prairies of Colorado. The cold winds of a blue norther were starting to race from the tops of the Rockies across the prairie to the east. A servant adjusted the drapes which billowed slightly behind sealed windows. The ranch house seemed to shudder. Outside, snow fell in a random pattern across the graves of Benton and Hanna Prowers. Winter had arrived on the prairie.

• • •

In the Abbot's house, Amy shivered and put both hands around the cup of coffee to warm herself. She thought about Sun Tzu's quote which said no one could see the strategy from which victory evolved. She found the Shroud, which was her father's last request.

As she listened to the Abbot explain why the Shroud was important and about her parents' life in the Balkans, she knew both were pleased with her life. She wanted to hear every detail the Abbot knew of their life during the war, knowing he would consciously or unconsciously filter facts.

The only way to get the truth was to be in control. Joining the Committee would give her control. She wanted to laugh but would have to explain what was funny. Her father and Sonora had won. She would become a part of their legacy. She couldn't believe after all the years how simple joining seemed.

Could the Abbot's story change her life? She didn't think so, but she looked forward to tomorrow. Maybe those tomorrows were what her father had in mind in his last request.

THE END

Turn the page for an exerpt from
the latest Katherine Burlake mystery.

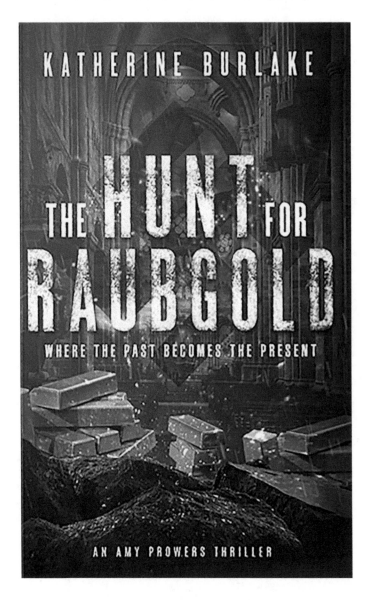

KATHERINE BURLAKE

THE HUNT FOR
RAUBGOLD

WHERE THE PAST BECOMES THE PRESENT

AN AMY PROWERS THRILLER

Preface

All generations share the same obsession, finding gold. Nazi Germany was no different. Gold built the Third Reich's war machine, guaranteed economic power, and financed Nazis who escaped at the end of World War II to build the Fourth Reich. How much gold did the Nazis confiscate? How much has been found? No one knows. Today, in the twenty-first century, the search to find the stolen gold, Raubgold, continues.

CHAPTER ONE

The Search for Stolen Gold Begins

The cascading snow had turned the base
of the mountain into a winter wonderland.

2019 ASUNCION, PARAGUAY

"We are broke. The dream of a Fourth Reich is dead. Simon Bell we may be dead if you don't find the gold."

The man, called Old Fritz, raised his beer stein in a toast. "To the New Nazi party here in Paraguay. Drink up. You have a long flight to Germany."

Simon finished his beer and looked around the bar of the Blue Boar restaurant on the outskirts of Asuncion, Paraguay. *I'm a German, and here, thousands of miles away I am surrounded by a room full of young, physically fit men of German descent."* All of the men were passionate believers in the New Nazi Party though few had ever been out of Paraguay or South America. What they needed was gold to finance the Fourth Reich.

He touched the letter in his pocket. He'd found it after his grand-father's death and knew the contents by heart. The Nazis had planned to ship the gold out of Germany, but he knew it was still hidden in Germany because World War II had ended sooner than expected.

For now, he sipped his beer. Old Fritz was right. The flight back to Germany was a long one.

• • •

VAIL, COLORADO

Amy Prowers heard the rumble, then what sounded like thunder. She opened her eyes to darkness and looking at the clock saw it was four in the morning. Before she could move, she felt the shudder almost as if the townhouse moved. Only it didn't.

She turned on the outside lights and opened the blinds. The cascading snow had turned the base of the mountain into a winter wonderland. The truth was something else.

A wall of snow and ice had careened down the mountain and across the decks smashing into the back of the townhouse complex and crushing the teak decks. Unable to get on the deck, she opened the door to the garage. The back of the garage was blasted open.

Knowing it would take some time for a contractor to repair, she started shoveling the snow out. As she did the back wall collapsed.

I'm lucky, she thought, *my jeep was in the adjacent space.*

Suddenly she stopped shoveling.   *What am I looking at?*

Lodged in what had been the backwall of the garage was a dusty leather bag. Looking at what was left of the wall, she could see a hidden space concealed behind the wall.

Amy managed to smile at the irony of finding the satchel. It had been missing for twenty years, just how long Vince had been dead. She thought the bag was lost when he was killed.

She opened it and saw wrapped in waterproof packaging what looked like papers. She knew what the papers were, a diary and a map. Before he was killed, Vince had been using them to hunt for Raubgold, the stolen Nazi gold. Everyone thought the book and map were lost when he died. *Obviously, we were wrong.*

She started to call her Aunt Sonora in Germany, but she was flying to Berlin for an extended visit the end of the week. Instead, she'd surprise her aunt with the bag.

Out the window, the sun was shining on the snow, making a picture-perfect Colorado ski day. She looked at the bag. What secrets did the map and diary hold? Afterall the years, maybe now she'd find out.

• • •

CHAPTER TWO

In Berlin

She looked at the bag holding
Vince's last adventure.

Amy Prowers watched her Aunt Sonora pour German brandy into
crystal glasses, and looked around the library, her favorite room in
Sonora's nineteenth century Berlin mansion. The late fall days were
chilly, and oak logs crackled in a stone fireplace that filled one wall.

She needed her aunt's help in figuring out the past. But it could
wait. Drinking brandy was a Prowers tradition. *And to think,"* she
thought, *we are really just two girls from the plains of Colorado.*

"So, what's in the box? My gift?" her aunt asked.

"Something from the past. Something we thought was dead and
gone."

Amy pulled the leather bag out.

"Oh my god. Is that what I think it is? I thought that bag was gone
when Vince died. Where did you find it?"

"It took an avalanche to find it. Vince kept every piece of junk he
ever found, but hiding the bag was unusual even for him."

Sonora looked at her. "And to think twenty years ago, we thought it was destroyed when a terrorist gang blew up his truck in North Pakistan. Why he put the bag behind the wall, or why he went to such an extent to conceal it, we'll never know."

She paused and laughed. "I made it sound like something out of a spy novel."

Amy laughed. "Everything Vince did was like a spy novel."

She opened the bag taking out the diary and a map. She was reminded that Vince never had a grave. She'd scattered his ashes in the Karakorum Range where he died. With that Vince was gone. Now he was back. Somehow, she was not surprised.

Sonora opened the map. "I hope there is a place marked with an X."

Amy looked over Sonora's shoulder at the map. "Berlin is the only city I recognize. The map is just lines, but it must show the location of the gold mentioned in the diary."

"The language in this diary is a mixture of German and old Latin," said Sonora. "It's an odd combination, and will take a linguistic specialist to accurately translate, and I know one at the Berlin Museum. Simon Bell is the grandson of one of my husband, the Count's long-time employees. I see him from time to time at the museum, and he attends my parties for museum staff. He is the guy who worked with your father and Vince so many years ago."

Amy picked up the diary. "What I remember Sonora, was that Vince always said he was looking for gold."

Why had Vince hidden the bag behind the false wall? What other secrets had he hidden? After his death, she had found nothing. Now she realized he had deliberately hidden his research before he went to Pakistan.

"Amy, after leaving Vail, Vince spent the last month of his life, here, in Berlin. "

"Yeah," said Amy with regret remembering she'd been in Mexico working on oil leases. "The price of oil had taken a dive and I was renegotiating leases. He and my father were here. Doing what?"

Sonora said, "They were secretive, which I never understood. Now, I think they were afraid of something or someone. Simon Bell might remember more details. He helped them with the ancient translations."

Amy hoped Sonora was right about this German. When Vince was alive, she wasn't involved in his search for missing antiquities. Someone had to run the family business while he and her father traipsed around the world.

She looked at the bag holding Vince's last adventure. He didn't live to finish it but now after all the years, she would try to find where the map and the diary lead. Maybe she could bring closure for him as well as herself.

When he was alive, she thought his search for gold was fool's gold. Now she had a concrete reason for the search. And to think all it took was an avalanche in Vail.

Sonora brought her back to today. "One of the last things your father and Vince did before leaving for Pakistan, was to go to Vilnius to meet a monk. Why the trip to the capital of Lithuania? Maybe the monk they met knows. I'll call the Abbot, who is his younger brother, in real life, and be sure the monk is alive and still lives in Vilnius."

"If he is alive, I'll go to Vilnius," Amy said. "Will do my best to find out after so long what Vince and my father were doing."

She had no idea what that might be.

• • •

ABOUT THE AUTHOR

Katherine Burlake

Katherine qualified as one of the first female Air Force Officers to attend the Air Force Navy Intelligence School and serve in the Vietnam War.

Living in Thailand, Peru, the Ivory Coast, England, and Germany led her to the Department of State and Broadcasting Board of Governors reporting on embassy operations globally. She has traveled to over 130 countries including Afghanistan and Iraq.

Katherine has been published in the *Macguffin*, The Face of War: A Baghdad Woman. Her vast experiences plus her four years in Riyadh, Saudi Arabia working in the embassy bring in the trench experiences to her engaging novels.

Colorado is now her home.

Katherine wrote *The Last Request* to show how events that happen with seemly no impact on a person's life, can change the direction of a life. It's the second book in the Amy Prowers mystery suspense series, joining *The Bystander*, a political thriller set in Saudi Arabia.

Discover **The Bystander,** the first book in the Amy Prowers mystery thriller series.

There's more to the desert than scorching heat ...

The desert of the Middle East combines with Saudi political intrigue in this intricately woven story of Amy Prowers close friendship to Princess Hassa of the Saudi royal family.

Her deceased husband's friend Prince Rashid, asks her to assist his wife on an excavation to validate a major finding. Although not an archeologist, Amy's aunt's private international organization, the Committee, has access to experts who will validate the excavation at the ancient city of Ubar in the Empty Quarter.

Eager to help her deceased husband's friend, Amy arrives and discovers there is more at stake than ancient cultures. Rashid is not what or who she and her husband believed him to be.

With a series of unexpected twists and turns, Amy's life is quickly at risk as she realizes there is a price to be paid for maintaining her values in a changing world.

The Bystander is one of those books that when you start reading it, you don't want to stop. Katherine Burlake has used her knowledge of Saudi Arabia and its inhabitants to create a masterful mystery.

—George Skarpentzos, retired foreign service officer

Anyone who enjoyed [the] thrilling tales of "Indiana Jones" will enjoy this book...
—David A. McCormick, reviewer

The Bystander is a mystery thriller set in Saudi Arabia where political power, religion, and oil money intersect.